Praise f[...]

Also by M.L. Buchman

The Night Stalkers

The Night Is Mine
I Own the Dawn
Wait Until Dark
Take Over at Midnight
Light Up the Night
Bring On the Dusk

The Firehawks

Pure Heat
Full Blaze

To the librarian at the Museum of Flight at Boeing Field. You know why, and all my thanks for it!

Chapter 1

THE SHARP WARNING BUZZ OF A CRITICAL SYSTEM'S FAILURE crackled through Vern Taylor's headset.

A momentary panic hit him as palpably as the time Mickey Hamilton had gotten drunk and decided that plowing a fist into Vern's chin made some kind of sense.

Vern had just flown his helicopter down into the critical "death zone." Helicopters that broke between fifty and four hundred feet above the ground were in a really bad place—too high to safely crash and too low to stabilize and autorotate in.

A glance out the window didn't improve the news. The Mount Hood Aviation firefighters' airfield was still two miles ahead. Below him was nothing but a sea of hundred-foot fir trees covering rugged, thousand-foot ridges.

So screwed!

Meanwhile, the more rational part of his brain—that the U.S. Coast Guard had spent six years investing so heavily in training and that four more years of flying to fire had honed—was occupied with checking his main screen on the helicopter's console.

He located the flashing, bright red warning. Hydraulic failure in the primary circuit.

He smelled no burning rubber or hot metal.

Several things happened simultaneously.

The first thing was being seriously ticked off that the helicopter was trying to kill him.

Vern had been type-certified in the massive, ten-thousand-pound firefighting helicopter for precisely thirty-two hours and—a glance at the console clock—seventeen minutes. It simply wasn't fair to be killed on his second day flying this sweet machine.

The second thing that happened was he actually read the flashing message: #2 PRI SERVO PRESS. The backup hydraulic-pressure warning system wasn't reporting any problems, which meant it was still running to cover the failure of the #2 pump's pressure.

Vern double-checked.

No secondary alarm.

He wiggled the cyclic joystick control with his right hand, which altered the pitch of the blades to control his direction of flight.

His chopper wiggled exactly as it should. The back pressure of the controls against his dry palm felt normal.

He tried restarting his breathing. That worked as well.

Then—with the practice of a hundred drills that had felt like a thousand under MHA's chief pilot Emily Beale's watchful eye—his left hand came off the collective control alongside his seat long enough to grab the correct circuit breaker among the eighty other breakers, switches, and controls that made up the overhead console attached to the chopper's ceiling.

He pulled on the breaker that shut down the #2 Primary Servo pump.

The alarm went silent, and the blinking red warning on the screen shifted to a steady red glow. Then his hand returned to the collective, completing everything that really needed doing.

The third thing that happened—all in the same

moment, as far as he could ever recall—was the thought that Denise Conroy, Mount Hood Aviation's chief mechanic, was going to kill him even if the helicopter had decided not to. Breaking one of Denise's birds on your second day flying it solo and expecting to survive unscathed was downright foolhardy.

The pilots generally agreed that upsetting the head of MHA's helicopter maintenance team was not to be considered a life-prolonging experience.

Nor was disappointing Emily Beale, who had only certified him in the Firehawk yesterday morning. The four years he'd flown the little MD500 for MHA wouldn't count for squat if he dinged up their newest twenty-million-dollar bird.

He followed the other two Firehawks back into camp. They were the massive Type I juggernauts of the heli-tack firefighting world, able to deliver a thousand gallons of water and foam or retardant to a wildfire. Only a few helicopters could carry more, and those were all far less agile machines. This chopper ruled the wildfire helitack sweet spot.

The Mount Hood Aviation Firehawks were painted gloss black, and with the red-and-orange racing flames of the MHA logo running from the nose down the sides, they looked as cool and powerful as they really were.

The Firehawks were built from Sikorsky Black Hawk helicopters. Each one was an eight-foot-high, ten-foot-wide, and forty-foot-long nasty-looking machine. Black Hawks, no matter how prettily painted, always appeared to be looking for a fight. They were the tough boys on the block, even if the two in front of him were flown by women: Emily, ex-military and kind of terrifying, truth be told, and Jeannie, one of the most competent and prettiest fliers he'd ever met.

How in the hell had some photographer guy snapped her up? Jeannie was awesome. Not that they'd ever done more than fly together—it wasn't like that between them—but seeing her look so damn happy emphasized how totally lame his own relationships had been.

Closing his eyes for a moment, Vern braced himself. Stepping on the rudder pedal, he twisted the tail of the five-ton helicraft to the side, then shifted the cyclic joystick in his right hand to compensate. Again, it felt completely normal, proving that the backup hydraulic system was indeed operational, even if his breathing still sounded harsh over the headset and microphone system he wore. He remained in formation with the other choppers but now flew mostly sideways in order to look behind him.

He opened one eye. A cloud of black smoke was streaming from his chopper. No sign of a fire warning on the instrument panel, so it was just the burning off of some hydraulic fluid that had spilled before the pressure loss was detected and he'd shut down the pump. They were under two minutes from Mount Hood Aviation's Hoodie One base camp.

Not enough time to burn everything off. Thankfully none of the fumes—nasty, astringent stuff—had leaked into the cabin. Vern realigned the controls to once again face forward and retain his position in the flight. He also managed to convince his breathing that he was back in control.

The MHA airfield and base camp lay less than a mile ahead now. They were perched low on the northern side of the towering mass of Mount Hood—eleven thousand feet of dormant, mostly, ice-capped volcano. The airfield was easy to miss among the towering fir trees and the vibrant yellows and reds of September aspens and maples.

It was the end of day, so the mountain's shadow already lay long across the camp, and the grass airstrip was not empty like he'd hoped. The four smaller choppers of MHA's seven-bird fleet had already returned, parked along the north side of the strip close to the towering Douglas fir trees that defined that side of the base. Pilots and ground crew were milling around them.

Along the other side of the field were the low buildings of the long-defunct kids' summer camp that MHA had taken over. Though much of the structures' dark wood was covered with green moss, like so much else in the Pacific Northwest, the buildings were dry and warm inside.

But were the other pilots, ground crew, and smoke-jumpers tucked away safe and warm?

No such luck.

They seemed to think that just because it was a beautiful, late-September afternoon, everyone should be out at the cluster of picnic tables that served as the camp's main hangout. As he neared, he could see the dots of their bright faces turning like damned daisies following the sun—all tracking the path of his smoking flight.

And sure enough, the nightmare awaited.

There at the end of the row of four already-parked choppers and the two smokejumper delivery planes was the maintenance truck. In front of the truck stood five feet and four inches of livid woman with dark blond hair down her back—her feet planted as if part of the mountain's basalt shield. Though not close enough to see, he knew she'd be standing with her arms crossed over one of the nicest chests he'd ever seen.

He could feel the burn of her glare at a thousand yards out.

Vern followed the other two Firehawks in for a landing, Denise coming into focus as he approached. Jeans, T-shirt, and a canvas vest that had once been beige before it spent years being worn around broken helicopters. She wore a tool belt like an Old West gunslinger. Damn, she was gorgeous and cute at the same time. And about the most unapproachable woman he'd ever met.

A single drop of salty sweat dripped into his eye and stung. He sniffed the air again—no smell of fire other than the bit of wood char that you always picked up flying over a wildland fire.

A glance back as he hovered, spun into place, and set his bird down on the markers. Yep, still smoking black.

Denise was going to do more than kill him; that would be too kind.

She was going to outright annihilate him.

He hoped that she at least waited until after he was done landing before she did so.

—⁂—

"What did you do to my poor bird?" Denise Conroy heaved open the cargo bay door and spoke to Vern Taylor's back in the pilot seat. She reached up and pulled down on the gust lock in the middle of the rear cabin's ceiling. That would keep the rotor blades from turning unexpectedly once she climbed atop the helicopter to check the engine.

"Broke it," was his sassy reply.

"I guessed that much. Confirm ignition key in the off position," she called out even though she could see forward between the seats to the center console that it already was. Outside the front windscreen she could see Mickey and Bruce pressing their faces up against the windscreen and making funny faces at Vern, blowing out their cheeks like puffer fish or three-year-olds.

"Confirm off and out." Vern pulled the key free and dropped it on the center console of radios that ran between the pilot and copilot's seats. Then he gave the finger to his juvenile buddies who laughed and moved on. She made a mental note to wash the outside of the pilot's side windscreen—while wearing gloves.

She stepped back outside, slid the big door shut with perhaps a bit more force than she should have, and climbed on top of the Firehawk helicopter using the notches built into the section of the helicopter's hull that had been covered by the door. Denise began peeling off the cowling of the Number-Two turbine engine, being careful of the still blazing-hot exhaust. She could feel the radiant heat on her cheeks as soon as the sheet metal was shifted aside.

The stink of scorched, high-temp phosphate hydraulic fluid made her glad for the slight breeze that was wafting it away. She pulled on goggles and neoprene gloves so that the acidic fluid wouldn't splash in her eyes or sting her hands.

The cause of the failure was instantly apparent from the spray pattern. The side of a hose had split and shot out a broad fan of pressurized fluid. Some of it had puddled, and some of it had struck the engine and been vaporized.

Vern finished filling out his log as if everything was absolutely normal before climbing down from his seat.

"You do know, Vern, busting a bird when you've had it less than two days really puts you on my bad list." Denise jerked out a wrench to loosen the blown hose, but in her nervousness, she scattered several other tools as she did so. She gathered them back up as quickly as she could. How had she even spoken that way to a pilot?

Vern didn't sound the least bit put out by her tone. "The few, the proud, the helitack firefighter pilots of MHA. We're all in the crapper with you, Wrench. How are we supposed to fly to fire without actually using your helicopters? That's the puzzle, isn't it?"

She shifted her scowl from the engine and aimed it down at him.

Vern leaned with his back against the pilot's door of the helicopter, staring off into the distance as if completely unconcerned about the midair breakdown and oblivious to her conflicted emotions.

It was her fault that the pilot had been placed in danger.

And Vern was teasing her about it. He was tall enough that the top of his head was almost close enough for her to swing down and rap it sharply with the wrench in her hand, which might cheer her up a bit. But he wasn't the problem, so she rammed the wrench back into her tool belt, knocking a few other tools loose that she then had to retrieve from the helicopter's innards.

She really shouldn't be aiming her anger at him; it was she herself that she was furious with. She'd sent a bird aloft that had broken in the sky. That was wholly unforgivable. Her pilots counted on her to provide safe, airworthy equipment, and she'd failed one of them.

Firehawk Oh-Three had been in the Mount Hood Aviation inventory for less than a month, and now it had blown a hydraulic line. Thankfully, Vern hadn't been in any danger from the failure—the backup system had taken the load. But she'd thought the bird was clean when she signed off on the airworthiness certificate, something she'd done every day for a month.

It definitely wasn't clean at the moment. In addition to the blown hose itself, hydraulic leaks were messy and took time to clean up. Furthermore, the fluid that sprayed into the engine, which hadn't cared in the slightest, had caused the trail of acrid black smoke that had scared the daylights out of her. She'd had to wrap her arms around herself to hold herself together until Vern set the bird safely on the ground. The burn-off of fluid had also added to the mess with sticky exhaust particulate sheathing the rear half of the pretty black-and-flame paint job.

"I can feel you aiming nasty thoughts down at me." Vern rubbed a hand on the top of his head as if it was getting hot. Then he turned to look up at her. His lean face was rich with a summer's tan. His mirrored shades hid the dark eyes that matched hair that, in her more psychotic moments, she'd occasionally fantasized toying with. "Anything I can do to help?"

"Not unless you're planning to break something else on my helicopter, Slick. Go away. You're distracting me." And he was. Denise had some principles, and those included not getting sucked in by the charm of a handsome flyboy. The last time she had let that happen was…a long time ago, and it wouldn't be happening now.

"Yes, ma'am, Wrench, sir." Then he saluted, hitting his forehead hard enough to pretend he was knocking himself silly.

No matter *how* handsome and charming he was, she would *not* be tempted.

She lifted the exact implement that had earned most mechanics the Wrench nickname and he stumbled back, raising his hands in mock terror.

He pulled a black, Mount Hood Aviation billed hat out of his back pocket and tugged it on before shooting her one of his cockeyed grins. The blazing red-and-orange MHA logo offered her a tempting target. Maybe if she had a tennis ball handy she'd bean him one.

"Make me proud, Wrench."

"Fall down a gopher hole, Slick." Again? Had she really sassed a pilot? That wasn't anything the Denise she knew would ever do.

He tipped his hat and headed across the narrow grass airstrip of the Hoodie base camp. On his third step he stumbled badly, pretending to fall into a gopher hole.

Denise laughed. Of the many jokers among the crews, Vern was the only one who consistently made her want to laugh. Though not usually out loud.

She watched him walk off. Had she just been flirting with him? She'd never been any good at it, so she couldn't be sure. He didn't fly a Huey UH-1 "Slick" helicopter, but she liked how the nickname fit him. Nicknames were another thing she rarely used correctly. Yet another reason not to become involved with flyboys who seemed to live by them. For example, Mickey was usually... She couldn't even remember. Hopeless. Absolutely hopeless.

Pilots also had all these unspoken rules and codes that the women they picked up in bars seemed to already know. It was as if every one of them had gone to the same training course, but no one had told her she needed to enroll to understand men.

Denise understood none of them.

Once he was gone, she could relax a little. She sat back on her heels atop the helicopter. It was one of her favorite times of day, and she took a moment to enjoy it.

Malcolm shot her a wave when he noticed her watching. He'd finished servicing one of the Twin Hueys and was moving to the other one. Brenna, her other assistant, was deep in an MD500 and didn't look up. No need to worry though. Brenna could handle almost anything on the smaller birds; she was good.

The sun was setting into the Oregon wilderness over the massive shoulder of glacier-capped Mount Hood. You could practically taste the pine-sharp chlorophyll on the ice-clean air. The birds were coming home to roost, the seven helicopters and three airplanes of her firefighting fleet.

The flesh-and-blood birds were also dancing in the last of the sunlight as they headed into their own nests among the towering Douglas fir trees on the north side of the runway. And if even one of them pooped on her helicopters, there'd be hell to pay.

By U.S. Forest Service contract requirements, right on the stroke of a half hour before sunset, all of the aircraft were out of the air and lined up on the grass. For the next dozen hours, the crews still fighting the fire on the ground would be on their own.

Emily and Jeannie were certified for nighttime firefighting, but that was awfully expensive and wasn't called for except on the very worst fires. Also, if the pilots flew at night, they still needed the mandatory eight-hour break out of every twenty-four.

Better to let them sleep and fly again at a half hour past sunrise rather than miss part of the morning.

Jeannie climbed out of Firehawk Oh-Two and waved at Denise. She treated her helicopter with the most respect of all the pilots. Emily in Firehawk Oh-One was so skilled after ten years in the Army that, while she didn't baby the firefighting Black Hawk, she never stressed the bird.

They were home safe now.

The two small MD500s for hitting spot fires were parked at the west end of the runway. A pair of the midsized Bell 212 Twin Huey choppers were lined up next, then her three Firehawks parked neatly down the side of the grass-strip field at midfield, directly opposite the main camp buildings. The seven choppers looked so pristine and glossy in their black-and-flame paint jobs. All glossy, that is, except Firehawk Oh-Three with a dark smudge down the tail section from the scorched hydraulic fluid.

Denise sighed. She really shouldn't have harassed Vern. It wasn't his fault the line had cracked and sprayed the compartment with slimy, silicone-based goo. At least it hadn't been the old hydraulic oil. That stuff would have burned rather than merely scorching and caused a major mess, if not an engine fire.

She finished the repair in ten minutes and was about halfway through the cleanup when the dinner bell rang. Her hands would reek of the cleaner for hours despite the gloves. She hoped it was a knife-and-fork dinner tonight.

Betsy, the camp cook, had brought the bell back from when they'd been fighting fire Down Under in Australia over the winter. The old, brass, twelve-inch fire-truck bell announced the exact moment of sunset, spooking aloft the last of the birds who were just settling into the trees. You think they'd get used to it—Betsy rang her new toy every night at this time. It echoed from one end of the airstrip to the other, calling the helitack and smokies to come eat.

From her high perch atop the Firehawk helicopter, Denise had a clear view of the whole field. Malcolm and Brenna downed tools and checklists from the nightly inspection they performed on each aircraft and began wandering across the grass strip toward the cluster of picnic tables. Mark Henderson's twin-engine Beech King Air, the Incident Commander—Air's aircraft, had landed without her noticing and was parked by the DC-3s used for transporting the smokejumpers when they were needed.

Actually, some part of her brain *had* noticed.

She could recall that the engines had sounded clean, nothing to trigger her internal alarms to hurry over to inspect them immediately. Mark's landing had been as immaculate as you'd expect from a long-term Army pilot. Like his wife, Emily, he flew smooth and clean every minute of every day. So no other warnings arose in her head, and she knew it would be a normal nightly inspection.

All routine.

That was good. That's what it was supposed to be when she wasn't creating a failure like Oh-Three.

She set up a pair of work lights so they'd be ready after dinner when it was dark. She laid her flask of cleaner and her gloves across exactly the spot where she'd left off so she'd be sure to start in the right place after dinner.

Today's fire had been a grassland range fire seventy miles to the southwest. Only the helicopter crews had been out today to help the local ground crews who'd been able to drive trucks to the fire. The MHA smoke-jumpers had the day off, so a lot of them were in town and the tables were less full than usual.

Most of the pilots, support crew, and ground personnel were already sitting around, reading or playing cards held in place by small stones against the light evening breeze that wandered lazily through camp. Thankfully, that same breeze washed away the bitter smells of cleaners and the sharp kerosene scent of Jet A fuel that the pumper truck had dispensed down the row.

As Denise headed for the chow line, Emily and Jeannie came up to her. They were out of flight gear and looked casually pretty. Someday she'd like to find the nerve to ask how they made it look so effortless.

Of course, MHA's first two Firehawk pilots wanted to know what had gone wrong with the third craft.

—◦◦◦—

"Damn!" Mickey, Vern's bunkmate and one of the twin-Huey chopper pilots, let out a low whistle of appreciation. "I've got to say...Da-amn!"

Vern glared at his poker hand a moment longer, puzzled because his own cards certainly weren't worth any such statement. He saw that Bruce and Gordon were both still in the game, so he folded and tossed his cards into the pile, careful not to drop one between the boards of the battered wood of the picnic table. Then he glanced up and offered a low appreciative whistle of his own.

"Da-amn is right."

Denise, flanked by Emily and Jeannie, was strolling across the green grass airfield in the light of the setting sun. The sky was orange behind them, and the lights above the chow line illuminated them like a Maxfield Parrish painting—kind light and impossibly beautiful women who belonged exactly where they were.

The image did strange things to his heart, as if it had caught and stumbled on something it had never seen before. Or perhaps seen but not noticed.

Maybe his pulse was still stutter-stepping from that pressure alarm.

Bruce and Gordon turned to look over their shoulders and didn't turn back too quickly. Bruce was a very careful card player, except when women were involved or even in the general vicinity. Vern saw enough to be glad he'd folded.

"Every time," Mickey whispered. "Every single time they come walking toward you side by side like that it takes your breath away. It's like you never get used to it. If Carly joins them, I could die a happy man."

Vern hadn't actually been commenting on the group; it was the diminutive mechanic who he would never tire of watching. He idly wondered if she'd ever been a dancer, or if she'd always walked as if she was floating just above the earth.

The trio moved into the chow line. Except when it was raining, Betsy always set up a long table outside. MHA ate buffet style, but their cook made sure it was the best quality.

The three looked so earnest that his ears were buzzing. He'd make a totally safe bet that they were discussing the smoky failure of Firehawk Oh-Three. Three beautiful women talking about him, but not. Yeah, that sounded about right.

Then Carly came out the door of the kitchen and joined the others. Mickey was right. They really did take your breath away. That they were hanging together was a common enough phenomenon at camp, but you still never got used to it. The noise level among the guys' conversation fell off by half across the entire chow area.

Emily Beale, with her toddler daughter riding on her hip, was the commanding cool blond—more than a little terrifying in her quiet control. Carly, MHA's fire behavior analyst, was as tall and slender, her Nordic light hair and pale skin aglow like a shining flame—the woman was also seriously intense. Jeannie was a sharp contrast with her dark hair, black leather jacket, and black jeans. She was as splendidly figured as the first two women were trim, and yet was as casual and easygoing as the other two were completely daunting.

But it was Denise who was really knocking him back tonight.

She was always around—she'd been with MHA for the last eighteen months of his four years here—but it was as if he was seeing her for the first time. She stood shorter than the others. As wonderfully built as Jeannie and with dusty blond hair that fell well past her shoulders and offset the softest imaginable tan that came from having immensely fair skin but living most of the summer out of doors.

"Yep." Mickey sighed. "Seeing that much female beauty in one place is a burden that a man has to bear if he works at MHA. Now that's a serious perk."

Vern nodded. It was. Three were married and Denise presented a bastion of pure steel to repel all boarders, but the women were amazing to look at. Far be it from him to deny himself the pleasure of enjoying what millennia of species-based conditioning had trained, nay, bred him to appreciate.

There was something about Denise though.

He squinted the way his mother had taught him when she started studying painting. The four women were in line to get their fried chicken and mashed potatoes, which he could smell from where he was sitting, and it was making him really hungry because Betsy made killer fried chicken. The women looked the same when he squinted, but now he could see them a little differently.

MHA's chief pilot Emily Beale was actually the one with the spine of steel. Her military training made every motion appear both effortless and meticulously planned. Carly was the driving force, a brilliant spark, and Jeannie the soft, steady one flustered by nothing.

But green-eyed Denise eluded him. As if she had a cloak of invisibility over her character.

"I'm hungry." Vern started to get up, but Mickey pulled him back down. It was probably just as well. His knees felt no steadier than after the landing when he'd had to lean against the chopper to remain upright. He'd lost three buddies to a mechanical failure when he was in the Guard. Thankfully he hadn't remembered it was five years ago today until after he was on the ground.

Denise had laughed at him as his knees almost gave out when he walked away—not a sound he was used to hearing from her. But it had sounded like a kindly laugh, not a cruel one. He'd been kinda pissed, but he didn't think there was a cruel bone in the woman. Maybe he'd missed some joke.

"Gotta finish this hand." The other guys turned back to the game at Mickey's prompting, but Vern had already folded. There was no money on the table anyway; they had been just killing time until dinner, not getting serious about poker. The only bets were who was buying the first round next time they went to the Doghouse Inn.

So he stayed put but still watched Denise as she moved through the line. She'd exchanged her work vest for one of soft leather that wrapped and showcased her figure. He watched how the ends of her hair curled down the back of the dark leather, mirroring the curves of her splendid behind that invited a man to dream of…

He shook his head. Who in the world was he kidding?

Getting the hots for Denise Conroy was about as useless as getting the hots for some movie star on the big screen. Sure, a guy could lust after Zoe Saldana, but that didn't get him on the bridge of the *Enterprise*.

No way it was ever going to happen with Denise Conroy. To make it even more unlikely, she'd been dating some townie for almost a year, which struck

him as pretty damn serious. And her attractiveness
level was off the charts. Vern usually did pretty well—
occasionally very well, though those occasions always
surprised him—but Denise was up at a whole other level
of amazing.

Vern turned back to the game. "Come on, you losers.
My stomach is grumbling."

Mickey flashed his hole cards at Vern. Vern slapped
his roommate on the back in a friendly way. It was a
good thing that they were only playing for drinks. No
matter what last card was turned up, Bruce was about to
kick Mickey's ass.

And boy did he ever, getting a three-drink raise
before driving the hammer down.

Damning himself for a fool, Vern swung wide as
he and the guys threaded their way toward the chow
line. The others bucked their way in the straightest line,
weaving and dodging among the tables, occasionally
goosing somebody as he was about to take a drink. You
could easily follow the wake of turbulence they left
behind as they went.

Vern followed the line of least resistance, walking
outside the perimeter of the clustered tables. A flight
path that just happened to pass close by where three of
the four women had settled.

Carly and Denise sat with their backs to him. Denise
was half a head shorter than Carly, even sitting down.
But the way her hair caught the last light of day and
shimmered with each tiny shift of body position was a
siren call.

He might have crashed right up on those rocks if
Jeannie hadn't been facing him from across their table.

She watched him, puzzled for only a moment, then offered him a knowing smile.

Shit!

The woman was too smart for his own good. Well, hopefully she'd have the common decency to keep her mouth shut or he really would be crashing on the rocks.

He cut farther to the outside to get clear. That had him passing close to Mark, Emily, and their daughter. Tonight their island nation was slightly isolated to one side from the rest of the group.

He passed behind them just as Emily spoke softly to her husband.

"Honduras?"

Vern suppressed a shiver across his shoulders and paused at their table. "Honduras? If you're thinking of a vacation now that the fire season is almost over, you can do way better than Honduras."

Emily closed a folder that was sitting on the table before they both turned to look at him.

"You know Honduras?"

"I do."

Tessa sat at the end of the table beside Emily, beating on a small bite of chicken with the back of her spoon and the enthusiasm of a two-year-old.

He circled around and sat next to her, starting the airplane game with a small french fry to get her to eat it while he spoke to her parents. She was a bright, shining girl who looked much like her mother.

"In 2009, I was serving on the Coast Guard cutter *Bertholf*. We were coming out of San Diego as the Honduras coup d'état of that year was kicking into full gear. Five months of political train wreck."

He managed to land the french fry, which Tessa began cheerfully chewing away on. He selected a bit of beaten chicken for the next flight.

"The Navy felt that they didn't have enough assets in the area, so they called us. Full steam south. Mine was one of the two MH-65C Dolphin helicopters they had on board. I had search-and-rescue gear, but they had an airborne use-of-force package ready for me if I needed to arm up. We were on constant patrols, stuck offshore from June through September. Back a year later for flood relief following Hurricane Paula. Honduras sucks. Highest murder rate in the world there just as a bonus. Try Belize or Costa Rica. Much friendlier."

The flight of the chicken was a crash and burn. As soon as the bit of food in question finally made a soft landing on the plate, it was beaten once more with a spoon to ensure its complete suppression.

After they chatted for a few minutes and another successful french fry landing, he headed to the line for his own meal. Glancing back at the table, he saw that Emily had managed to fly some chicken in safe, but her attention wasn't on the task.

She and Mark had reopened the folder and both were studying its contents.

It was full dark outside as Denise sat in the pilot's seat of Firehawk Oh-Three and cycled down the hydraulic pumps. Everything checked out. As long as she was here, she turned on the Health and Usage Monitoring System and checked the readouts.

The HUMS tracked most of the problems and worked

as a fair predictive tool for maintenance. It didn't like surprises though, and it took her a few minutes to convince the computer that the line failure had been fixed. The HUMS was quite certain that the pressure drop and subsequent return to normal was a problem rather than external service done by a human it knew nothing about.

Then it convinced itself that due to the pressure loss, the rotor was on the verge of imminent failure even though they were sitting on the ground and the engines were off. She didn't start the twin turbine engines or even let them have any fuel, but she started the Auxiliary Power Unit and let the APU cycle the engines once. That cleared its miniscule computer brain. She shut down the power. The HUMS, well, hummed at her, happily green across the entire screen. She shut that system down as well.

The large LCD screens across the control panel went dark, and now the only light was the soft glow beside the few mechanical instruments that were there in case the electronics were blown. Beyond the windshield, night had fallen. There were still a few lights over at tables across the runway and small groups gathered around them.

Denise threw the last switch. The lights died, and now she sat alone in the dar—

"How's it going?"

She yelped. She didn't mean to, but she did. A totally girly sound of surprise.

"Sorry, sorry." Though she couldn't see him, Vern's voice was right outside the open pilot's door, not more than a foot from her elbow. For an instant he rested a steadying hand on her arm.

"Vern, you jerk. First you break my new helicopter, then you sneak up to scare the daylights out of me? What's up with that?"

"Sorry." His deep voice did sound really contrite. He was long, lean, and had a voice to soothe wild animals. The man should not be allowed to run around loose.

"You owe me!" He did. A new heart. Because her present one was cranking at liftoff speed and still might fly away without her at any moment.

His silhouette crossed in front of the camp lights outside the windscreen as he did that lazy mosey thing that pilots did so well and circled around the chopper's nose to the copilot's seat.

She didn't leave, didn't gather her tablet computer with its checklists, didn't... She simply waited until he'd climbed aboard beside her and then leaned back against the seat. The seats were comfortable enough—they had to be for the pilots to fly the hours they did every day—but they weren't loungers. They kept the pilot upright and facing forward.

Vern somehow managed to lounge in the seat anyway.

She became intensely aware that she was in his normal seat. Her toes could barely reach the rudder pedals because they were set for his long legs. She'd need to raise the seat several inches for a clear view over the top of the T-shaped console. The base of the T started on the deck between their two seats. After curving up until it was above their knees, it then branched to either side at the height of a car's dashboard. His hands would rest right on the controls that—

Denise jerked her hands into her lap milliseconds

before she rested her hands over where his would normally be.

"Like we're at a drive-in movie." A hint of reflected light showed the joystick was moving. Vern must be nudging the cyclic around with gentle taps of his fingertips. The one rising between her legs brushed the inside of her knee.

She didn't move, but she did shiver. Curiously, her nerves insisted it was a good shiver, one that warmed rather chilled her skin.

The two controls were linked together so that either pilot could fly the craft at any moment. It was as if he were somehow sitting on her side of the cockpit as well. If she reached out and touched the cyclic, she'd feel his small motions…which was way too personal.

"I'm not your girl." She'd never been to a drive-in movie. She hadn't been…wasn't the sort of girl that boys took to "the movies."

"Seem to have noticed you weren't." His tone had a definite *duh* quality to it. "How's Jasper?"

"Okay," she guessed. The relationship had fizzled and finally died a quiet death a month ago, but she hadn't told anyone. She didn't like failure in any form, not even when it was mutual. Subject change. "I'm really sorry. I should never have certified this chopper for flight without—"

"What did you find?" With a wave of his hand that she could barely see in the dim light coming through the windshield, he brushed her apology aside as if it hadn't been her fault.

She reached into her work-vest pocket and offered him the six-inch piece of offending hose line. It was about as big around as her thumb. She braced her eyes for the shock of a cabin light, but instead he held it out before him. He was holding it so that the camp lights across the runway would glance along the surface.

"That doesn't look right."

"Duh!" She felt pretty good about the casual sound. It came out correctly instead of her normal too-awkward-to-live sound when she tried such things. "There's a split blown right through the sidewall."

"Not that, this." He didn't hand it back to her. Instead he leaned over until their shoulders were almost brushing and she could smell the soap he'd used to shower. He held the hose out in front of her and twisted it back and forth slowly. She had to shift her position to get the distant camp lights to shine along the surface. A millimeter more and they'd be rubbing shoulders. It was so tempting to let herself take some comfort in—

"What's that nick?" And how had she missed it and a pilot caught it?

"This bird used to be Army before we picked it up used and converted it, right?"

"Sure, though it was the Sikorsky factory that converted it for us." She winced and clamped her mouth shut to stop herself. She was always correcting people to get things exactly correct, which she'd been told very clearly was one of her less charming habits.

Denise was torn between studying the hose and considering whether or not to lean against Vern and feel human contact for even a moment. She didn't miss Jasper.

Not at all.

Which was information she'd only just processed at

this moment—a feeling supported by the fact that she'd thought in the general terms of their relationship ending a month ago rather than counting the twenty-seven days that had actually passed. Or was it twenty-eight? While she might not miss him, she did long for the casual intimacy of being with someone. She'd liked the human contact while it lasted and missed it.

But this was Vern Taylor, the handsomest flyboy in MHA and one of her coworkers—an absolute recipe for disaster. Men like him didn't notice women like her when they could have any cute girl passing through Hood River, Oregon, to windsurf the Columbia Gorge. What was she thinking? He always hooked up with the tall, loud, flashy ones who laughed brightly and easily. And probably gave the same way.

Personally, she'd never found sex to be the least bit easy. Occasionally good, but it complicated all matters and everything connected with them.

Like easing right on the cyclic to tip the rotor swash plate, she pulled away from Vern enough to create a small distance between them. But she didn't shift so far that she couldn't still see the hose…or sense the warmth of his closeness on her cheek.

"This Black Hawk…" Denise actually had to swallow to clear the lonely taste her thoughts had left in her throat, as if the emotion was a bad flavor. "It served with the 101st Airborne, the Screaming Eagles. Three tours, I think."

Jasper had always been on her about how precise she was about everything. Four miles, not three miles to the nearest restaurant—rounded up from 3.85. "Sixty-five degrees outside," not "in the sixties." "It's seven thirty-eight," when asked the time. She wasn't being fussy; it was simply how she thought about things. She'd slowly been forced to append most of her conversations with "I think" or "about" or "somewhere around" until she stuttered like a mistuned radial engine.

Well, she was done with that.

"Three tours." She repeated definitively, then added the beginning and ending dates of service because she knew the history of every one of her birds from the moment they flew off the assembly line—and to hell with any man who didn't like it.

Except for Firehawk Oh-Two. Something very strange had happened to that helicopter last winter, but she'd never been able to uncover what. And when she'd pushed, she'd not only been stonewalled. She'd been told flat out that questions were unwelcome and were a job-level "didn't need to know." Finally, when she still didn't back down, her questions were deemed a security-level risk.

With no explanation and a maintenance record that displayed odd discrepancies, she didn't trust the craft. Without telling anyone else why, she'd had her team help strip the bird down and put it back together, but it was as flawless as any aircraft she'd ever seen. Yet it still wasn't the bird she'd sent to Australia last year to fight bushfires.

She wondered if Vern knew what had happened, but she'd guess not. He hadn't traveled with the two Firehawks when they'd split off from the rest of the MHA team to fight a different bushfire.

Vern didn't comment about her elaborate precision and total command of Firehawk Oh-Three's service record. Instead he was once more inspecting the hose in the distant camp lights.

She no longer had any excuse to remain leaning so close, so she sat back in the pilot's seat. But now she could feel his shape in the shapeless pilot's seat. How pathetic was she?

"That's a bullet crease."

"It's what?" She rapped his ribs hard with her elbow as she leaned back over to see.

"Easy there, Wrench. You could hurt a fella. See?" He held it out again.

"You're right. It looks like the bullet cut through the first layer or two of the hose. How did you know?"

"Flying Coast Guard isn't only about pulling idiot tourists out of riptides."

Coast Guard? How had she not known that about him? If he'd been one of her choppers, she would have.

Denise tried to see Vern more clearly. His dim silhouette looked the same. Mr. Casual and Easygoing being a former U.S. Coast Guard helicopter pilot was pretty hard to reconcile.

Though it did make a certain kind of sense. He'd been steady as a rock while his chopper trailed smoke. The sideslip to check his smoke trail and then straightening out without ever breaking formation spoke of lots of practice with emergency situations.

Maybe there was more to Vern Taylor than just being a charming flyboy with nothing but sex on his mind.

—◦◦◦—

Vern had to make a joke. Something—no matter how feeble—before Denise's proximity totally overwhelmed

his common sense and any shred of decency a man had
to maintain around such a woman. This wasn't some bar
babe. This was Denise frickin' Conroy.

"Your precious helicopter had a rough childhood."

Yeah, there was a distraction that had possibilities.
He'd been hyperconsciously aware of her from the
moment he'd touched her arm after spooking her. Which
was not a good thing. First off, Jasper was an okay guy,
mostly. Though Vern had never much liked him. But if
he was Denise's choice, he must be okay.

"You know"—he patted the chopper's main console
as if soothing an unruly child—"street thug, gang wars,
drive-by shootings. It's a tough life being an Army
chopper, but, hey, someone has to do it."

He let his mouth ramble as he breathed her in. Her
scent, a crazy mix of woman and mechanic's grease, of
hot metal and warm female, was making his head spin
worse than when the #2 PRI SERVO PRESS warning
had blinked on.

"This hose…" She brushed a long, delicate finger
across the bullet crease as if to confirm its existence.

He felt the motion through his fingertips where he
still held the failed piece of hose. It felt as if he'd been
electroshocked where, well, you weren't supposed to
feel for another man's woman.

"It must have caught a nick, but not bad enough to
fail. Just enough to create a weak point. It was on the
side away from what I could see with a visual inspection." Denise had a soft voice, all out of keeping with
the tough exterior she projected. There was a gentleness
to it he'd never noticed before.

"Right." Vern kicked his brain to keep it running

because his own personal Auxiliary Power Unit was thinking thoughts that made him glad it was dark in the chopper's cockpit. "It was lurking until the time was right."

"Until the time was right? For what?"

"Sure." He swallowed hard and wished she'd lean back in her seat. He wished he was still in the predictable poker game he could see continuing under the camp lights. If he had stayed there rather than coming over to check on how she was doing, she wouldn't be mere inches away making every nerve jangle on full alarm. "It, uh, was waiting for a chance to really embarrass me on my second day solo."

"You think this bit of hose was lying in wait for you before failing? You are going to take it personally? It's just a hose."

"I take everything personally."

By the shimmer of glistening hair shifting and catching the reflection of distant lights, he could see her tilt her head sideways to inspect him.

"Especially when it tries to kill me," he added.

Which is exactly what she was doing to him. He slipped the bit of hose into his pocket to give his hands something to do.

Chapter 2

UNABLE TO SLEEP, DENISE DROVE BACK FROM HER TOWN house at the foot of the mountain a couple hours before first light and started working on Firehawk Oh-Three. The night was cool but not chilly, one of the last warm fall nights. No one here except her, her helicopters, and the sleeping forest. She could unwind and focus in the silence.

It didn't take her long to find the patch over the hole made through the hull's skin by the bullet that had nicked the hydraulic hose. After that, her inspection went much faster. She went to every single patched hole and poked around until she could figure out the trajectory of whatever had punched it. This craft had endured a rough life. She cataloged thirty-four hits that penetrated the hull and several dozen grazes that had only creased the metal skin. Maybe that wasn't much by Army standards, but it was thirty-four too many in her world.

Bullets really creeped her out. Her mom had been shot in a grocery store holdup and had died in her dad's arms. It was months before he stopped flinching if Denise dropped something, like one of her schoolbooks. She went from a precocious nine to an adult ten in those same weeks with no one noticing, not even her.

Well, this helicopter had been a weapon of war, and it had been shot. She hoped that whoever had flown in it was okay.

One by one she traced each of the thirty-four lines of impact. By the inside shape of the penetration—behind the outside patch—she was able to estimate the angle of trajectory on each hit. She found scuffs and creases where rounds had hit secondary surfaces and finally spent the last of their energy. No fragments or leftover rounds. The Army mechanics had done a good job of it.

There was a long scrape on the shaft that drove the rear rotor, but it was utterly meaningless. No damage done beyond the cosmetic. Around sunrise she found a spot where bullet number thirty-two had taken the insulation off a wire for a weapons' system harness that no longer had any weapon to connect to. She replaced the wire anyway.

"You been here all night, Wrench?" She'd spotted Vern when he was halfway across the field from the bunkhouse, so his silent approach didn't alarm her this time. He came up to lean casually against the nose of the helicopter.

He wore an unzipped fleece jacket against the cool morning. The open front revealed a fire T-shirt from a blaze two years ago that had seen a few too many washings. The material was so thin that it took no great effort to imagine the man underneath. None! So she looked away and returned her attention to the last two bullet trajectories. That didn't stop her from thinking about how nice six feet and one inch of lean and casual pilot looked in the first light of day.

"Only for a few hours." When he asked what she'd figured out, she eyed him carefully. "Do you actually want to know, or are you merely being polite?"

His grin was easy. "Bit of both. I'm interested,

though I don't expect to understand a tenth of what you do. I'm a lowly pilot who breaks choppers, not some, you know, 'Goddess-Incarnate Mechanic'"—he put air quotes around the title—"who can actually fix them."

"I should get a bumper sticker."

"I'll get it for you. The polite part is terribly self-serving. If I show interest in what you're doing to my helicopter"—he let it drag out making it absolutely clear that he knew it was the first half of a really lame pickup line—"then you're just that much more likely to take really good care of my chopper. Anything that makes you take more care of the chopper is good for the preservation of my skin. I'm rather attached to my skin. I like having it intact."

She had to laugh. Okay, so he hadn't gone for the pickup line about him showing interest to make her like him more. Which actually did make her like him more. She'd bet that he knew that too, but found she didn't care.

He was an attentive student as she used the last two bullet holes to demonstrate what she'd been doing. She really did appreciate a pilot showing interest in what she did; so many of them didn't. The mechanic, male or female, blended into the background for most pilots.

Mickey and Gordon might not even have known she existed if she'd been a guy; though they were both such hounds that she'd have to be seriously "plain Jane" not to have them notice her being a woman. Bruce was no better. Vanessa was still so overwhelmed at being hired by MHA—to fill the MD500 that Vern had vacated when moving to the Firehawk—that a mechanic was still wholly invisible to her, male or female.

Mark Henderson treated everyone with equal respect, so equal that Denise felt invisible to him too. Emily and Jeannie certainly knew who took care of their birds, and she'd count both as friends, as much as she ever had friends.

But Vern saw her.

Really saw her, which was both uncomfortable and interesting. And both emotional responses were for the same reason: they evoked the question of "Why?"

She studied him without really looking at him as he held the last panel in place for her to screw back down. If she had an emergency and needed help, Vern was probably the one she'd call without thinking about how she might be imposing. That too was a revelation she wasn't expecting.

Everyone's life was a checklist. Like the inspection list on her Firehawk repair report, like her dad's tally of what chores were owed or skipped when she was a kid. Everything had been a balance sheet with Jasper. It was how life worked. Though with him, she'd always been on the losing side for reasons she still didn't understand. Some failure in her attempts to be a woman when she was actually just a mechanic.

Except Vern didn't work that way. He simply gave. She'd witnessed it a hundred times. Someone was moving and Vern was the first to volunteer to haul boxes. Someone was down sick? Vern would fill in no matter how nasty or dull the chore.

Even yesterday's flight. He'd flown at the back of the returning Firehawks' formation. She'd bet it wasn't because he was the newest. It was because he hadn't thought it was of any importance where he flew. Emily would always take the lead, part of being an ex-Army major, and Jeannie would always take Emily's wing position. Vern was fine with bringing up the rear.

A guy with no ego on the line, which ranked most unusual in her experience. Unusual? Totally unheard of.

She focused on anchoring the last of the screws to finish her inspection on bullet number thirty-four as Betsy's bell announced breakfast. Its peal heralded the sunrise and flushed the early-bird crows and jays abruptly into the morning sky.

Vern's hands remained steady and patient while she finished her work, even though they stood close enough that she could hear his stomach grumble when the vagaries of the morning air wafted the smells of bacon and coffee across the field.

"Coffee," he moaned quietly like a pitiful child, but he kept the piece of bodywork in place as she drove the last screws home, then double-checked that she hadn't missed any.

She finished, signed the bottom of the log on her tablet, then made her dad's hand sign for "okay to fly" as she did at the end of every repair.

"What was that?"

"What was what?" No one had ever noticed or asked about that. Vern was noticing everything about her. Jasper sure hadn't. By the end of their relationship, she'd been near enough invisible. Might have been pretty invisible at the start, now that she thought about it. It was as if even being around Vern was slowly shining a flashlight on quite how pitiful her relationship with Jasper had been. "It's a hand sign my dad made up."

"Do it again."

She wanted to refuse. It was their private sign, only her and Dad, but she did it again.

"Slower."

This time when she made the gesture, he copied it fairly accurately.

"What does it mean?"

"It means everything is okay. It comes from American Sign Language."

He leaned back against the just-repaired panel, crossed his arms, and made it clear he wasn't leaving until she explained. Irritating man.

"Fine. You know how to make an 'I love you' sign?"

"Sure. Everyone knows that." He held up his palm facing her with index finger and pinkie raised, the middle two fingers folded down, and his thumb to the side. Then he realized he was aiming it at her and jerked his hand down so quickly that he rapped his elbow sharply against the chopper and winced.

"If"—she spoke to cover her smile—"you turn that palm down and jab it forward twice, you have the sign for an airplane. Dad turned it sideways, thumb up. When he swings his hand to the side and up, it indicates an airplane repair is done and the plane is ready to fly."

Vern did the gesture that way. Then inspected his hand. "No. You did something different."

"Do you have to be so damned observant?"

He simply grinned down at her. "Mom's wanted me to be an artist. I was terrible, but I must have picked up something. Now give."

She sighed, seeing no way out other than telling him

to go jump. "Fine! I add the middle finger tight beside the index finger, which makes the letter *H* for helicopter. It says everything's okay in my 'happy helicopter land.' Ugh! Please tell me I didn't say that aloud."

"You did."

No condescension that she could detect, but a grin worthy of Dennis Quaid it was so big.

"Or are you telling your helicopter that you love it? They like that, you know. It makes them want to fluff their little rotors."

She shook her head to bring her hair forward and mask the heat rising to her cheeks. Denise could feel him grinning down at her. "So?" She knew she sounded like a petulant child.

"So," Vern drawled out easily, "you love your helicopters. That's a good thing."

A glance up at him showed that he wasn't teasing her, or not much. If he was, it was kindly. He understood. No one, not even her dad, had understood that about her.

Then Vern stood up and nodded toward the tables, which were rapidly filling up with people cramming down calories before the morning flights took off at thirty minutes after sunrise. As simple as that, he invited her to eat with him and they fell in together to head for the chow line.

She usually ate with her team and discussed upcoming maintenance or the latest FAA service bulletins. Or by herself.

She had a sudden urge that she couldn't explain to herself to make her "all okay in happy helicopter land" sign.

Vern knew he was being utterly ridiculous as he hovered over Brewer Reservoir east of Madras, Oregon. He was a dozen feet above the water, and the downwash of his Firehawk's rotors was tearing the water white with an outward-expanding wave of sparkling ripples. The hot midday sun that had baked the semiarid desert especially dry this season was also beautiful to watch as it lit the water. This was one of those moments that his mother would love to come and paint—that mixture of beauty and powerful change.

He lowered the Hawk's twenty feet of six-inch siphon hose into the water and hit the pumps. Forty seconds to take on a thousand gallons. And he was counting the gallons by the hundreds in a singsong voice that sounded silly even to him. MC Hammer had probably never in his life rapped about gallons of water loading into a helicopter. Good thing he was alone so that someone didn't lock him up for foolishness.

He often whistled or hummed while he flew. The beat of music lent itself well to the pulse and rhythm of flying. In the little MD500, he was more likely to whistle something quick and upbeat, maybe some of his mom's rock and roll. Music was her main career; he'd grown up sitting on his dad's knee watching her play at dances, in bars, and at small concert halls around the Northwest.

But the Firehawk called for something more serious and substantial, like Gregorian chants maybe. Except he didn't know any, and MCH didn't feel right, so he switched to Little Big Town because, damn, those women could sing even better than they looked. "Pontoon" was instantly stuck in his head in a way that he knew he'd be screwed for the next several hours, if not days.

He shut down the pumps and began winding in the siphon as he headed back to the fire—"on the pontoon." Crap!

At least he was getting the hang of doing two things at once. He could feel himself shaving precious seconds off the process with each pass. Yesterday Emily and Jeannie had outrun him by almost twenty percent for number of loads, and it had stumped him. Today he was running only about ten percent behind and he was starting to understand why. Yes, they were damned good, but so was he. What they had that he didn't was practice in doing *three* things at once in the Firehawk.

But there was more cheering him up than achieving a higher drop-per-hour tally than yesterday.

For one thing, he'd seen how Denise had fine-tooth combed his chopper and how personally she took the hose failure from yesterday. It gave him a confidence in the Firehawk that he'd lost at the failure. Actually, he felt safer now than he had before. The woman was meticulous to the point of being compulsive, something he really appreciated in his mechanic.

"Hey, Mark." He keyed the ICA frequency. "Where away?"

"We're sounding way too cheerful, aren't we?" Mark's voice was backed by a girlish giggle coming from his two-year-old daughter who often rode copilot in his command plane circling high and safe above the fire. "Remember, there is a wildland fire down there burning things." Mark tried to sound serious, but Tessa belied that with another giggle.

Vern leaned forward to look up through the wind-screen toward the ICA's Beech King Air circling high overhead. He caught a flash of sunlight reflecting off some part of it. "Just glad to be flying and beating down the flame. Can't that make a man happy?"

Mark snorted. "Drop on the inside of Emily's line. She's got the north end of it stopped for the moment; now I want you to kill it."

"Consider it dead, boss."

Okay, maybe he was feeling excessively cheerful. He spotted Emily's Firehawk pulling off the leading edge of the fire. Any question that it might be Jeannie was removed by the transponder code showing up on his radar sweep and the large "01" painted on the side of the chopper. He turned to head toward it.

Ten thousand acres of scrubland had been scorched black by the fast-moving fire. Yesterday had been mostly about steering the flames away from homes and farmland. Today was about killing it before it hit the fuel-rich rugged hills of the Ochoco National Forest.

Mark and Carly had decided that water and foam were needed at the moment rather than retardant. That decision was their job.

It was Vern's job to bring it, hard.

The flames had scorched most of the fuel out of the black. The fire looked like a fat, orange snake slid-ing sideways across the landscape: achingly dry dun-colored grass and brush to the left side, black sear to the right. The evil serpent spat a dark sheet of smoke aloft as it ate.

Vern approached over the black, away from the smoke. The black wasn't uniform. There were patches of green that the fire had left untouched and others that still burned orange where it had struck some fuel-rich pocket. Even as he spotted one, Vanessa—the newest MHA pilot—flew at it in Vern's old MD500. She doused the flare-up with two hundred gallons from the bright orange Bambi bucket that dangled on a long line below her bird and snuffed it out.

He double-checked. A good enough drop. If she'd hit it another dozen feet to the left, she'd have killed the whole thing. She'd learn. It took a lot of practice to nail a fire with a giant bucket swinging on a line a hundred feet below your chopper.

Vern returned his focus to the problem at hand and came down low, a mere hundred feet above the flames. Unlike a forest fire, scrubland didn't typically create massive and dangerous downdrafts, and despite how much it was eating, this fire hadn't done anything night-marish. So it was safe to come in reasonably low and really pound the fire. And his beautiful Firehawk had a belly tank rather than the bucket and line. Which meant he got to fight fire up close and personal.

Emily had soaked the leading edge of the fire, tempo-rarily freezing it in its tracks. He felt it, felt that moment for the first time in the Firehawk when he simply knew that he was dead-on over the heart of the flame. He triggered the dump doors on the belly tank and followed the smoke line, just enough upwind of the flame that his load of water and foam would land directly on the most active heart of the fire—and that his air conditioner wouldn't suck in lungfuls of smoke. The foam expanded the water's volume by a factor of ten and slapped the fire down hard.

"Nice," Mark offered.

Coming from a man who rarely gave compliments, that told Vern he was really getting the hang of the larger craft. If both of his hands weren't busy on the controls, he'd do a fist pump. Of course, with Mark, he might get another compliment six months from now if he was lucky.

"Now put some hustle on it this time."

So much for the honeymoon period. "Yes, sir!"

He managed not to giggle into the mic. Grown men didn't giggle, even if they were busy trashing a wildfire with a sweet twenty-million-dollar machine…and getting paid to do it. He turned for the reservoir to reload.

Of course breakfast this morning had given him some reason to at least chortle. It had been him and Denise and no one else. By chance in the ever-changing swirl of groups at MHA, there had only been the two of them at their table for a whole meal.

They'd talked of nothing much, mostly about the Firehawk, and he'd enjoyed every damn second. She was so… That's where words failed him. The woman with steel barricades hadn't been anywhere in sight. He had flown the machines she maintained for a year plus, and he'd never before met the woman behind those towering walls she kept raised against the world.

He really couldn't recall much of what she'd said; a lot of it had been awfully technical, and his coffee had been slow to kick in. But he'd enjoyed listening to her and had done his best to ask at least quasi-intelligent questions.

Vern bumped his cyclic side to side to rock the helicopter in a wave as he passed Jeannie returning fully loaded from the reservoir and headed back to the fire.

This time he remembered to lower the siphon over the shining water as he arrived so that it was fully extended by the time he hit his hover height. Another ten seconds shaved off each run. He popped on the pump switch and again sang the hundreds of gallons aboard.

———

Denise couldn't breathe right until she saw all seven of the choppers come back over the horizon in the late-afternoon light. No long trails of dark smoke like yesterday.

Oh-Three was at the tail end again; she could tell by how Vern flew. Emily Beale flew the straight-arrow course, not a single wasted motion. Jeannie's bird always wandered a bit across the sky, as if she were reaching out to feel every little air current with her rotors.

Vern must be rock 'n' roll beatboxing to get that odd bob and weave in his path. It was subtle; had he been flying alone she wouldn't have seen it. But with Emily's razor-edge straight flight for comparison, you could see his funky pulse of rhythm as he came in for a landing.

Beatboxing or an issue with the controls? She went to Firehawk Oh-Three the instant the wheels touched, before he had a chance to even shut down the engines.

"Everything okay?"

"Give a guy a break, Wrench. I'm not dumb enough to break your bird two days in a row. I don't have a death wish."

It wasn't until he was aloft this morning that she realized he'd barely said a word over breakfast. She'd babbled at him about the differences she could see in the three Firehawks. The Black Hawk might be a production machine—the most produced medium-lift helicopter other than the Russian Mil Mi-8—but Emily's bird was ten years older than the other two and improvements had been made. Denise had spent breakfast processing aloud which upgrades were sufficiently worthwhile improvements to implement on the older craft.

Dull as dust. That was her. If she ever wanted to impress a guy, she'd proven exactly how *not* to do it.

She'd learned early on never to talk about her work with Jasper. Whereas this morning over eggs and toast, Vern *had* kept after her with questions that forced her to clarify her own thinking on several points. The synergy between them had left both her mind and her body buzzing throughout the day.

"We beat the fire"—Vern stepped down—"which is a good thing."

"A very good thing." Denise hadn't ever noticed quite how tall he was.

He was six one to her five feet four, which meant the top of her head would just about tuck under his chin.

Dumb-as-a-thumb! She was so dull and dumb that it was a shock he was even speaking to her. She covered her own stupid thoughts by finding something to say. "It's a very good thing because you're probably going to be in it tomorrow."

"Really?"

She nodded downfield. It only took him a moment to notice that both of the DC-3 jump planes were gone.

"Where?"

"They jumped in Lolo National Forest about an hour ago."

"Ouch! Rugged Montana wilderness. Where are the Zulies?" Lolo was the Missoula Smokejumpers' home turf. They were considered the top team out there. Even the MHA jumpers gave the Zulies respect, at least in their less-arrogant moments.

"The entire team jumped California yesterday, the Hard Creek Fire."

"Double ouch for them!"

"Yeah, I know. That's already a really bad fire headed right into Pasadena. You know some of those homes up in the Wildland-Urban Interface are going to burn, and the firefighters are going to be blamed. It's a real no-win scenario. But we're off the hook for tonight because it's too late for our choppers to be on the move, especially after a full day on a fire."

"Well"—Vern patted the nose of Oh-Three—"at least I know we'll be ready. You were flawless."

Denise could feel herself wanting to smile at the compliment. Vern made it clear that he meant her, even if it was the helicopter he was anthropomorphizing.

"If we're headed into the boonies, we should enjoy civilization tonight. Want to get dinner in town?"

"Sure." Denise wasn't clear on which of them was more surprised, Vern that he had asked or herself that she'd accepted. "I"—*really need to cover my embarrassment*—"need to check over the choppers first. In an hour?"

Vern nodded too quickly. "I'll catch a shower. Take all the time you need."

Her team kicked through the full inspection of the

machines in under thirty minutes. Then she faced the question of whether or not to freshen up or dress up or…

She really didn't have any options. Unlike many of the MHA Hoodies, she'd gotten an apartment down near the base of the mountain. Vern lived on-site, sharing a bunkroom with Mickey.

Denise didn't even have a change of clothes in the car. She'd switched out her canvas work vest and tool belt for her leather vest. She'd managed to get several streaks of lube grease on her jeans. At least her T-shirt was clean, except for the small hole over her ribs where she snagged a sharp edge while crawling under Firehawk Oh-Two's belly tank to inspect the cargo hook. At least her vest should cover that. Mostly.

Well, she was already in over her head, so there was no help for it.

Vern was waiting at one of the picnic tables. He sat backward on the bench, leaning against the table, his legs stretching out forever to rest on the bench of the next table over. His short hair was still slick from his shower, curling a little as it dried. He was so lost in his book that he didn't even notice her until she shadowed the pages.

"What are you reading?"

—⁓—

Vern didn't have a clue what he was reading, so he turned the book cover to Denise in answer. He'd been surreptitiously watching her across the field—had purposely sat so that he would appear to be reading from behind his sunglasses but had a good field of view.

Despite the time he'd had to sit here, he still couldn't

figure out quite how he'd asked MHA's chief mechanic to dinner or what to do about it now that she'd said yes. Still, he'd enjoyed studying her while pretending to read.

He'd actually been irritated when people kept stopping to ask if he was coming down to the Doghouse for a drink. Bruce had completely blocked his view across the field and almost received a boot in the butt for it. Finally the others had cleared out or sacked out—tomorrow would be an early day.

The numbers had dwindled until it was Vern on one side of the field, Denise and her service crew on the other. There were still a few strays. He heard a couple voices behind him, people sitting at one of the other tables or headed out to the parking lot. He'd ignored them all and watched Denise work.

She inspected the three Firehawks and Mark Henderson's Beechcraft herself before checking in with her two assistants on the other four choppers. Moving no faster, she'd covered twice the ground Malcolm and Brenna had—on far more complex aircraft. And he'd wager that her inspection had been more thorough than theirs.

He'd noticed a pattern. She did each one exactly the same way, as if she'd found the most efficient path and then followed it precisely. He was half tempted to follow her around and see if she placed each foot in the same spot as she inspected successive aircraft.

Vern had maintained some idea of the book he was reading until she finished, set down that damn sexy tool belt that hung across her hips like a gunslinger's rig, and came stalking toward him across the field. She wore jeans and work boots, a tight, red T-shirt from last year's Grindstone Canyon Fire, and a worn leather vest, unclasped in the front and soft with age, that tantalized the eye as it swung open and closed.

Even now it swung open and revealed a tiny tear in the T-shirt over her lower ribs. It was just big enough to expose a fingertip-sized spot of skin. He was thankful when the vest flapped closed over the distraction.

The vision that was Denise Conroy had totally shorted out his brain. Though he wouldn't be mentioning that to the lady standing before him; she might pull out an electrical meter and a wrench and go rooting around for the cause of the cerebral malfunction. He already knew what that was.

When Denise walked, it was as forthright and efficient as everything she did, but her body belied her intent. He'd wager that she thought she was striding purposefully across the field to get from point A to point B.

Her hips knew better.

They belonged to a shapely woman as they swung slightly side to side and her hair billowed along after her, dancing and twisting in the wind like a smokejumper's crepe-paper streamer tossed out of a jump plane to test the air currents.

"Conrad?"

"Who?"

She pointed at his book. "You're reading Joseph Conrad."

He looked at the cover, Conrad's *Typhoon*. "It's Dad's fault. Don't blame me. I was trying to pick up my Catwoman comics and got Conrad by accident. The big letter *C* on the cover fooled me. I did think the plot was kind of heavy going. You see, Dad's a sailor, runs a small marina on Vashon Island in Washington.

He's a terrible influence." *And you're a babbling idiot, Vern Taylor.*

"Vashon?"

He couldn't read what was behind the question. Surprise? A smile? A joke? She didn't explain herself, but instead nodded toward the parking lot, asking if he was ready to go. Again, maximum efficiency of motion.

He rose to his feet, tucked the thin paperback in his back pocket, and ended up standing mere inches from her, as close as they'd been last night. So close he'd almost grabbed her and kissed the living daylights out of her, and damn the consequences.

Vern looked down into her face and was even more tempted to earn a hard slap. In the bright sunlight of the afternoon he could see what last night's darkness had hidden. Her eyes didn't merely give the impression of green, the almost colorless blue that some women called green. No.

Denise's eyes evoked the Coldplay song "Green Eyes" that his mom sometimes sang when she was in a mellow mood. Against Denise's tan and flawless complexion, her eyes really stood out, and they were inspecting him curiously.

"Ready when you are." He managed to sound normal, or at least not totally Neanderthal, and she led the way. Following behind her, he really was walking as if he'd stepped in a gopher hole.

And then it clicked. Yesterday she'd laughed thinking that he'd made a joke about her wishing he'd fall in a gopher hole. The reality was that he'd barely been able to stand up after remembering the loss of his friends to a shattered swash plate in a Coast Guard MH-65 Dolphin.

It only reinforced his guess that Denise didn't have a mean bone in her body. Which was a really distracting thought because she wielded one hell of a body.

She led the way to her Fiat Spider two-seater convertible sports car—one of the few cars besides his own Corvette left in the parking lot. There was a bunch of the smokejumpers' trucks, left here when they flew out. Everyone else had pretty much scattered for the evening.

Denise apparently just assumed that she was driving. That was probably a good thing since at this point his attention span was deeply involved in resisting the urge to reach out and stroke the shining mane of hair floating within easy reach.

The car's black paint was a perfect gloss. The red leather bucket seats were immaculate. He'd always appreciated the image of this woman in this convertible whenever he saw it, but he'd never really noticed the condition of the car itself. It was an absolute showpiece. Restored to new condition even though it must be forty years old.

He was tall enough that, with the top down, he could simply step over the door and slide down into the seat. The leather was as comfortable as it looked, once he moved the seat back. Even the wood paneling of the dash looked freshly oiled.

"This is beautiful!"

"Thanks. Her name is Irene." Denise pulled her hair over her shoulder as she sat down. With a dexterous flash of nimble fingers that held him mesmerized, she trapped her glorious mane in a thick French braid secured by a neon-red hair tie—like a danger warning sign at the end of a long load—before tossing the braid back over her shoulder. A pair of dark sunglasses soon hid her green eyes, and she fired off the engine. You didn't do something as mundane as "start" an engine like this one. It rumbled and roared to life.

"Irene? Like in 'Goodnight, Irene'?" Had he taken his life in his hands getting in this car?

Denise backed it out carefully over the gentle crunching of the heavy gravel in the parking lot.

"Irene as in Irene Adler." She shifted it into first gear, revved the engine, and popped the clutch. With a gravel-spewing, fishtailing jolt, they shot past his bronze-colored Corvette convertible that glowered with jealousy at being left behind. The Fiat launched out of the parking lot and onto the narrow two-lane that wound down the mountain.

"Crap!" was all he managed as the car carved the turns, gripping the road at least as well as his Vette. He managed to relax his desperate grip on the wood-and-leather dashboard because hanging on made him look decidedly feeble and not the least bit calm, cool macho. Though he was sufficiently wise to retain his tight hold on the inside door handle.

She slammed into third and laid into another corner, then did a double-clutch downshift to rocket up a short but steep grade in second.

"Why her?" The one woman ever to outsmart Sherlock Holmes.

"Because Irene is tricky, but when she's running clean, I'll bet that even your fancy Vette can't catch her, any more than Holmes could."

Of course she'd know what car he drove. One, it

was one of the hottest cars in the lot. Two, she was a mechanic through and through and probably knew the cars better than their owners.

And he'd bet that while his Corvette probably could catch her—it had like a jillion times more power and road traction than this little Italian dream—he'd never be able to keep up with this car if Denise was at the wheel.

He glanced over at her. Her left hand, fine-fingered and delicate looking, handled the leather-wrapped steering wheel like a chopper's cyclic, twisting them easily down the winding road. Her right hand worked the five-speed stick with an effortless confidence to edge the most out of every curve and straightaway.

Vern cruised in his Corvette with its automatic transmission; Denise flew.

Stray strands of hair had escaped the quick braid and danced about her head, catching the sun like a halo. This was a side of her that he'd never imagined. She was always so quiet and unpresuming, caring only about her helicopters and nothing else, never revealing an emotion. At MHA, Denise seemed the sort of woman to drive a Toyota because of safety, probably a Prius for mileage or a Camry—a staid and careful choice.

Instead she'd transformed into the sexy babe in a high-powered Italian sports car. And the more she drove it, as much as he hated to admit it, the more he saw that she was a better driver than he was. He'd have to get her up in the Firehawk someday. Then he'd show her a thing or two. Of course, if she kicked his ass when they were aloft as well, he'd have to turn in his manly club membership card, so maybe better not to risk it.

The warm wind, rushing so furiously by, made it

hard to talk. That, and she'd plugged her phone into a wire snaked under the edge of the dash. Florence and the Machine's "Howl" was, well, howling out of the car's speakers. Denise had definitely done some serious work to the sound system while she was making the car so perfect.

Any illusions he'd had about the town of Hood River being a half-hour drive from MHA's Hoodie One base camp were completely blown apart.

They tore past the orchards thick with apples, pears, and late peaches.

They flew past vines lush with grapes and wineries thick with tourists.

Traffic wasn't a nuisance, despite the road being just two lanes; it was a challenge. She slalomed better than Lindsey Vonn medaling in the Winter Olympics. And looked better too, which was saying a lot, 'cause Vonn was model hot and world-class-athlete fit. His libido briefly wondered if Denise also shared Vonn's habit of modeling skimpy bikinis in snowy settings. He told it to shut up and go away, he was busy at the moment— hoping he'd survive the car trip into town.

In twenty minutes flat, they rolled into town despite the heavy fall traffic along the route. She hadn't achieved it by speeding, well, not any more than he would, but rather by not wasting a single second during the entire passage.

She parked with the same efficiency and speed that she drove. Had there been two fewer inches, they wouldn't have fit. She nailed the parallel parking on her first try without hesitation. That was just creepy; nobody did that.

By the time Vern was able to release his stranglehold on the door handle and climb out of the car, Denise had transformed back. No race-car-skilled driver in evidence, no rock and roll; she was once again the quiet woman he'd thought he knew at least a little.

He rested a hand against the slender trunk of a handy maple tree to make sure that the world had slowed down enough to be grasped by normal human perceptions. The people on the busy sidewalk moved at a rational pace as well. And the sidewalk pretty much stayed in place. His world had returned to normal speed.

"That was"—he searched for an appropriate word— "unexpectedly intense. Have you been a member of NASCAR for long?"

She aimed a smile at him that definitely weakened his knees. The smile was as beautiful as the woman. "I do like to drive."

"No," he corrected her as she circled to him and they joined the people walking farther into town. "I like to drive. That was a whole other thing again. It wasn't racing. I need a new word for it. I'll have to work on it."

"It's sort of my alone time. I didn't mean to be rude, if I was. Was I?" She looked worried and hurried along before he could respond. "Behind the wheel is when it's just me, the machine, and the road. I get kind of—"

"Not rude." Vern got the words in edgewise and stopped her rolling apology. "Miraculous" was more what came to mind. One of the camp rumors was that Denise was as cold as the steel machines she maintained. So not! "You were…passionate." That was the word he hadn't found a moment earlier. He liked to drive, but she was passionate about it. And that peek into Denise

Conroy was as surprising as going to work one day to fly his MD500 and finding out he was the next MHA Firehawk pilot. Bruce and Mickey had shrugged off that he'd been the one Emily chose to promote, but he knew there was still envy behind their sincere congratulations. It had been a huge step.

"No, I just like to drive."

Vern desperately needed to cover what he'd said, because it evoked other images of how "passionate" might look on Denise Conroy that were wholly inappropriate, especially as she had a boyfriend. "Well, if you ever want to discover what driving is really about, I'll let you try my Vette."

"Feh!"

"Feh? You actually said 'feh' about my Corvette? It's a 2006 Z06 convertible with five hundred and five horsepower. Have you ever driven one?" They turned a corner toward the restaurant and were nearly run over by a family of five, each toting a major sugar-rush worth of ice cream cones. He considered offering his arm to escort her. Then he considered that he'd completely lost his mind.

"No, but—"

"Nope." He cut her off. "Not another word until you've tried it."

She nodded. "Fair enough." Then she flashed that radiant smile at him. "Of course that means that you'll have to drive Irene as well. That way we can both be impartial. And you'll see what driving is really about."

"Deal." They shook on it.

He'd expected her hand to feel small and dainty. Instead it felt strong and warm. It was the first time they'd touched in a year and a half of knowing each other. He liked discovering that she was strong in addition to being powerful. Even for that brief moment of contact he liked how her hand felt in his. He decided maybe it really was okay if he disliked Jasper, if only for being with Denise.

She'd parked on the edge of the town, which wasn't saying much. The heart of Hood River was perhaps six blocks square of tree-lined streets and low buildings. For whatever reasons the town had begun, it really only had three reasons for existing now.

It drew massive numbers of tourists to the best windsurfing in the world on the Columbia River Gorge, which meant there'd be no parking in the core, not even for the short Spider. Second, from the town up to the base of Mount Hood itself was some of the best fruit-growing country around in a state known for its orchards and wine. And third was the high-tech factory that made small surveillance drones like the one MHA used for observing fires.

They strolled side by side past busy tourist kitsch shops and crowded bars. It was early evening and people were spilling out onto the sidewalks sipping beers while waiting for a table.

Of course, being MHA Hoodies, there was no question where they were going.

The Doghouse Inn was a decrepit, old brick building that was going to be the first thing to collapse if the big earthquake ever hit—or even a small one. The harsh winds and alternating drenching by the Pacific Northwest rains and baking hot sun of eastern Oregon had aged the exterior until one could imagine that it was held together only by the dried glue of stale beer and old nicotine that must be on the inside. Even the sign was disreputable and a third of the neon was out.

When asked why the outside was such a disaster, the owners claimed they hated tourists—though they took outsiders' credit cards with a minimum of disdain. But word of mouth packed the place regularly despite the bar's crusty exterior.

Those who braved the dark entryway entered *the* prime pub in town. It was brightly lit, with an old wooden floor and solid tables and chairs. The windows were so few that there was little impression of the outside world, which only made the inside all the more friendly and welcoming. This was a place that neither the patron nor the proprietor wanted to leave quickly.

The first thing that hit in the cheerfully appointed room was the noise. No wall of heavy rock and roll. No brain-piercing country wails. The playlist was modern, soft, and easily ignored. What hit you was the sound of laughter and happy conversation.

Right behind that was the smells of Gerald's awesome little kitchen in the far corner. The man was like an eighteen-star chef in the world of burgers. He might do only one thing, but he did it so well that you never tired of it. Vern's mouth watered over more than the delectable woman at his side.

If you were a real regular, the third thing that hit you was Amy, the spunky and totally hot redhead who ran the bar. She was busy with a big order so all Vern got this time was a hasty wave, instead of a small-tornado-style hug. Denise received an assessing glance that Vern really hoped she'd missed.

Gerald, who was also Amy's husband—and massive enough that even a lunatic didn't mess with his wife— shot a wave.

The highly polished oak bar ran down one side of the room, boasting enough regional microbrews to satisfy even the most dedicated beer taster. The floor was packed with cozily close tables so that conversations crossed from one table to the next as easily as to the person seated beside you.

Despite all of that, the walls and ceiling were the best and definitely the most unique feature of the pub. Every surface was covered with overlapping postcards, ads, and photographs from around the world of dogs in their doghouses. Miniature show-dog poodles perched in pink pagodas, a bulldog in his boxing-ring-styled bed, a team of racing huskies with their heads peeking out of the rows of small doors on their whole-team dog-box truck—complete with a sled on top and icicles hanging from the truck's bumper.

"Hey, let's grab that one." Vern moved quickly to the prize table right as it was vacated. It was a table for two under the big drawing of Snoopy atop his doghouse and wearing his full "Curse you, Red Baron!" World War I fighter ace getup. Rumor had it Charles Schulz himself had drawn it years before, but there was no signature, so Vern kind of doubted it. Of course it would be high treason to express such an opinion in the Doghouse. So rather than risking a long walk off a short plank, he sat down and waved hello to Rikki, the waitress, as she worked another table.

It was only as Denise was sitting down that he realized what he'd done.

Mickey and Bruce had landed with a couple of the ground support guys at the big central table that MHA always grabbed when it could. It was made for six, but they often crammed eight or ten around it, with beer and conversation flowing freely. It also put the primarily male MHA crew within easy firing range of any cute windsurfer babes at a large number of neighboring tables. And when the smokejumpers were on the ground, it got even wilder.

Mickey gave Vern a look of flat-out, wide-eyed astonishment.

Vern shrugged a "What?" For not sitting with them?

Mickey tipped his head sharply toward Denise, then mouthed, "WTF?"

Jeannie wandered in with Cal and dropped down at the central table. Jeannie offered Vern a smile and a nod of approval.

Unsure which he found more irritating, Mickey's disbelief or Jeannie's easy certainty, Vern turned away. He'd have to go with Mickey because he too had no idea what Denise was doing here with him, and he really didn't need his bunkmate echoing the sentiment.

But isolating her? Was that fair?

"I should have asked." Vern faced Denise. "Are you okay with being here rather than...?" He tipped his head to indicate the central table without turning to see whether all of the guys were now eyeing him oddly.

In a momentary lull that sometimes swept across a crowded room, he heard Bruce asking, "What's he doing with Stainless-Steel Conroy?"

It was one of her many nicknames, and Vern did his best to make a throat-clearing noise so that she wouldn't hear Bruce.

"I'm not that good in groups." Denise looked down, hiding those green eyes as she inspected the tabletop. Maybe she had heard. He was going to need to beat the crap out of Bruce.

"Then we're good here?" Vern had spent far too much of his youth in bars or backstage at Mom's bigger concerts to care much about who he ran into and how big the group was. But he rather liked having Denise to himself.

She nodded without looking up.

———

Denise *was* good here. Sitting alone with Vern below Snoopy's protective gunfire. Before Jasper, she'd sometimes come along with the MHA groups that hit the Doghouse. It was expected, though it wasn't something she'd really choose to do on her own. But once here, she'd always liked the feeling of belonging in a group, even if she didn't really.

There were always whisperings like Bruce's. "Stainless-Steel Conroy" was actually among the nicer things said about her. Better than stuck-up, frigid, dyke, and a dozen others that had been aimed her way before she'd joined MHA. At least here they always gave her respect. They appreciated the mechanic enough not to disparage the woman, even if they wholly discounted her. The "stainless-steel" epithet was as bad as it ever got around MHA.

Well, she didn't exactly radiate womanly virtues, so that reaction didn't surprise her much. Though it didn't make the memory of the old ones hurt any less.

During the Jasper era, they'd only come here the

one time. The Hoodies hadn't taken to him, nor he to them. Which in retrospect probably should have told her something. He didn't understand a comfortable bar filled with good people. He was a rich-kid windsurfer with a torn knee turned successful windsurf shop owner, turned aspiring yuppie with a BMW and an attitude. She'd been too polite to leave him until the relationship really did completely die and neither of them could even remember why they'd gotten together in the first place.

But sitting here, in the group but separate, with only Vern to deal with, was pretty close to ideal. The general hum of conversation and shouted greetings actually made their table quite private, like a sound isolation booth afloat on the cheerfully noisy sea that was the Doghouse's atmosphere. Now she would be included without being crowded. Rikki dropped off a couple of menus and took their beer orders.

The best parts of the Doghouse were the smells and the laughter. This wasn't a bar that you came to so that you could get drunk or have a fight. It was a place where friends laughed over mountains of nachos, potato skins, and burgers. It was a place for tasty craft beer and good company.

Denise needed a conversation starter. Vern was feeling awkward about something. Maybe her driving or the way that she'd tried to apologize or… She could feel herself spinning into her "stupid" place; going all mental was something she was far too good at.

"Vashon?" She leaped at the lifeline. He'd mentioned something about his dad on Vashon Island and it seemed a good place to start.

"An island in Puget Sound a couple hours north of here. Born and bred." Vern latched on to the topic as well. He sounded easy and casual with that lazy drawl of his, but she could see the relief as plain on his face as it must be on hers. "Dad runs the marina, in a place called Quartermaster Harbor. Mom was a rock-and-roller, retired about ten years back except for the occasional local island stuff. She picked up painting, decided maybe that the reason she kept giving me art supplies as a kid was that she was the one who wanted them. I think she's even sold a couple at the island gallery—under a pen name. She's really done with the whole tour and fan thing. Maybe you've heard of Margi Taylor?"

Margi Taylor! She pulled out her phone and scrolled down her playlist before turning it to him. Four albums on her playlist. Both the music and the lyrics were intelligent. And it wasn't merely good rock; they counterpointed each other until neither element could stand alone. As neatly as her Fiat's synchromesh.

"Okay, that's kinda embarrassing. I guess you have." He didn't look embarrassed. He looked amused. "Mom…" He had to raise his voice to be heard over a loud delivery of plates nearby. "Mom seems to be my calling card. I'm twenty-eight, and I never seem to introduce myself unless I introduce my mom as well. You'd think I'd have outgrown that by now."

She stuffed the phone away. "Sorry, I didn't mean to—"

"She's like that. A cool mom who takes up a lot of space." Then he narrowed his eyes at her.

She wanted a mirror to check there wasn't helicopter grease on her face or something. She glanced up, but

Snoopy was fighting other battles off in the distance over her head.

"You apologize a lot. Why—" Vern looked up at Rikki's return and ordered something with the word "hamburger" in it.

Did she? She suspected that she did. It felt as if she was always apologizing for something. During her long year with Jasper, their relationship had been nothing but one unending apology. And it had been entirely on her part. Not his…ever. What was—

"Denise?" Vern and the waitress were looking at her.

She hadn't even looked at the menu yet, so she held up two fingers.

They both looked at her as if she'd lost her mind.

"The double teriyaki burger is about as big as your head. You that hungry?"

Denise held up one finger and tried not to be embarrassed when the waitress nodded and departed. Before she came here again, she'd memorize the menu; it was bound to be online.

A quick glance around the restaurant showed that the portions here were firefighter huge. The MHA table was practically mounded with onion rings, nachos, beer, and burgers. The table was packed solid with fliers now, and she was so glad she wasn't crammed in there. Brenna was right in the center of the mayhem. Denise suppressed a shudder; she was so glad to be at a table for two.

Jeannie looked completely at ease in the madness, even sent a friendly smile Denise's way which she did her best to return.

Mickey and Bruce were working a table of obvious

windsurfer tourists. The fact that it appeared to be three couples already didn't even have them hesitating. The guys were utterly shameless. Well, she didn't spot any wedding rings on the women, but still.

"I'm glad you like Mom's music." Vern's voice drew her attention back to the table. "She's great. 'Course I grew up listening to her play."

"Do you?" She was so glad he'd dropped the earlier question because she was starting to suspect that she really wouldn't like the answers once she found them.

"Do I play?" He shuddered. "Mom tried to teach me. She gave up after like the fifth instrument. Claimed I was on the verge of giving her ears a coronary. Do you know her cut 'Bad Man-Music'?"

She did. It was funny. Gentle and kind, but definitely making fun of a bad musician.

He tapped the center of his chest and made a small bow. "I did play backup guitar in the studio version. A sad attempt to redeem myself that is only tolerable because I think they unplugged my cable."

Denise felt her laugh bubble forth and covered her mouth with a hand, but that didn't stop it. Not really.

"Yeah." He grimaced. "Totally pathetic attempt. After that I was thinking I could maybe grow up to be a shepherd or something and never have to show my face in public again. Dad tried to make me into a boat mechanic. I liked to sail, but I can't do the kind of things you can. Machines despise me in almost every way you can imagine except when I'm flying them. Where did you learn that anyway? You're like freaking hippo-in-a-purple-haze good."

"I'm what?" Of the many things she'd been called behind her back, that wasn't one of them.

"It's from an old *Bloom County* cartoon. The guy who drew it lived on our island for some time. You've got a rep that goes right up to my neck of the woods."

"All the way to Vashon?" It was a good joke, even if she could feel her cheeks heating up. She was never good at jokes, and she was bound to ruin this one. But it seemed good.

"Actually, yes. Old Yuri McKinnon, a crazy old coot with a Russian mom and a Scottish dad, mentioned this wizard female chopper mechanic. I'm guessing that's you. Not a lot of female wrenches in the helicopter business."

"Flies a military 1953 Bell 47G-2A that never saw action in Korea." She made it a flat statement. She'd worked on Yuri's rotorcraft several times.

"Flew. And how the hell did you know that?" His voice had gone cold and angry. No. Sad.

"I'm sorry. I didn't know." She'd definitely screwed up the joke. And Yuri had been such a sweet old man. The world was a dimmer place for his gentle teasing now to be nothing more than a memory.

Vern took a slug of his beer and looked around the room for a moment.

She saw him take a deep breath, searching for equilibrium of some sort, and felt sorry she'd said anything. Maybe if she stopped speaking. She wished their food would come so that she'd have something to do.

"You knew Yuri?" His voice was steadier.

She nodded without looking up.

"How?"

"He'd bring his Bell over to Boeing Field when I

was still working there. That's where I got my A and
P—airframe and power plant certification."

When he didn't speak, she glanced up out of the
corner of one eye. He didn't look upset. As a matter of
fact he looked amused.

"What?" She couldn't imagine what might be funny
about this conversation.

"Yuri is the one who taught me to fly."

Now, too late to save her earlier embarrassment,
Rikki delivered their burgers, offering Vern a smile that
spoke of a past. Well, apparently he'd left her happy,
whatever had happened. She was nice enough to offer
Denise a friendly nod that just might be interpreted as
"Well done getting him; he's a good one."

A moment later, she had whisked off and Denise
looked down at the plates. There was no way on this
planet she could have finished the monstrous meal that
had landed in front of Vern. Even without the double
sizing of her own order, she'd be taking at least half of
her own burger home.

"And"—Vern nipped a french fry between his teeth,
having apparently missed the whole exchange—"Yuri
always told me there was this AME I really had to meet.
Like I'd be interested in meeting a stodgy, old aircraft
maintenance engineer who would discover in the first
thirty seconds that I couldn't even change a car tire, much
less fix a bird. He never let up on it. I'm guessing the
old bastard meant you, but he never let on. Well, doesn't
that beat all. You're a Seattle local, and I didn't know."

"Closer than that. Fauntleroy." It was the neighbor-
hood where the Vashon-to-Seattle ferry landed, old
houses and towering trees, mostly maple and oak. And it

was funny how small the world was. "You know that big oak, kind of across from Thistle Street in Lincoln Park?"

He nodded, looking more than a little dumbfounded. The traffic off the ferry ran right along one side of Lincoln Park.

"I spent a lot of time up in that tree with a book. We lived about two blocks from there. No view of Puget Sound, so it was affordable, I guess, but right near the park which was all I cared about." She'd probably watched him drive by at some time or other.

"That's…wow. You're not making all of this up?"

She didn't bother to answer. Yuri had loved teasing her about taking her home. At first she'd assumed it was the harmless flirting of an old man. But it wasn't, and now it made sense. A crazy kind of sense, but it fit together nonetheless. He'd wanted her to meet…Vern.

"Well"—Vern rubbed one of those large hands over his face as if trying to manually change his expression— "if you ever want to fly in it, he left the old Bell 47 to me."

It was horrid that Yuri was gone, but that his old helicopter had ended up with Vern was wonderful. It was such an immaculate old machine that it would be a pity if it went to a lesser place. She felt a little better about Yuri being gone. "You said he's the one who taught you to fly?"

Vern nodded. "Taught me to *love* to fly. Did six years aloft in the Coast Guard because of him." Then he bit into his burger and chewed before mumbling around his food. "Of course if you want to fly in it, you'll have to fix it up first. I can't do a thing with it."

The laugh burst out of her yet again. She couldn't

help it. How could a man who flew as…flew as…beautifully as Vern Taylor did, not know how to maintain something as simple and reliable as a Bell 47?

─∿∿─

Vern cursed as Denise laughed at him in her Spider later that night. Clearly it was becoming a thing with her. The laugh would start small and bright, often masked behind a covering hand. Then it built until it sparkled in the air. And each time it was because he was being a complete idiot.

"I know how to drive a goddamn stick shift," he growled. "Irene hates me. You're right. She's a tricky woman." He wanted to blame it on being drunk, but he'd had only one beer over the two wonderful hours spent with Denise Conroy telling dumb-things-I-did-as-a-kid stories. He wanted to blame it on the drugged feeling coursing through his nervous system just from being near her. Maybe he could blame it on the weather. Nope. Nothing above but stars on a warm, cloudless night.

Without an excuse of any kind, he was sitting out here on the streets of Hood River and totally humiliating himself by stalling her car three separate times in the first two blocks. If Bruce and Mickey caught him doing that, he'd receive a Bambi-bucket sized load of shit for it.

"Irene is a 1973 Spider," Denise said as if that was somehow helpful.

"Which means what?" He tried not to snarl as he restarted the engine. With a silent plea, he begged Irene to please stop embarrassing him in front of such an attractive woman. This time he made it a block, then he foolishly tried for second gear and almost ate the windshield as the stall flailed him forward. "Switch," he ordered as he set the brake and climbed out.

"The 1973," Denise explained as they passed each other in front of the car, the flash of headlights shining bright against their legs and reflecting enough light upward for him to see her green eyes and far-too-amused smile, "has a hardware linkage for a throttle rather than a wire. One end is mounted on the frame and the other end on the engine. When you accelerate, that torques the engine and the engine twists slightly on its mounts, lengthening the throttle linkage. That in turn slows the engine, which detorques it, shortening the linkage, and it accelerates again without you touching the pedal. It takes a practiced touch to get a smooth start. You shouldn't feel bad."

"No. Why would I feel bad?" Just because he hadn't been able to drive a beautiful woman's car that she drove like a racing dream.

Just because she'd left him feeling like a panting schoolboy the entire evening, neither one mentioning Jasper. What was up with that anyway? She wasn't flirting with him. Denise Conroy did not flirt. But she's been as friendly as if she'd never earned a reputation for possessing battlements of steel.

Then she proceeded to make him look like a complete idiot by making the car launch in a perfectly smooth leap from a complete standstill to racing back up the mountain road.

He slid down lower in his seat and mumbled below the volume of the engine's roar, "Irene hates me."

Denise's laugh was whipped away as she slammed up into third and they shot out of town.

Chapter 3

FOUR A.M.

Vern, Jeannie, and Emily huddled around Mark with to-go cups of coffee clutched in their hands. Vern was actually on his second cup, but it wasn't enough. He didn't know what was wrong with him this morning. Between the years as a Coastie and now MHA, he knew to anticipate chaos in his sleep schedule. So that wasn't it.

The dark night air had a damp chill to it. Fall was definitely coming; the weather felt as if it had arrived last night. Hadn't he been riding in an open-top sports car with a beautiful woman about six hours ago? Now he'd have the top up and the heater on high. Though he'd still be sure to put her at the wheel. Irene hated him.

Of course, he totally despised Jasper now. The one time Vern mentioned him, Denise had looked so sad, as if some of the light had gone out in her. He'd done his best to steer the conversation anywhere but there throughout the evening. And it had been absolutely great. It killed him that she was involved with someone else.

The stars were out above. A few lights were on in the compound. Actually, that should cheer him up. When the Firehawks went aloft in a few minutes, they'd wake the entire camp. He'd make sure to pass directly over his and Mickey's room on his flight out. That way, if he wasn't getting sleep, at least Mickey wouldn't be either.

They stood midfield, staying out of the way of the

ground crews loading the choppers. The smokies had sent back requests for additional gear and Chutes, the paracargo loadmaster, was getting it aboard.

The three of them were certified for night flight, so they were timing their departure for arrival at the fire just after sunrise. Vern wasn't certified for night drops from the Firehawk yet, but that wouldn't matter; it would be daylight by the time they arrived.

Mark was giving them the rundown. "Emily, you've got Carly and Steve as usual. You'll under-sling the drone's launch trailer so that we can set it up in Montana. We're not expecting anything unusual, but, Steve, you should grab the second bird anyway."

The MHA Unmanned Aerial Vehicle, the UAV that everyone except Steve called a drone, had proven to be a fantastic tool for tracking hotshot teams on the ground and seeing fire conditions in places they didn't dare send a manned aircraft. They were pretty much the only outfit that the FAA allowed to fly drones.

When Mark's words registered, Vern looked up from staring at his coffee cup and begging the caffeine to kick in sooner rather than later. "Nothing 'unusual'? What second bird?" The other two pilots had nodded curtly, once.

Mark ignored him.

Fine, whatever. A normal fire, though it was an odd way to say it. But it wasn't. The second bird meant something to everyone except him. Like Honduras. Mark and Emily hadn't reacted right if it were a vacation spot. But they weren't browsing a folder. They were studying it. He was about to ask a question, but something in Mark's look told him it wouldn't be welcome.

"Jeannie," Mark continued as if Vern didn't exist, "Cal is with you."

Cal was the ex-hotshot MHA wildfire photographer, media specialist, Jeannie's newfound husband, and an all-around decent guy. Too many of those here for Vern's taste. It made Vern want to be foulmouthed and crappy.

Damn Jasper! Vern had never considered trying to take a woman away from another guy. Even Mickey and Bruce's antics last night were outside his normal operating procedures. He'd always waited for the ones who were obviously looking and made a really clear offer. The formula had worked wonderfully over the years.

But Denise had slipped into his bloodstream through some doorway he knew nothing about. Even the memory of her reluctant but merry laugh made him feel better. Then worse because it couldn't be for him. God, he was such a damned mess.

What was it with MHA and couples anyway? It was like the Firehawk helicopters themselves went around making people marry each other right and left.

Steve—in addition to being the drone guy—was a cocky-as-hell former smokejumper who'd snared model-gorgeous Carly. Mark and Emily had been happily married back in their military days. Now Jeannie and Cal.

The morning air was thick with the reek of contented matrimonial harmony. He would be perfectly content with a cheerful cohabitation, but that was his outer limit.

"Chutes," Mark continued to Jeannie as if the presence of Vern's morning mood wasn't polluting the atmosphere as badly as a wildfire, "is loading your bird to capacity with gear and food for the smokies. They're promising a clear helispot by the time you arrive. You'll stop off on your way to Missoula to unload.

"Vern, you've got Denise, and you'll under-sling her service container. So, you two will fly direct to the Missoula airport along with Emily before you hit the fire. It's a ten-hour drive, and I want Denise on-site faster than that. When the other choppers follow after first light, they can bring the other two mechanics. We clear?"

Okay, Vern was feeling less morose now. The morning—despite the obscene hour—had taken a sudden turn for the better. A three-hour flight with Denise Conroy sounded great. Even if she was someone else's, at least he'd get to spend the time with her. Then he thought about it again. For three solid hours she'd see every single technique he didn't do perfectly in his flight.

Dismissed, he headed over and started the preflight on his chopper, wondering if he'd regret a third cup of coffee before a three-hour flight. There were no rest stops along the way.

He decided against the coffee, figuring he'd find enough other ways to embarrass himself during the flight as it was.

—⁓—

"I haven't made a night transit before." Denise leaned forward as if to look out the window.

"Stay inside your helmet," Vern told her.

That was the problem. Her eyes didn't want to. They'd been aloft about fifteen seconds. Vern had climbed to hover five feet over her shop-box. It was a twenty-foot steel cargo container sitting on a flatbed truck. Inside the container was MHA's mobile service shop. With the tools and spares she had stocked inside, she could service almost anything on any MHA aircraft.

Malcolm then climbed atop the van and slapped the head loop of the steel long-line into the cargo hook on the bottom of the Firehawk. The cargo-hook indicator light went on briefly, indicating the hook was down and open. Then the light blinked out again as the jaw closed over the wire loop.

Once Malcolm was clear, Vern hit the arming switch on the emergency load-hook release. Then he went straight up, hesitated at the moment the line came under tension at a hundred feet up, then continued aloft in a clean motion lifting the three-ton steel container off the back of the truck so gently that a stray screw might well remain in place on the workbench inside the shop-box.

And just that fast, they were in darkness. She leaned her head into the rounded window built into the door. The laminated glass bulged out far enough that she could lean into it and see straight down past the structure of the helicopter. She shifted until her helmet bumped the window and got only the briefest glimpse of the lit MHA airfield as it disappeared astern.

After that, there was no real sense of motion without the visual aids of the helmet display. She knew in her brain that the helicopter was now tipped nose down as it raced toward the Montana fire. She could see the read-out on the inside of her visor that showed they'd rapidly climbed until they were moving at 150 knots.

"This feels wrong."

"It does, doesn't it?" Vern was absolutely calm.

She'd never flown with him before, not in the MD500 and not the Firehawk. She felt absolutely safe…and had nothing to base that feeling on. When she flew with Emily, she felt secure enough, but with Vern she didn't feel any underlying tension that something she'd overlooked might break. Somehow Vern calmed the part of her brain that worried for a living.

The helmet projected information onto the inside of her visor, but most of it was meaningless. She knew enough to understand the helmet was working properly. But more than half of the information conveyed nothing to her. Attitude to the horizon, air speed, heading—those were obvious. The navigation codes, not so much. She was a Visual-Flight-Rules pilot. Under her VFR license, she could bop around an airfield to make sure everything was working properly, but she did little more.

She reached out and tentatively tapped the Heads-Up Display toggle switch on the front of the cyclic, doing her best not to jar the joystick control. A vast array of engine information flashed across the visor. At least this she understood. Everything looked well within operational ranges including a solid green "HUMS" in the corner of her display. The chopper's health management system wasn't seeing any problems either.

Another tap of the HUD button and the world jumped into sharp relief, forcing her to gasp in surprise. A thousand shades of green painted the landscape roaring by below them. She could see the terrain's shape as ridges rose to greet them, then were left below and behind.

Her vision was narrow, limited to thirty degrees ahead, which made her feel as if she were roaring down a tunnel at ten times normal speed.

"Found it, did you?" Vern chuckled. "Turn your head side to side, or it gets nauseating."

She did and was able to see in any direction she looked. Always the same width, but a sweeping view. It was as if she had her hands cupped to either side of her eyes.

But she could see…right through the console as if it weren't there.

As if her legs, her seat, even the floor weren't there.

She was sitting in the air with nothing holding her up.

As if she was going to fall and fall and never land until—

"Look back up!" Vern order was sharp and she did.

The world slowly made sense again. Though her heart still pounded.

"It takes some practice. The cameras are on the out-side of the bird, so they don't see the dashboard or the hull and it feels—"

"Incredibly scary."

"Right. Like last night when you were driving back up the mountain."

God, but he made her laugh.

―⁓―

Vern wanted to take Denise's laugh and wrap it around himself. He wanted to wrap himself around Denise. He wanted…

No! What he *needed* was a distraction.

"You know"—which had to about the lamest conversation opener ever discovered by man—"there's something weird going on."

"You mean other than the two of us flying across three states in the middle of the night?"

He really liked the way "the two of us" sounded. "Yeah, even stranger than that." Vern double-checked their course off the Columbia Gorge VOR radio beacon. It matched his GPS position neatly. "Do you know anything about Steve having a second kind of drone? I thought he just flew the same thing every time."

"Maybe." She didn't sound very sure about it.

"Maybe?"

"I'm thinking."

Vern kept his mouth shut. Using the infrared image projected on the inside of his helmet, he looked down toward his belly. Locators inside the cockpit noticed the movement of his helmet's position. Outside, on the nose of the chopper, the infrared camera shifted to look down and a little back to offer the view below.

Denise's shop-box was visible. It hung smoothly at the end of the long-line, dragging through the air a hundred feet down and twenty back. All looked good. He looked forward again.

"Last year…" Denise began. "You remember the New Tillamook Burn?"

"Not really. It was only three weeks of hell to kill the worst Oregon wildfire in half a century."

"Sorry." She went all meek.

"Denise, stop apologizing. I was teasing. I know about it because you kept my chopper in the sky for three straight weeks without a single fault when everything else in the world was going wrong."

"Sorr—that's a hard rule to follow."

He could hear the lightness return to her voice. What in the world was in her past to make her apologize for everything? And just how completely was that none of his goddamn business?

"Do you—" She cut herself off and started again. "You remember that Jeannie's chopper went down after a tree exploded and took out her rear rotor?"

Back then Jeannie had been an MD500 pilot just as he had. One moment they'd been aloft fighting spot fires, and the next she'd been spinning down toward the fire mostly out of control. He shuddered. Jeannie had, by some miracle of piloting, gotten down in one piece, but it had been awful to witness. "Yeah." He remembered.

"Well, when I was over servicing her bird that night, they were meeting around a picnic table. Very serious. They seemed to be talking about a special drone, but I couldn't quite hear them and I had enough troubles rebuilding that chopper's tail section. Forgot about it until you asked."

"Who was there?" A sleeping Pasco slipped by below, then Walla Walla slid by beneath them with no one the wiser.

"Mark and Emily. Steve and Carly. Jeannie. And some woman I've never seen before or since. An Asian woman with a really serious body."

Damn it! Now he was thinking of Denise's body. While not built with a "really serious body," she possessed a body that was plenty serious enough to satisfy him. She had—

"You know, that's the same group that left us in Australia, although Cal had joined them by that time. That's when they replaced Firehawk Oh-Two."

"Huh." Vern picked up the signals at Spokane and Coeur D'Alene, Idaho. He ran the vectors to keep his hands busy. After this many years aloft, he could do the work of double-verifying their position without bothering his thinking processes.

That group had been pretty tight. When he was named to Firehawk Oh-Three, he'd thought he'd be welcomed into that inner circle of Type I heli-pilot camaraderie. Not so much. Civil, friendly, but there was no inner sanctum. Yet the people Denise had just named felt like a team that he still stood on the outside of. They had some common—

"Wait! What? When did they replace Oh-Two?" The chopper had flown in some direction different from the rest of MHA in Australia, but Oh-Two had come back with them.

"The chopper I sent was not the one that came back. The service on it was meticulous, but it wasn't the same bird. I know when a repair is mine and when it's someone else's."

—◦◦◦—

Denise waited for it. Waited for Vern to deliver that off-the-cuff denial or dismissal. "Oh you're just being paranoid." "Don't worry your little head about it." Had she actually put up with such language from Jasper? She had, and it was embarrassing. Even shaming.

"But—"

Here it came.

"Jeannie would have to know. And anything she knows, Cal knows. And that means... But then all of them are in on it? Whatever it is?"

Bless Vern. She could really go weak in the knees over this man. He was gorgeous, funny, and not only did he listen to her, but he believed her. It made her feel at least six feet tall. Well, maybe five feet ten.

"Do you have any idea what 'it' is?"

"No!" And Denise could taste the bitter memory. She recounted her inquiries into what had happened.

"Total loss, nonmechanical failure" was the only answer she'd ever been given. Mark had informed her it was strictly "need to know" and then had done that arms-crossed thing with the neutral gaze from behind his ever-present mirrored shades. It was hard to argue with him when she didn't even reach his shoulder and was about as big around as one of his legs.

Jeannie had simply blanched pale when Denise had asked about it, then shook her head, refusing to speak. Even MHA's chief pilot, Emily, had stonewalled her.

"Mark told me it was a security-level matter, and I could be fired for discussing it with anyone. Or worse. And he left that dangling." Mark had left a chill in her that day, and six months later it still hadn't gone totally away. When he was a military commander, he must have been truly terrifying.

It was a huge relief to share her fears with someone. She loved doing the work at MHA, but it had begun to feel creepy and she'd thought it was all just her.

Vern told her about the strangeness of the Honduras conversation.

They chased it around right through the second hour of the flight but didn't make any headway about what was going on at MHA. There was obviously something, but it was extremely well hidden. They were both long-term employees and all they had were a second drone, a switched-out helicopter, and a conversation that could have been about a Latin American beach holiday.

They fell into an easy silence. In addition to the relief of finally talking to someone about it, she felt much closer to Vern because of the conversation. He was sharp and thoughtful. He'd suggested many ideas that were unlikely in the extreme. Some serious, some having to do with the secret hideout for the X-Men.

He'd made a space where it was safe for her to voice ideas at well. When he laughed at some of them, she could see that they were indeed funny. She'd almost never experienced that level of comfort in a conversation. With anyone.

"We're passing over into Idaho. We're just over Moscow."

Denise looked around out the windshield but didn't see it.

Vern took his hand off the collective for a moment and touched her lightly on the arm, then pointed down.

The touch tingled even as she looked straight down. The city was painted across the inside of her helmet's visor. It lay directly below in a thousand shades of green. Perhaps twenty blocks square, the city ended abruptly in black.

"Farmland," Vern informed her when she asked. "Not a lot of variation thermally, so most of it just looks black at this time of morning. Sunrise is still an hour off."

She could see the occasional cars, but nothing else

was moving. She'd never been there, but it looked sleepy and pleasant from above. Denise was aware that she'd grown used to the odd view and wasn't freaking out over watching the world pass by from her bird's-eye view.

"What's Jasper up to?"

She bit off a sharp breath. Suddenly she felt like really freaking out.

—∿∿—

Vern couldn't believe he'd asked that. In the interminable silence that stretched farther ahead of him than the rest of the night passage to Montana, he considered releasing the controls so that he could strip off his helmet and box his own ears.

Of all the tactless, clumsy, awkward…

"I wouldn't know." Denise's voice was soft over the intercom. Her boom mic captured a definite note of distress and fed it straight into his helmet's sound-insulating headphones.

"Wait. What?" He hadn't meant to say that aloud, but he'd been so startled that his brain was being very slow about catching up with the conversation.

"We broke up a month ago. It actually ended way before that, but neither of us even noticed. At least I didn't." She sounded on the verge of tears.

"Hey, none of that. Women's tears are strictly forbidden on my helicopter. Tears of joy, sure. Anytime. But no weeping women." Could he sound like more of a jerk? "On the ground, okay. But not aloft. We clear on that?" He did his best to make it funny, but it didn't work even to his ear.

In his peripheral vision, he saw her nod by the

movement of her helmet shifting up and down. When he looked sidelong at her a moment later through the terrain topography projected on the inside of his visor, he could see her raise her own visor and wipe at her eyes.

"Sorry," he apologized. "None of that came out right. I didn't know. You look pretty broken up about it." Good, Vern. Real frickin' smooth. A part of him was thrilled that she was no longer with Jasper because—

"Go ahead and say it." Her voice was steadier, and he returned his attention to the images of the two choppers flying ahead of him over the ghostly green terrain.

Emily's was marked by the launching trailer for the surveillance drone dangling far below. Jeannie's was apparent by the large pallet of gear for the smokies, also dangling two hundred feet below her chopper. With the short container of Denise's workshop hanging from his own machine, they made quite the picturesque flight.

"Go on," Denise prompted him again.

Vern knew he should keep his mouth shut. Never criticize a woman on her choice of men.

"Say it, Vern." Denise didn't use her chief mechanic voice designed to daunt assistants and totally cow mere pilots. Instead, she sounded tired.

"I always thought you were too good for him." Damn it! He really shouldn't have said it out loud.

"That wasn't quite what I was expecting."

Vern flicked through the modes on the HUD and saw that everything mechanical was fine. He had enough fuel to make the crossing with no stops. No weather ahead. The only bad storm was a firestorm, and that wasn't his problem for another hour. That and being a certifiable idiot.

"No one at MHA seemed to like Jasper much." Her voice was soft, and he wished he could reach out a comforting hand.

I don't. Vern kept that statement to himself. Finally learning from his own maddening stupidity.

"I guess that should have told me something." Her voice didn't sound upset, just sad. And the tears appeared to be gone as quickly as the storm had threatened—except for the occasional sniffle.

"Then why the tears earlier?"

Denise was silent a long time before she spoke. They'd flown over the Saint Joe National Forest, the trackless Idaho wilderness. He climbed an extra five thousand feet to clear any of the peaks.

They had traveled from darkness into pending sunrise as they raced across the landscape at two hundred miles per hour. The sky offered a soft pink, followed by a warm glow and then a bright one. They were high above the sharp-edged Clearwater Mountains of the Bitterroot Range, with the sun cracking the horizon and stabbing at them, before she spoke again.

"They were for myself." Her voice was little more than a whisper. "That I'd think so poorly of myself that I thought Jasper was worth staying with."

"Don't you have any damned idea how amazing you are?" *Shit!* How could he put his foot so deep in his mouth when it was resting on a rudder pedal?

Her silence, even deeper this time, lasted until Missoula was in sight. As they descended after clearing the Bitterroot, the sunlight ducked out of sight again behind the Rattlesnake Mountains. The higher peaks were already white with early snow. They continued to shine like beacons once he was down in the valley's shadows.

Jeannie peeled off to deliver the supplies to the waiting smokejumpers. The tall plume of smoke above the Lolo wilderness was clearly visible, though they passed twenty miles to the south.

He followed Emily in. The Zulies usually didn't need much help; other than MHA, they were probably the best smokies in the business. So, he wasn't particularly familiar with their site at the Aerial Fire Depot off in a corner of Missoula International. He followed Emily's lead. Thankfully she'd called them into the control tower as a tandem flight so he cruised by the four-story tower, which looked as if they'd killed a whole lot of trees to side it, and slipped up to the Smokejumper Center at the north end of the field.

There was room for four planes to park in front of the low white-and-wood buildings. And two large pads of white concrete stained red with the inevitable spills of retardant that always happened in loading areas. The red of the retardant would clearly mark which trees they'd hit and treated, and which still needed fire protection.

"Where do you want your shop-box?" He held back while Emily lowered the drone-launch trailer onto the grass verge beside the parking lot.

Denise, who still hadn't spoken, pointed to an empty parking space close beside the hangar.

He brought it in. He leaned his head into the bulbous window of his helicopter door so that he could stare straight down. He had shoved the data-projecting visor out of the way just before sunrise. Not nearly as useful in broad daylight and he'd always found it restricting—even back in the Coast Guard days.

Twisting slowly above the parking space, he rotated the container so that the big double door would be facing toward the aircraft and not out toward the car parking lot. He dropped it as cleanly as he'd picked it up. Rather hoping Denise might notice.

Once he had it down on the ground, he hit the cargo-hook release and was an instant too late to stop his mistake.

The heavy four-point lifting harness, a hundred feet of thick wire cable, and the top loop were dropped all at once. They landed atop Denise's service box with a crash. Definitely scraped paint, probably some dents as well. He should have descended another seventy-five feet before he let the harness go.

He focused on getting the bird down on the tarmac. He'd need fuel and retardant and to drop off Denise.

He'd cycled down the engines as they each climbed out of the cockpit and tested sore bodies against hard tarmac. The fuel truck was rolling up as Denise came around the chopper and stopped so close that he could smell her. That warm woman mechanic filled his lungs.

She rested her hand on his arm for a moment. "To answer your question…"

His question? "Oh, the one about how incredible you are?"

Denise nodded. Didn't blush, only nodded.

He liked that about her. She wasn't embarrassed by who she was, but rather accepting of herself. A lesson he could definitely learn.

"My answer is no."

"No?"

"No. I can't imagine myself as being incredible, but, and this does surprise me, I find that I rather enjoy that you see me that way." Then she flashed one of those stellar smiles at him before turning to inspect her shop container. She managed a dozen steps before his wits gathered enough to shout to her.

"Hey, Wrench?"

She turned and looked at him. The sun had cleared the horizon of mountains and now shone full upon her, lighting her hair up in blond glory.

"Start imagining it. Because you are beyond incredible. Get that straight in your brain. You hear me?"

"Yes, sir, Mr. Pilot, sir!" She snapped a salute, pretending—as he had—to knock herself silly, then sashayed off to get to work.

He heard the clunk of the fuel nozzle as the serviceman behind him began reloading his bird. The bite of Jet A fuel on the air did nothing to diminish the sweetness of the morning.

Chapter 4

DENISE HID IN HER SHOP CONTAINER FOR A FEW minutes, trying to gather her composure and wrap it around herself.

"Incredible?" She said it softly, but it rang off the steel walls of the box as if her echo was mocking her. She had nice hair. Men had a weakness for her hair, but then so did she. It was the only thing about her that was feminine other than her body shape. She often reeked of sweat, oil, and grease. For a living she wore a tool belt and jeans. She talked about machines. She was about as alluring as an anvil with a nice wig.

By some autonomic reflex, her hands—with their short-cut yet still-ragged nails—began the task of inspecting the container's contents. MHA had given her a free hand in making sure it had everything she needed. With the contents of the container, which was twenty feet long and eight wide, she could almost do anything to a helicopter.

Down the left-hand side ran a deep bench. Above it were racked tools; below, the heavy parts in case something serious broke. Almost the entire right-hand side was filled with drawers. Everything she needed was here—from screws small enough to secure console instruments to spare hydraulic hoses, air filters, and drive belts. A small section by the door had welding tools, the specialized high-temperature hydraulic fluids, and a small service cart. She'd need to borrow a crane if she had to dismount and rebuild an engine or a rotor shaft. Otherwise, short of a new rotor blade, she had it covered and in stock.

And Vern had delivered it so delicately that nothing was out of place. It felt like a steel cocoon wrapped about her, a safe haven from the rest of the world.

She looked up at the new dent in the very center of the ceiling, where the outline of the cargo line's Flemish eye splice was vaguely recognizable. It had surprised her, but when she'd turned to see the deep chagrin on his face, he looked like he'd killed her cat, not dented a steel box. It had taken all of her control not to laugh.

She knew he'd been bothered when she'd laughed at him about not being able to drive her car. He'd get it next time; it just took a bit of practice. Even though he'd been good humored about it, she'd try not to laugh *at* him again.

Everything here was in order. Only yesterday she'd reviewed the stock list, so she couldn't use that to distract her.

If she was so incredible, why did her shop suddenly feel so confining? She wanted to be out where she could breathe.

But stepping outside the container was no better. The fire's smoke had begun to settle over Missoula in a thickening smog, trapped in the narrow valley. The fire was up in the Lolo forest to the west, and the prevailing winds were blowing right toward town. The morning sky was a light brown rather than a bright blue. The taste of smoke tickled her nose and made her want to sneeze. It was only going to get thicker until they beat this fire.

The Zulies' smokejumper buildings were ranged around them. Some admin and clerks had come out to greet them. Handing out paper sacks of food and fresh water bottles.

The resident ground crew had snapped to life with the arrival of the Firehawks. Even the Zulies didn't have these beautiful birds. They descended to fuel and gawk. The roar of the fuel-truck pumps blocked all other sounds except for the basso roar of a jet taking off from the Missoula airport in the background.

Steve and Carly were setting up the drone trailer.

Denise considered going over and offering her help, but she could see she'd be in the way. They had it down to a science. Every move orchestrated, no motion wasted. In moments the trailer's front end had been jacked up to steepen the launch rail. The tall, articulated arm held the landing rope aloft—the drone landed by flying into the rope and snagging it on a wing. They'd have it aloft before the big choppers.

Then they'd be in their normal positions, Carly riding copilot to Emily so that she'd have the best view for analyzing the fire's behavior. And Steve seated right behind his wife at the drone's control console mounted in Firehawk Oh-One.

As soon as Firehawk Oh-Two had finished delivering the supplies to the smokies, Jeannie would be in here for the same treatment. Then she and Cal would take to the skies. His photography from the copilot's seat had already graced newspapers and magazine covers from *Time* to *National Geographic*.

As soon as the fuel truck moved aside, a couple of the Zulies ran retardant hoses to each of the Firehawks, pumping their belly tanks full with the thick, red goo so essential to fighting forest fires. They'd be airborne in minutes. Aloft and racing to the fire.

Vern and Firehawk Oh-Three would be aloft and she'd be...

Useless. Sitting here on her backside. The three big choppers would be preoccupied with the fire, and the four smaller craft would only be leaving MHA's airfield about now. They were easily four hours away.

Four hours. What in the heck was someone who was supposed to be incredible going to do for four hours?

Her feet were in motion before she even thought it through.

The APU on Vern's bird and then on Emily's screamed to life. In moments, the massive four-blade rotors began to spin, sluggishly at first, but then picking up speed as the Auxiliary Power Unit shut down and the twin GE T700 turbines took over the job with their deep-throated roar.

The climbing pitch as the engines gained RPMs sent her scurrying the last few yards to grab Vern's door before he pulled it shut.

"Want company?" She felt breathless, light-headed. In her year and a half with MHA, she'd never flown to a fire.

"Sure. There's extra gear in back. Climb aboard and you can get dressed on the way. We're going right now."

She looked at Vern. He now wore full firefighter's gear. Black fire-resistant cargo pants and a yellow Nomex jacket with a safety harness across his chest. A big work knife at his hip, a fire-shelter bag stuffed into the door pocket beside him. He looked so damned handsome and manly sitting at the controls of his big helicopter that she couldn't stand it.

Without thinking, she grabbed the big D-ring on the front of his harness that would be used to lift him out if there was a crash. She pulled him toward her and did what she'd spent most of last night's dinner thinking about. What she had found herself having to resist doing on their flight this morning.

His surprise at her kiss froze him for a moment. He didn't move. His hands remained on the cyclic and collective.

Then he snapped out of his momentary paralysis, and she wondered just what she'd unleashed.

Her idle whim in a moment of excitement took more than a second—but less than two—to morph into an enthusiastic kiss that seared her with its heat. Her heart rate raced upward as rapidly as the turbines continued to climb toward full RPMs.

Vern's kiss didn't caress; it took. He kissed her with such sudden hunger that she really could believe—in that moment—that she was incredible.

He pulled back abruptly. His eyes were wide. He opened his mouth. She could see the apology coming.

"One word of that," Denise cut him off, "and I really will whack you with my wrench."

He nodded once. Then nodded again a couple of times.

After that kiss, would she feel awkward spending the rest of the morning aboard with him? Maybe she shouldn't go. Maybe she should politely back away and—

"That thing I said earlier about no women's tears in the helicopter?"

She nodded, confused.

Then his infinitely reassuring smile broke out. "No kissing the pilot once we're aloft either. A kiss like that could make a guy faint with sheer joy. Very dangerous there, Wrench. *Incredibly* dangerous. So are you coming or not?"

The turbines were up to speed. She could tell by the note of their roar that the temperature was up to spec and the chopper was ready to fly.

On the other side of his Firehawk, Emily's rotors shifted and dug at the air to drag the retardant-laden bird aloft.

Denise took one look at Vern's smile and matched it with her own. She slammed his door shut and grinned at him again through the pilot's window. Moving a few steps aft, she slid open the chopper's big cargo-bay door, climbed inside, and then slid it shut behind her.

"Get us out of here!" she shouted at him. Then she began pulling on one of the sets of fire gear stowed in the back of the cargo bay.

She braced herself as the deck tilted forward, then banked when they climbed and headed toward the fire. She overlapped the coat's lapels as well as she could, but the gear swam on her small frame.

Didn't matter. The pounding of her heart would fill the extra space.

Denise's emotions had been through a lot of changes this morning. Flying to a forest fire in a Firehawk helicopter was both exciting and horrifying.

As they approached the fire, the hazy air become thicker and thicker beyond the windscreen. Even the few minutes to get dressed, double-back for the water bottle, foil shelter, and hard hat that Vern required, and then clamber into the copilot's seat without stepping on a radio in the center console had been long enough for a significant drop in visibility. The air quality was even worse by the time she was buckled in and had the headset positioned.

"I really only use the helmet for night flying. Or hot-spot work for the infrared feed. For the main fire, I still like directly seeing what I'm doing."

She preferred the headset too. She liked being able to see his profile, see his smile when he glanced over to check her harness.

The visibility at Missoula had spanned the valley, barely. Ten miles from the airport to the rise of the high peaks along the southern edge of town. Now, as they neared the fire, the view was under a thousand yards.

"Oh, man, this is gonna suck." Vern didn't sound put out or worried, rather a bit disgusted. So she would trust him to keep them safe.

A helicopter came out of the smoke headed almost right toward them. It flashed by so fast she barely had time to spot the large "02" that identified Jeannie's Firehawk. Denise almost gave herself whiplash trying to follow it.

A glance down at the instruments and she saw they were traveling at 150 knots, 173 miles per hour. With Jeannie going the other way, the choppers had passed at almost four hundred miles per hour—well, 345.2, but for once that felt too fussy even for her. Denise herself only occasionally crossed fifty knots during integrity tests lapping around the airport.

"How close were we?"

"What? Oh, to Jeannie?" Vern shrugged as if the close call was of no interest. "Three or four rotors."

"Rotors?"

"Sure." He descended to stay below the smoke. The high, sharp ridges of the Bitterroot Mountains rose to meet them. It was a narrow space to fly in.

She wanted to pick up her feet to keep them clear of the treetops.

"'Rotors' is the best way to think about distance between helicopters. At three rotor diameters out, fifty-four feet times three, there is no way our rotor blades can collide. No real turbulence either. No hassle." He pointed with his left finger at one of the screens on the console without removing his hand from the collective. "You can see the other choppers on that screen there."

The screen, about as big as a laptop's, was a cluster of symbols. She was working on how to straighten them out when the radio sounded loud in her ear.

"We've got the smokies in deep," Mark Henderson, the Incident Commander—Air, called down from his King Air. "Be cautious, everyone. We're in high and rough country. You clip a tree on a ridgeline, and your body is going to wind up two thousand feet down in the valley before you stop tumbling."

"Really?" Denise felt her voice choke in her throat, and her response came out as no more than a squeak. She was glad they were only on intercom; she was only embarrassing herself in front of Vern and not her boss as well.

Mark continued with a wry tone as if he had indeed heard the squeak and began giving them vectors for their first attack. All gobbledygook to her ears, but Vern seemed to be taking it in.

When Mark finished, Vern transmitted an acknowledgment before glancing in her direction and remarking over the intercom. "Look out the window." He was so casual that he sounded practically blasé, whereas her nerves were wondering why she'd ever left her nice, safe steel shop-box in the first place.

Denise did look out…and down. Way down. One moment the forest was close below them, the ridge stretching side to side as they crossed above it. Then it dropped away with an alarming abruptness, so sudden it gave her vertigo.

When she thought she might actually be ill, the tree-covered slope rocketed back up until she thought they would run square into the cliff face. After the third ridge and valley passed safely below the chopper, she decided that looking downward was a really stupid idea. At their current speed, a half-mile-deep valley slipped beneath their feet every thirty seconds.

"Oh man, those things are steep." She lay back against her seat and closed her eyes. *Incredible women do not barf on helicopter consoles.* She repeated that several times, focusing on the steady sound of the rotors and the smooth flight of the Firehawk.

Then the chopper dropped from under her and for a moment she floated off her seat, held in place only by her harness before she slammed back onto her seat.

Her eyes snapped open and she saw the fire now close before them.

This had been a really bad idea.

"Vern…" She managed to keep the panic out of her voice, mostly.

"We have to keep it from rounding the south end of the ridgeline," Mark's voice continued, passing on instructions. "The smokies are atop the ridge, so it's up to you guys to hold the lower slopes. Lay the retardant from the top down."

"Roger, boss." Vern wasn't panicked, running, arguing…nothing. "And so you know, I'm one mechanic heavy."

"She suited up and strapped in?"

Vern glanced over at her and nodded for her to respond, as if they were merely cruising down the highway in her car.

She wanted to curse him when he nodded again. "Damn you!"

Vern chuckled, to her complete annoyance. See if she'd be kissing him again anytime soon.

She rested her hand very lightly on the cyclic control and pulled the microphone switch. It changed her from intercom communication to transmitting over the radio. "Yes and yes!" she snapped out at Mark and let go of the switch but left her hand in place.

"Good," Mark came back, terribly amused about something. "You might want to hang on anyway."

"Why? I—" And gravity disappeared. And the horizon along with it. Her hands convulsed on the cyclic and again pressed the radio switch. She heard a scream through her headphones, again that weird girlish sound of shock and surprise.

They stopped dropping and she managed to release the mic switch.

"Oh God!" Her hands were shaking. "Everyone heard that, didn't they?"

"Everyone with an eardrum left anyway." Vern's tone was light enough to nudge her sensibilities loose. "Easy on the controls, Wrench."

Once she eased off, she could feel the smooth confidence with which Vern maneuvered the cyclic and the five tons of helicopter carrying that same amount again in retardant.

They rolled over almost onto their side in a steep bank and dove down along a ridgeline. Gravity came back during an ear-popping twist. No more than a few hundred feet—four rotors, she corrected herself—beyond her door, flames were roaring aloft, far higher than they were flying.

Vern kept them nose down and began counting down seconds. His voice soothing in her ears.

Which was exactly why he was doing it aloud. She was so thankful that maybe she would kiss him again.

Though not right now.

The next change she felt right through the soles of her feet resting on the steel decking. A buzz of motors actuating the dump doors on the Firehawk's belly tank.

She stuck her head out into the bulge in the window and marveled at the long, red spray that poured out of their craft. It splatted down into the trees, coating them with the sticky fire retardant intended to keep the oxygen away from the fuel. No oxygen, no fire.

If the coating was perfect…that's why it was retardant and not fire-stopper.

The buzz of the closing doors, again tickling up through her feet, indicated the first thousand gallons was down on the fire. Abruptly 4.4 tons lighter, the Firehawk roared back aloft like the best roller coaster on the planet.

Her pulse was ripping at her chest. Her breathing was shallow and rapid; her trembling hands reminded her to keep them away from the radio switch.

"Holy shit!"

That was exactly how Vern felt watching Denise. The Woman of Stainless Steel was nowhere to be seen.

Stainless Steel?

Ha!

She didn't kiss like steel.

She kissed like wildfire, flashing to full heat in the blink of an eye. She'd kissed him barely ten minutes ago, the fire line only twenty miles and six minutes from the Missoula airport, and his body was no closer to recovering than the moment she'd hauled his lips down to hers.

He was glad she'd been in back long enough for him to make a few discreet adjustments to his clothing or he'd have been in pain.

Did she have any idea what she'd done to him?

Did he?

It was the fantasy of the gorgeous woman in the Italian sports car come true. The unadulterated joy she revealed in her driving had been nowhere to be seen this morning.

Then, *pow*!

She'd come running toward the chopper—like in one of those movie scenes. Then, for reasons he still didn't dare ask about, she dragged him down into a blazing-hot kiss.

He really needed to pay attention to what the hell he was doing. They were descending back into the Missoula Aerial Fire Depot for another load of retardant, and he didn't remember how he'd gotten here.

He talked to the tower and settled beside Emily's Oh-One.

The Zulies' ground crew clearly had this down to a science. His chopper was still rocking on its shock absorbers when he heard the loud clunk of retardant hoses hooking up to it. They ran dual two and a half inchers, which meant...

"You've got seventy seconds if you want off," he informed Denise.

"Are you kidding?" She sounded breathless, wound way up. "I thought roller coasters were fun. I had no idea."

He kept his attention on the tank fill. He needn't have bothered. The loading team roared up to twenty gallons short of filled, then topped off at a thousand exactly using the reaction time to shut down the pumps. Three seconds later he heard the double-slap on the outside of the chopper, signaling that he was good to go.

He had the rotors humming even as the verbal confirmation came in over the headset.

A dozen feet aloft, Denise spoke over the intercom, her voice so calm and steady that it wholly belied the breathless gasp of moments before. "I really liked kissing you."

Beautiful, charming, and spoke her mind without games. Who the hell was she?

Another part of him answered with, *What the hell do you care?*

He didn't. He'd be perfectly content to answer that particular puzzle as they went along.

"Well"—if she was going to be so forthright, he couldn't return less—"I'll admit to counting the seconds until I get to kiss you again."

"Forty-two thousand, three hundred and sixty."

"Say what?" He reached cruising altitude, high enough to clear the peaks en route back to the fire, and nosed down for best speed.

"Local sunset is eight-oh-two tonight, minus thirty minutes earlier that you're required to be down per U.S. Forest Service contract. Seven hundred minutes times sixty, plus six more minutes."

Not many people made Vern feel stupid, but this woman could make a good try at it. "Wait, no way you had that on tap." As they cleared the second major ridge, he glanced over to see her smile.

"While you were flying us back to base, I got to wondering how much longer I'd get to stay aboard. Same amount of time until I can kiss you again."

Vern could feel himself grinning as he lined up for the next run down the ridgeline, right on Firehawk Oh-One's tail. "There's always lunchtime."

"Thirty minutes mandatory," Denise agreed. "Feeling lucky, flyboy?"

Damn! Lucky didn't begin to cover it.

Chapter 5

At lunchtime, Henderson called a pilots' meeting and flew down from his station above the blaze. The smaller choppers had arrived and gotten in a half-dozen runs each.

Vern landed right behind Emily. He'd managed to keep up with her, barely. Damn, but the woman flew so smoothly. He had the feeling that she was actually moving a touch slow to coddle his male ego. Or maybe to teach him.

Former military—well, so was he. But she was former SOAR.

The Special Operations Aviation Regiment was an absolute legend. Only the very best were given even the chance to take the tests that rejected three-quarters of the applicant pilots. He probably had a lot more to learn from her than how not to make a total fool of himself with a Firehawk.

So even if she was flying slower so he didn't feel totally hopeless, his male ego wouldn't complain about that bit of coddling. He didn't mind being outflown by two women; he just minded being outflown at all.

He stretched as he climbed down, trying to work out the kinks from flying mostly nonstop from 4:00 a.m. to noon. The Zulie Air Depot was cloaked in smoke now— visibility under five miles and falling. The quadrangle of buildings framed an area big enough to easily park

MHA's three planes and seven choppers. The tarmac was immaculate except for the two filling stations, their white concrete stained bright red with the dribbles of ten thousand loads of retardant.

He'd always enjoyed the energy of a firebase. Even when everyone was too exhausted to breathe, there was a unified front—everyone working to stop the fire. He'd seen fuelies and loaders catnapping on the concrete even when the choppers where running just minutes apart. He'd seen smokies, pulled off the line for a break, almost impossible to wake from where they'd fallen asleep sitting up in a chopper's cargo bay.

And then he'd seen the woman who had sat beside him for the whole morning's flight. His overwhelming relief at Jasper's passage from Denise's life was offset by the more he learned about her. Denise was sufficiently daunting that he was again buying into her steel-like reputation.

When he'd been a young teen reading John D. MacDonald thrillers and picturing an endless line of easy women and vigilante justice, she'd been reading Patrick O'Brian and Tom Clancy.

The old sailing ships and the modern military, she'd patiently explained her reasons, both authors gave such exceptional descriptions of how and why the equipment works.

He'd graduated from high school a year early and bummed around the sailing circuit for a couple of years. He'd been in some oceanic races as a crewman and done some big crossings. He'd finally gone Coast Guard, because Yuri had threatened to kick his butt if he didn't, and ended up flying choppers all over the waters of the

Pacific coast of the Americas. Had drifted around afterward and ended up fighting forest fires.

Denise had gotten her airframe and power plant certification before she was twenty: fixed-wing and rotorcraft. Spent three years at Sikorsky, but hadn't liked Connecticut. Had walked right into the new expansion plans at MHA.

He thought kissing her still sounded like a pretty good idea, despite her incredibleness. But she'd rushed her team into an inspection of the air filters, and Mark had monopolized the lunch break by laying out his plan of attack on a large, plastic-coated map rolled out on a picnic table with bags of burgers and fries pinning down the corners.

Back up they went, and six hours later, Vern didn't know if he was ever going to move normally again. He set the chopper down in front of the Zulies' buildings and shut it down. Digging deep, he tried to find the energy to pull out his log, but his nerves were powerless.

He pulled off his headset and rolled his head enough to glance down the row. At least Emily and Jeannie were equally hammered, still sitting slumped back in their seats.

Denise whisked by outside his windshield so fast he could barely follow her. She'd shed the harness and jacket. Her T-shirt clung and outlined, and even that wasn't sufficient to get him moving. A whole lineup of the easy Florida babes that John D. MacDonald had delivered for Travis McGee to enjoy wouldn't be enough to get him moving.

His door was popped open from the outside, and he almost tumbled out in his surprise.

Denise was standing there, tablet computer in hand. "C'mon, Taylor. I need you to finish your log before I can start my end-of-day inspection."

He considered whining. He considered pulling the door shut and going back to sleep; he'd been so close. He considered Denise's compact form and generous chest so splendidly outlined in stretchy material, her flowing hair, and her beautiful eyes glaring at him from that lovely face.

Okay. That last one did it.

He hauled out the paper logbook and recorded the vitals: hours in flight, number of drops from his tally, number of gallons—cool! "Beat the crap out of yesterday's drops."

Denise leaned in to see the count, leaning against him as casually as if they were dear friends completely comfortable with one another, rather than near strangers who'd known each other for a year and a half and had just kissed for the first—and only, damn it!—time this morning. Sitting here, he was only a few inches taller than she was standing on the outside ground.

To hell with it.

He turned until his nose was buried in her soft hair and breathed her in. Now that his hands weren't on the controls, he slipped one into that blond glory and turned her to him.

———

Denise groaned against his mouth as Vern kissed her. They were on display for the whole line, and she didn't care.

He didn't taste of fire and reek of smoke. He tasted of

heat. As if the fire that he fought with his helicopter ran inside him but was such a contrast to his cool exterior.

Would she ever be able to match his unflappable manner as he flew? She rather hoped not. The last flight had been as amazing and adrenaline-worthy as the first.

And the second kiss was proving that the first had been no fluke.

She melted against him. Denise never melted against anyone. But apparently her body didn't know that about Vern Taylor.

Part of it was the way he saw her.

Part of it was the way his eager hands held her so. He wasn't gentle—as if she were a goddamned delicate china doll—the way her few boyfriends had treated her. He wrapped his arms around her and pulled her close as if she was a strong woman.

That word "incredible" floated by her consciousness somewhere but slipped away. His mouth on hers took and gave.

When the kiss finally broke, he didn't step her back, which was a good thing because her legs were a long-forgotten concept lost in a land far, far away. Instead, he buried his face in her hair and breathed her in. She could feel his chest expand beneath her hand, which had come to rest over his heart. He breathed her in as if he'd never stop, as if she were the finest tonic in the universe.

"Damn," he whispered softly against her neck. "That's all I can think to say, Wrench." He breathed her in again and exhaled another soft "Damn!"

Denise knew in that instant that they weren't going

to stop anytime soon. They weren't going to kiss a few times and move on. No. They were going to sleep together, and that wasn't going to be particularly far in the future.

She'd never known it so early on or known it so assuredly.

Leaning farther into the helicopter, she rested her head on his shoulder and let herself simply enjoy being held.

She also had never so looked forward to it.

———

Vern had thought he was in trouble before.

Ha! Not even close.

He finally managed to trade places with Denise, so that she was the one in the pilot seat with her checklist and he was the one standing outside the door.

Bruce and Mickey strolled by, especially slowly. Bruce looked somewhere between aghast and horrified. Mickey gave him a look that said, "Who the hell you kidding, Vern? Guys like us don't get women like Conroy." And Vern wanted to bury his nose in her hair again and smell the heady woman, mechanic, summer-afternoon scent of Denise Conroy.

"Anything I can do, Wrench?" He fell back on the familiar. It was the only way he could find to not simply ravage her where she sat. A nice kiss was a long way from an invitation to a tumble. Nice kiss? Shit! Who was he kidding?

"No. Go away, Slick. You're distracting me."

Vern nodded, managed to fumble on his cap, and turn for the showers. A really cold one.

"Don't make the shower too cold, Flyboy," Denise called from behind him as if she'd read his mind. "Save a little heat for me."

The smooth tarmac offered no excuse of a gopher hole or a stray tuft of grass to explain his stumbling gait as he moved away from her.

—⁓—

Denise finished her inspection as quickly as she could. The choppers had come in at a half hour to sunset. She'd lost a little time with Vern that she'd never, ever regret. And spent an hour going over the choppers. The ash and dust were taking their toll. She shifted a half-dozen items onto the "check daily" list and sent the update to Malcolm and Brenna. But for the moment, she didn't have to order any unusual maintenance.

She found Vern sitting in the Zulies' mess hall, drowsing over his half-finished dinner. The hall was a large, low room that could fit the sixty smokejumpers as well as their support staff. With the smokies still in the field, MHA was rattling around the big space.

The chow line ran down one end of the hall. Wooden tables—every single thing in Missoula was either made of wood or covered in it. Even the room's Sheetrock walls had wide-board trim. It must come from being at the junction of a half-dozen national forests. Steel chairs with faded red padding where the only break in the theme.

Denise grabbed her own meal tray quickly and moved to sit across from Vern. The small Formica table had definitely seen better days, but it was clean and the spaghetti and meatballs smelled heavenly.

"C'mon, Slick. Eat up, then you can go to bed."

When he didn't respond, she rapped his knuckles with the handle of her knife.

"Huh. Wha'? Oh, hey." He stared around, clearly uncertain of where he was.

"Eat up, Vern."

He finally spotted his meal and began to eat mechanically.

Denise looked around the room and could see that the other pilots each had their own attendees. They all looked hammered, but the three Firehawk pilots were beyond pale.

Emily's daughter, Tessa, clearly thought it was time to play and run around after spending much of the day aloft with her dad. One of the Zulie ground crew appeared with a teddy bear in her hands and whisked the girl away. Mark was practically fork-feeding his wife. He didn't look all that much better himself.

Even as Denise watched, Jeannie packed it in, curled up across three chairs—which looked terribly uncomfortable—and appeared to fall instantly asleep. Cal swept her into his arms with a tenderness that came right out of a girl's dreams.

Carly was in slightly better shape, leaning heavily on a limping Steve as they left. His injury might never let him walk normally again or carry his wife, but it made them no less a beautiful couple.

The rest of the MHA and Zulie crews were at least functional, but the chatter was low, no more than a soft murmur in the long room. The view of the parked choppers and failing daylight out the broad windows only reinforced that it was time to be done with this day.

Vern had lost the thread of his meal again while she'd been looking around.

Denise looked at his plate and decided he'd eaten enough.

She piled a couple slices of garlic bread on top of her pasta, stabbed a fork into it, and took that in one hand. With the other, she tugged on his hand. "No way I'm carrying you, Vern. Get a move on. Time to get you in bed."

His fingers slid into hers as he made it to his feet. No jokes about getting her into bed with him; yet more proof of the depths of his exhaustion.

She led him down the hall. Any attempts to imagine they were walking along romantically holding hands were belied when he clipped a shoulder on a doorjamb and nearly crushed her hand in his grip as he struggled to remain upright. It was a close thing, but she managed to save her dinner.

He'd been assigned one of the two-person bunk-rooms. The room was enough wider than the tiered bed to stuff in a chair, a set of drawers, and maybe set your boots on the floor where you wouldn't trip on them. An open window let in the very last of the evening light and a soft breeze that thankfully only hinted at the smoky haze now filling the valley.

Vern collapsed onto the bunk with only the barest guidance. She set her dinner on the dresser, closed the door, and began unlacing his boots. Denise hesitated at his shirt and pants, but he couldn't sleep in those. Managing to elicit a little help from him, she got him down to underwear and T-shirt.

Then the T-shirt was gone and his autonomic habits

almost hauled down his briefs before she was able to stop him. Clearly a man used to sleeping naked.

Six feet one of naked Vern Taylor. She definitely wasn't ready for that.

Denise had to take a steadying breath at the mere thought; not that the tight cotton underwear left much to the imagination. But even on its own, his chest was devastating enough. Jasper had tended toward the well fed. Not fat, but he showed definite signs of enjoying his food, and you could already see the suggestion of the beer belly that would arrive over the next five years, now that his knee had ended his windsurfing days.

Vern was as fit as any firefighter, even one who flew for a living. Just because he had a slender frame didn't mean that it wasn't sheathed in a smooth flow of muscle.

He settled in and she got a sheet over him, which was a blessing. She fetched her dinner and perched on the foot of the bunk, leaning back against the vertical support. She'd only stay until she was sure he was settled. At least that's what she told herself.

"You'd make a good wife, Wrench." His mumble was only half coherent.

A chunk of meatball caught in her throat and she barely managed not to choke on it. Light, she needed to say something light. "You shopping for one, Slick?"

"A wife? Hell no. Not old Vern Taylor." He rolled onto his side, reexposing his chest to the warm evening air that slid in through the window beyond her shoulder.

"Why not?" She wasn't disappointed. It wouldn't make any sense if she was. They weren't an item and she was a sensible woman. She wasn't disappointed... She only felt that way. Which was stupid because she didn't want to be a wife anyway. She just wanted... She had no idea.

"'Cause." His voice was no more than a mumble.

"'Cause why?"

"Come lie down with me and I'll tell you."

He hadn't opened his eyes, so she couldn't read his expression. He looked harmless and beautiful in the last light of day. His muscled chest was becoming a land of shadows and promises. His face fading even further into mystery.

It was stupid.

She set her half-finished plate back on the dresser.

Getting into bed with him was absolutely not a smart idea.

She took off her boots because climbing into his narrow bed wearing boots was even dumber than climbing into his bed to begin with.

One part of her brain acknowledged that she must be more tired than she'd thought if that last bit of reasoning had made any sense.

Yet the same rationale prevailed until she stood in the gathering darkness wearing no more than a T-shirt and underwear.

She slid into the small space between Vern and the edge of the bed.

His arm came around her waist and pulled her back to spoon against him. He didn't grab for her breast or anywhere else. He simply wrapped his arm around her and tucked his fingers between her ribs and the mattress.

Denise tugged the sheet over them and tried not to be overwhelmed by the sensations. He held her with an impossible surety and familiarity that made it feel both safe and normal. His flat chest against her back. His warm breath a mere whisper on her ear as he nuzzled into her hair.

"Hey, don't go to sleep yet. You promised." A final belated and hopeless flail for common sense, but she spoke it anyway.

"Promised what?"

"Why you don't want to be married?"

"Oh." He tucked his face down against the back of her neck as if hiding behind her hair. "My mom and dad. They're so perfect together." His words were dragging out. Slurring.

"I'd think that would make you want to get married." She had to shake him and repeat her question to elicit the final sleepy answer.

"Never be good enough for someone like you."

By the time Denise recovered from the shock of his answer and tried another question, she was answered by a soft snore against the base of her neck.

Denise had never wanted to get married either, but for wholly different reasons. She never wanted to make anyone suffer the loss that had so shattered her father. By keeping herself to herself, and only entering into shallow and relatively meaningless relationships, she had kept her vow to herself.

But that didn't fit into how Vern saw her. He saw her as important. He also had her up on a pedestal she could make absolutely no sense of. There was no way she'd ever live up to some unreal creation of his mind.

Yet she felt plenty real lying here against Vern's chest, his arm wrapped around her waist as if he'd never let her go.

She was awake a long time that night. Not worrying at some technical problem as she usually did. Nor reviewing some mental checklist to make sure she hadn't missed anything.

She simply lay in Vern's arms and enjoyed herself, feeling important to someone and listening to Vern's gentle breathing.

Chapter 6

VERN WOKE SLOWLY. AFTER YEARS OF FLYING TO FIRE, SOME-thing about the morning woke him before sunrise. Maybe it was the call of the first bird of the day. Or the first hint of light in the sky despite closed eyelids.

He liked this time of day, even if his brain insisted that coffee was necessary to actually face it. It gave him a chance to collect his thoughts, get oriented for the day. And when he was with someone, like now, it occasionally gave them time to—

With someone?

A woman...the smoke and summer smell of her hair nearly overwhelmed him...Denise. Denise Conroy lay curled up against him. Her head pillowed on one of his arms, a soft warmth against the inside of the other that encircled her trim waist.

How in the hell had...

Any thoughts of waking slowly were banished by his body's instant and intense reaction to holding her. He tried to shift his hips back away from where he pressed against her tight behind, but after about a half inch, his back bumped up against the wall behind the bunk bed.

Obviously still mostly asleep, Denise snuggled back into that tiny gap he'd managed to create. Now he was pinned back against the smooth wood.

Unsure what to do, he lay there unmoving as she slowly came to life in his arms.

A gentle sigh.

A bit of a stretch.

She turned her face into the pillow, taking the pressure off his arm which responded with a sharp tingle and sting of renewed blood flow.

Vern kept waiting for the moment she came awake and bolted from his bed. But it didn't come.

Instead, once she was most of the way awake, she pressed her back more solidly against his chest and slid her hand over his arm until she was holding it in place around her waist.

Then, with fingers partly laced into the back of his, she pulled his hand up and rested it over her breast.

He'd never felt anything quite like it. It wasn't only the way her breast filled his palm, or the way it responded and tightened against his fingers, something he could easily feel through her T-shirt. It was that she placed his hand there and held it against her chest, letting him know exactly what she wanted without the least hint of coyness.

Denise Conroy couldn't be an uninhibited lover. Could she? She was too careful, too distant, and…definitely felt too good.

He bent the arm that she lay on until he had her in a double-breasted cross-hold, and she groaned. It was a ripple of sound that he didn't hear, but instead felt riding up her back where it pressed against his chest.

She was guiding his hand down over the perfection of her flat stomach when a loud thump sounded against the door.

"Rise and shine. Shower if you need it. Airborne in thirty." Mark moved off and was pounding on the next door before he'd even finished the instructions.

Indeed, in the time Vern had been watching Denise awaken, the predawn light had brightened beyond the window. Time to shower, shave, eat, and prep for flight. Just. Maybe if he skipped the shower. And the shave.

She finished guiding his hand downward. He was glad she was wearing underwear, even if there wasn't much of it. A thin swatch of smooth cotton masking neither texture nor growing heat.

At her guidance, he cupped her.

And his reflexes took over.

He pulled her hard back against him. He leaned into her, pressing them both together until they both were writhing, their breath caught equally short and ragged.

"Oh God!" She clamped his hand in place for a moment between her soft, smooth thighs and the next moment slid from his arms and was standing before him. "That is such a fantastic way to wake up!"

Vern tried to speak. Even without his morning coffee, he tried to reach deep for words but couldn't dredge up any.

Denise, in a bright blue T-shirt and a tiny swatch of white cotton, looked like neither a china doll nor some miniaturized version of a larger woman. She'd been designed and built to exactly the height she was; her hips fit her frame as well as her breasts. Her legs were as long and magnificent as her hair.

She was dressed and gone, leaving behind a sweet kiss and the worst arousal of his entire life.

Then he thought about Denise. No shuddering release. No jerking breaths.

Well, at least he wouldn't be the only one suffering today.

—·····—

With her full crew on-site, Denise didn't join Vern for the flying.

Well, she could have, but too many things in her head needed straightening out.

Overnight the smoke in Missoula had thickened noticeably until it hid the helicopters before they were even a mile aloft. The hills ten miles away on the far end of town were relegated to myth and rumor.

Some of the locals began wearing white face masks, reminding her of her one trip to Beijing as part of a Sikorsky exhibition. The transport that had delivered them had to do an instrument landing despite their midday arrival, and they'd never left the airport. The airport hotel was part of the exhibition center. That had been her one foreign trip, other than Canada, before MHA's trip to Australia last winter, and she hadn't been able to see anything more than a thousand yards away through the smog. An air show where you couldn't see the aircraft flying overhead. Only the Chinese teams had even bothered going aloft.

Figuring the Missoula locals knew the score, she had her crew put on masks as well.

Once the choppers were aloft, she corralled Malcolm and Brenna. At a battered mess-hall table, they reviewed their extreme-conditions plan. Check the filters at three hours, fully prepared to replace immediately. Review the high-temp readings captured by the HUMS during each refueling. Air compressors to blow out errant ash and grit, especially the carbon of char, which was highly abrasive on moving parts.

A heavier cleaning could be done over lunch.

She made a quick radio call to Mark to stagger the big chopper pilots' lunch breaks by a half hour so that her team could really hit each bird in a unified effort. The littler birds staggered at the fifteen-minute marks.

Her team was up to it. Mal had been with MHA a year, and Brenna was new this season but had shaken down well. Remarkably well.

Mark had asked Denise if she wanted to make any changes before the winter season. Most fire-fighting outfits laid off the bulk of their crews over winter, mothballing their aircraft. However, MHA had been approached by several countries for off-season work.

Malcolm wasn't eager for travel, so this could well be his last fire of the season. He had a winter gig lined up at Columbia Helicopters as soon as MHA's season was done. Columbia had acquired a bunch of retired military equipment and purchased another outfit. They needed a team to convert each one to Columbia's specs, which were as stringent as MHA's own.

Brenna was up for travel though, and Denise had given the tall Eurasian woman the contract extension a month ago so as not to lose her. Tall. Well, taller than her but way less than Vern.

Denise spent much of the morning wondering how she and Vern could fit together so well. He was so much taller, yet their bodies were as custom-made for each other as her Fiat's throttle linkage. It simply worked, even if common sense said it shouldn't.

She shuddered deliciously at the memory of their waking. Her judgment hadn't been slow to kick in. Vern had simply felt so good that she'd decided to revel in it for a moment. A long moment that had fired off nerves she didn't even know she had. So foreign they'd scared her. Not scared so much as…

Something that strong.

Was it pleasure? Or fear? She wasn't even sure how to tell the difference. All she knew was that it was huge and they hadn't had time then to investigate it further. She'd slid from his arms wanting to keep the wonderful part, just in case the next part did turn into fear. Like a cozy set of thick fleece clothes, she'd tucked the memory of those sensations around her through the morning and cherished them.

With the maintenance plan finally knocked into shape, Denise sent Malcolm and Brenna to scrounge up two additional service carts and stock each one with everything they'd need for a midday servicing by chopper type. Three models, three carts.

She set about stocking the one for the three Firehawks and let her mind drift again, while her hands did their job by rote.

Her body actually still vibrated from this morning. More than cozy, the emotions were shimmering through her as well as the physical sensations. She'd never before even considered doing the things that she'd done.

The man felt so good that he should ship with a warning label: "Caution! Dangerous levels of wonderful."

And she'd let an intensely erotic dream melt into the waking moment—both had to do with her and Vern Taylor.

She'd covered it with a cheerful thanks: "That is such

a fantastic way to wake up!" (Could she possibly be any perkier?) Then bolted from the room.

Vern made her want to be all of the things she wasn't. She wanted to be…bad. She wasn't even sure what that meant. It wasn't as if she were a naive and virginal sixteen-year-old, actually twenty before she'd—but she set that aside. She was a dutiful daughter and a dedicated professional.

Vern filled her with a desire to kick out the jambs and just see what happened. Maybe see who she would be if she wasn't always so damned careful.

She began working on a customized maintenance checklist for today's conditions and loading it onto everyone's tablets.

At the same time, another checklist worked its way through her thoughts.

First, they'd kissed. Check.

Second, far sooner than she'd imagined possible, they'd slept together. Check.

Third, heavy petting. They'd already gotten a pretty serious start on that as well. Big check mark there.

Fourth, oh damn. She was so not ready for what came next. Making love was not an area in which she received many compliments. She hadn't noticed it at first. Then she'd chalked it up to men just not being verbal, and then she'd finally concluded it was probably her. Maybe she was too analytical about it. Or too—*Bad place!* she admonished herself.

As she forced her attention back to the task of finishing the maintenance list, some small, rebellious part of her wondered how it would feel to make love with Vern.

—⁓—

"What's gotten into you?" Mark harassed him over the command frequency.

Vern triggered the radio to answer Mark. "Maybe I'm just this good." He was flying fast and clean this morning—so deep in the groove that no one could touch him.

"Nope," Mark replied cheerily. "Now punch the center of the saddle in grid S-34 and let's see if we can stop this section from jumping to the next ridge. Watch the winds."

Vern had been watching them but appreciated the extra warning. The fire was climbing the ridge face, sucking up cold air to feed the base of the flames with its powerful heat-driven upwelling. When the hot air and smoke crested the first ridge, it rode skyward in a massive plume that reached the jet stream another twenty thousand feet up. There the smoke was sheared off to the east, settling over Missoula, Butte, Bozeman, and Billings before moving out to shadow the Great Plains.

But at the crest of the ridge, the rising hot air separated from some of the cold air it had dragged aloft but not had time to heat. On the verge of the saddle—where a high mountain valley separated the ridgeline from an even higher one beyond it—a horizontal rotor of wind was forming. It was as if someone held a giant rolling pin made of wind horizontally over the valley and was beginning to spin it on its handle.

Curls of smoke were being dragged down past the ridge by the slow rotor. And where there was smoke, there were cinders able to ignite new fires in the valley

and up the next ridge. To stop it, they had to coat the area with retardant.

"Mark," Vern called over the radio, "I'm going to take this one a bit high. Jeannie, hang back and let's see what my drop does. I don't like the way this pattern is forming."

"Roger that." Jeannie might be a better pilot, he hated to admit. She was a bloody natural. But his six years of service flying and four years actually on wildfires to her two on fires made him a better flier when it got ugly. And this looked like it might be shifting toward ugly.

"Hang on," Steve called from his usual seat in the back of Emily's chopper. "Let me send the drone in ahead of you."

Vern held back and waited for the tiny craft to come zipping down from whatever section of the fire it had been observing. Less than a minute later, the tiny cross shape, six feet long with a ten-foot wingspan, zipped by overhead.

Vern tipped the cyclic forward and followed the drone in. He stayed back as far as he could and still see it clearly. The drone only had one speed, so he followed it in at ninety miles per hour, half what his bird could do. That was okay by him. It gave him a wide margin of power and maneuverability if he needed it.

Most of it was clear air. The edges of the smoke weren't doing anything violent; some wind shear perhaps, but he wasn't going anywhere near those. Their job was a series of runs down the back side of the saddle to coat the trees.

There was that strange curl again. Almost as if it was the clear air that was in turmoil, not the smoke-filled air.

At least he was far enough back that he'd have time to react if it—

The drone slammed down and sideways. No gentle shift; it was there one instant and flung into the saddle and the smoke the next.

At ninety miles per hour, Vern had about two seconds to react.

He hauled up on the collective, teasing the very edge of blade stall, and heaved the collective sideways to cut across the wind current. The wind roll that he'd observed had, somewhere in the last thirty seconds, become a microburst downdraft.

He felt his heavy bird fighting it. Shifting right though, he was pulling left. A swirl of smoke wrapped about him, cutting his visibility to zero.

At full lift on the rotors, his distance-to-ground radar was feeding him a strong negative even though the rate-of-climb gauge was pinned positive.

The air was descending faster than he could climb and taking him down with it.

He hit the tank dump switch and four tons of retardant spilled downward, gone in a matter of five seconds.

Lighter now.

Still going down despite full up on the collective.

A ground proximity alarm squealed to life.

He slammed from a hard left bank to a hard right bank. Sometimes you had to turn into the skid.

Four hundred feet above the ground level.

The one problem was that his skid had to end before he'd crossed the width of the saddle. Just beyond where the drafts were battering him, on the far side of this dip in the mountains, the ridge rose once more.

Three hundred feet Above Ground Level.

It was a near-vertical wall of chopper-killing conifers for another five hundred feet up.

He found the edge of the microburst.

Two hundred feet.

The rate of fall eased off, but he was still headed in the wrong direction.

Requests for status from the others rattled in his ears.

Vern ignored them.

A hundred feet.

He found clear, calm air down in the heart of the saddle.

Fifty feet above the trees, he arrested his descent.

He hovered in a tiny, fragile bubble of clear air. He glanced at the temperature gauge. The air was cold. That's why it had no smoke in it.

But dense smoke surrounded him on three sides and formed a capstone above. Inside his little bubble there was himself, the pointed shafts of towering pines clawing upward from the green forest below, and the vertical face of the next ridge—which was less than five rotors away.

It was the eye of the firestorm and it wasn't going to last.

"Coming out!" He hit the radio. "Aiming southeast, but no promises."

The scanning radar said he was good straight ahead, and the orange glow shining deep in the smoke to his right told him there was fire coming far too soon.

Cyclic up hard, nose down, and the belly tank empty.

The Firehawk leaped like a bird of prey.

At 190 knots, only three below the rated "Never

Exceed" speed, he pulled back on the cyclic and shot upward.

He punched a hole into the overhead smoke cap.

Visibility extended only as far as the thickness of his windshield. Now he was flying strictly IFR—Instrument Flight Rules.

The heat of the smoke curtain so close above the fire was intense and instantly overrode the air-conditioning.

The Firehawk was being dragged north by the wind vortices, so Vern carved the climb to the right. According to the instruments, he needed another two hundred feet up or he wouldn't be clearing the ridge.

Detritus flew by his screen, flaming branches torn from the trees and cast skyward.

If they battered his chopper, he didn't hear them. He was far too busy to hear anything. If he yelled at the heat shock, he missed that as well.

A wildfire tornado.

He'd heard of them, had seen Cal's award-winning photo of one from last year, but he'd never seen one himself.

And he sure as hell hadn't flown right next to one!

A dozen feet over and his rotor blades would be in the fire. A dozen more and he'd cook.

It reminded him of the storms off the Oregon coast when he'd flown Coast Guard. The Pacific Ocean regularly threw sixty-, eighty-, even hundred-knot winds at the shore. That basically meant that what the East Coast called a "category three hurricane," the West Coast called a "good storm" and sent out the chopper pilots.

One thing he'd learned from the storms: the way out of a hurricane was to circle and climb.

So Vern rolled into the wind and rode it until his ground speed was truly terrifying—his own speed added to the wind's cyclonic whirl. He skimmed along right outside the fire.

Then, moments before he would have eaten the cliff face, he slammed left and punched out into clear air to the northwest.

"Got him!" someone shouted over the radio.

Vern didn't acknowledge.

He ran into the still air as if he hit a wall.

He flailed against the double cross-shoulder harness that felt as if it was trying to cut him into quarters.

Out of the high-speed winds, he was suddenly moving at far past the "never exceed" speed.

The trailing edge of his spinning rotors lost all lift and his chopper tumbled to the right. With a hard kick of the rudder pedals, he managed to turn it into a corkscrew fall into the main valley, bleeding off speed.

When at last he could fly straight again, he climbed, getting above anything that could kill him without his permission.

Let Mark keep everyone out of his way; he didn't care where he was so long as it was up and out.

"Now that was the way to hustle." Mark's voice was dry and almost as filled with relief as Vern's suddenly drained body felt.

Not trusting his voice yet, Vern acknowledged with a click of the mic switch.

"You're done for the day, Firehawk Oh-Three. Take her home and put your feet up."

Vern wasn't going to argue.

He was thankful for three things.

One, that he was alive.

Two, that Denise wasn't with him.

And three, that she didn't need to know about this. Really didn't.

Denise had her team lined up on the tarmac and ready. The fear of what she would find was so thick in her throat and chest that she couldn't breathe. Couldn't drag enough of the smoke-laden oxygen into her lungs to function. Tearing aside the white dust-filter mask didn't help.

Vern didn't land in either of the retardant-loading slots, but instead settled his chopper in the corner closest to her service box.

Smooth, so smooth.

No beatbox dancing about the sky this time. He simply flew it in and set it down.

She was at the door before his rotors had stopped spinning. "Are you okay?"

He tossed his sunglasses up on the dash and offered one of those easy smiles. "You heard?"

She tapped the radio on her belt.

"So much for number three," he said cryptically. "I'm fine. Haven't flown something that nasty since the Coast Guard, but I'm fine."

"I can do the shutdown for you," she offered in her calmest voice, unsure which of them she was trying to soothe.

"No worries, Wrench. I'm really okay."

She watched him anyway. And he did start out fine. But his hands began to shake about halfway through the shutdown. He finished that, but she plucked the logbook out of his nerveless fingers and completed the day's entry herself. She tucked it back in its slot and rested her hand over his where they'd gone limp in his lap.

"Shit, that was close." His grip crushed down on hers. His face was drawn and pale as he leaned back against his seat with his eyes closed. "I'm really glad that you weren't there. Really glad."

"Could I have helped?"

He rolled his head back and forth against the seat. "Never seen anything like it before. None of us has. It was a whole new level of nasty. If Steve hadn't brought his drone in so that I had some warning, I'd be—" He managed a weak smile. "At least none of us will fall for it again. I'm okay, and I didn't break your precious chopper."

Like she gave a damn about that.

He didn't even make an attempt at a laugh to go with his comment; which scared her more than anything so far. It had been so bad it had blown the breaker on his sense of humor.

She helped him out of his seat because it was clear that his hands weren't going to work the harness releases yet.

He clambered down, landing steady, and looked down at her. He brushed a thumb along her cheek. "You're so beautiful, Denise. What are you doing hanging out with a joker like me?"

She did her best not to melt into a girly puddle of happy. But she kept her answer light for his sake. "Just slumming, I guess."

That earned her the low chuckle she'd been hoping for. She'd made a joke at the right time, and it had worked. This was good.

They both became aware of externals at the same time. The sounds of her crew going over Vern's chopper, the roar as Emily's bird came in for another load of retardant with Jeannie's close behind. A passenger jet shot down the main runway beyond the Zulie Aerial Fire Depot and took flight. The deep bass of its engines at full burn pounded against them as it climbed out of the smoky valley.

Brenna came up. "I think you need to see this one, boss."

Denise made sure that Vern was okay, then followed Brenna around to the other side of the chopper. She stumbled to a halt.

She heard a soft curse as Vern came up behind her.

The paint down the left side had bubbled and blistered with heat. The two big panes of laminate glass in the cargo bay door had been shattered, and the lower window on the copilot's side was star-cracked. A section of tree limb four inches in diameter stuck out of the rear fuselage, driven right through the metal as if it had been a spear.

"Didn't break my bird, Slick?" Where she found the bit of humor, she'd never know, because she was fighting against the urge to be sick over how close it had been. It might not be bullets, but the aircraft had definitely been to war. "What the hell was it really like up there?"

When she looked up at him, Vern was shaking his head. "I don't really know. I was kinda busy at the time trying to get out of it."

"If that branch had hit six inches higher, it—"

"Don't say it!" He cut her off.

It would have gone right into the main power trans-fer for the rear rotor. She'd seen the terrain yesterday. There'd be no nice neat autorotation into some meadow. Instead, Vern would not be standing here beside her. Ever again.

And suddenly, that he was standing just inches away was terribly important. Far more important than their shared bed last night could explain.

"You did good, Wrench. Your bird performed when it counted, and it got me home." Now it was her turn to laugh.

"I don't think you're the one who's supposed to be reassuring me. I think that it's the other way around."

"Whatever works." He pulled her against him with an arm around her shoulder, and for a moment she allowed herself to enjoy the sensation. He kissed the top of her head and murmured into her hair, "Whatever works."

She burrowed her face into his chest for one glorious instant. This. This definitely worked.

Then she snapped herself out of it.

"Okay, team." She patted Vern's chest where her nose had rested a moment before and then stepped out of his embrace. She felt a slight tearing in her chest as if she'd left a small part of herself behind. Denise won-dered if it would come back the next time she snuggled up against him.

Malcolm and Brenna came back from around the tail section where they'd been inspecting for other damage.

"This is a full teardown inspection." Denise plucked at a paint blister, and a six-inch patch of paint peeled off in her hand exposing silvered metal beneath. "This bird doesn't go aloft until we replace every piece of rubber on this side including the tire. I don't care if we put it in new yesterday, replace it. Then we fully inspect the other side.

"Brenna, you're on drive train. Malcolm, control systems and watch for any sign of melting in the wiring. I'll start with structural integrity and rotor blades. Let's go, folks. We want this bird aloft again. I want it perfect right down to the paint job, and we don't have a week to do it."

They didn't need any further instruction, but were headed off to the shop-box at a good hustle. It was a tight team, maybe the best she'd worked with outside of the Sikorsky factory itself.

She went up and tugged on the tree limb that was sticking out of the rear fuselage. Its surface was scorched, as if it had been flaming when it was driven in. It was firmly embedded; they'd probably have to drop the panel and cut it out.

Then Vern's big hands wrapped around the branch above hers. Together, they managed to haul it free. Three feet of tree limb reluctantly slid out of the Firehawk's guts.

"Spartacus," was Vern's dry comment as he hefted it.

"Like in the gladiator guy?"

"Heaving his javelin at me, but I survived."

She looked up at him. The sunlight, softened by smoke, lit his face. The joker wasn't there; neither was the easygoing pilot. Instead, for the first time, she could see the man who'd flown for the U.S. Coast Guard and knew more about flying to fire than anyone in Mount

Hood Aviation. Emily might have flown longer and be the chief pilot, but Vern had the most fire experience of anyone on the crew.

He reached out and rested a palm against the chopper and closed his eyes. It wasn't for support to stand up. It actually looked as if he was offering the damaged Firehawk his support, or perhaps thanking it for bringing him home.

She left him to it and went to fetch her tools, but the image didn't go away.

The man was so damn handsome, a military hero brought to life in a fire, and for some reason, he wanted her. Well—she felt a spring enter her step—she wanted him, so that worked out nicely.

She could feel the fear that had lurked beside her all day slide away as she set to work.

—◦◦◦—

At a half hour to sunset, the other pilots were down. Five minutes later, Mark Henderson called a pilots' meeting, and five minutes more after that, they were grouped around a set of tables pulled together in a corner of the mess hall.

Three hours later, Vern's head was whirling. Right through dinner, they'd reviewed every detail of both his flight and the drone's—which Steve had managed to save through some piloting almost as creative as his own. They pieced together what radar imaging and flight tracking they could, and slowly rebuilt each step of the fire and the flight.

Twenty-seven seconds. How so much could happen in twenty-seven seconds was beyond him. Looking over the final re-creation of what he'd done only made his successful escape that much more unlikely.

It also gave him a new level of respect for Mark and Emily. They extracted every nuance of his observations, getting him to report things he hadn't even known he'd seen, until they built a precise picture of what he'd done and also a protocol on how to recognize and avoid similar conditions in the future.

He found it hard to remember sometimes that these were two of the very best heli-pilots on the planet. They had both made it to the rank of major flying for the U.S. Army's 160th SOAR. The Special Operations Aviation Regiment flew those deep, dark, crazy missions like attacking bin Laden's compound.

So when Emily finally said, "I wouldn't want to try flying that route," Vern knew he'd done pretty well. Mark's "You didn't miss a single trick" made him feel even better.

Which was good, because despite the last lazy couple of hours—including one long, hot shower where he finally let the shakes out—he was hammer-down exhausted.

He did go out to check on his Firehawk.

Mickey tagged along for moral support.

They stood side by side in the darkness and stared at the chopper.

It sat alone. Only a few security lights were aglow. The main compound lights were off.

"How late is it?"

"Past eleven," Mickey responded.

A silence hung over the airport as thick as a smoke blanket, everything muffled, finally quiet.

"Man, she has really trashed that thing."

A line of "Do Not Cross" tape had been strung around his helicopter, and he could see why. His poor machine looked like one of those exploded-view diagrams that were so useless on "some assembly required" sets of instructions. But he could see there was a perfect order to it.

Starting from the tape line, Denise and her crew had laid out each section of the disassembled helicopter in order: scrap bits closest to the tape, next sheet metal, after that carefully arranged carts of new and rebuilt parts, and a big tool chest that had been closed for the night. She hadn't been kidding when she said full inspection.

Denise was nowhere to be seen. It was late and doing an all-night push on repairs was no safer than doing all-night flights as a pilot. Besides, even a full night wouldn't get his bird back together.

"You're actually seeing Denise? Like…seeing her?" Mickey's voice was as disbelieving as his own would have been even a few days ago.

"Maybe."

"*Maybe?* How can you not know?"

"Well, we slept together," Vern admitted.

"Well, duh! That means—"

"But no sex."

Mickey left a long silence.

The main airport's lights shut off, darkening the scene even further.

"That's just weird, Vern. You're not making any sense."

"Yeah, tell me about it." He stared upward, seeking the stars. Nothing but a smoke-hazed moon.

"Hey, glad I caught you." Mark arrived out of the darkness.

Not really a night for romance anyway; Vern was weaving with exhaustion and had no idea where Denise was bunked down.

"Hell of a mess," Mark observed, surveying Denise's handiwork.

Or perhaps it was a comment on the mess Vern had created.

"I need you tomorrow, if you're up for it."

Vern shrugged. He realized the gesture probably wasn't visible, but he was having trouble finding the energy to speak.

Mark apparently took his silence as sufficient assent. "Vanessa's training is coming along, but I think you could really help her. Do a fly-along instructional round with her."

"Oh man," Mickey groaned with envy. "Hot Italian babe in a tiny helicopter. You lucky son of a bitch. Her accent totally slays me."

Mickey was such a dog. Sure Vanessa was five ten of dark, sleek Italian. But when Vern tried to picture the moment the way Mickey was, he came up with five feet of shy blond instead.

"Sure, Mark. I won't be flying Hawk Oh-Three tomorrow. That's for damn sure."

The three of them surveyed the carefully organized mayhem spread across the tarmac before them.

"Well, you got that much straight." Mickey sighed. "Man, what a mess."

"In more ways than you think, buddy." What the hell was he going to do about Denise? And where was she anyway?

It was too late, and he was too tired to ask.

Resigned, he headed back to his room.

When he opened the door, it let a splash of light in from the hall. Enough light to shine off a flowing expanse of blond hair. Denise was curled beneath the blanket on his bed with her hair over the covers. Sound asleep, but here, of all crazy places.

He closed the door and let his eyes adapt slowly to the pale moonlight coming through the unshaded window. She'd gone to sleep close against the wall, leaving just enough space for him to join her.

Denise Conroy wanted him beside her.

The top bunk made more sense. All they'd shared were a few kisses and one brief awakening. Despite the implicit invitation, it would make more sense if they actually spoke and maybe got to know each other better before they went any further.

Resolute, he undressed, stopping at the last moment to keep his underwear in place. He folded down the sheet on the top bunk. Then, after telling himself he was a complete and total idiot who should be flogged for what he was thinking, he slid into the lower bunk.

Denise didn't wake…not really.

She slid against him and wrapped a leg over his, rested her cheek on his shoulder, and with a soft sigh settled back into sleep.

Vern stared at the shadowed bottom of the upper bunk. Never before had he slept with a woman who wasn't first a lover. Never before last night anyway.

With some chagrin, he laid his cheek against her ever-so-soft hair and thought back to the moment he'd broken the Firehawk while returning to the MHA base from the grassland fire.

No question, he'd been absolutely right.
Denise was killing him.

Chapter 7

VERN WOKE ALONE AND BLINKED AT THE SUNLIGHT SHINING in through the window. The bright, mid-morning sunlight. That meant the smoke was clearing out of Missoula. That in turn meant either a wind shift, which could be a very bad thing, or they were beating the fire. And he was supposed to be aloft with Vanessa at first light.

He rolled up out of the bunk. Right before he made it upright, he remembered that he hadn't been alone when he went to sleep. He turned to inspect the empty expanse of sheets, at the same moment his temple whacked hard against the upper bunk.

Collapsing back onto his pillow, his groan didn't make him feel any damned better.

When the stars had cleared and the spins stopped, he tested for blood. Nope, though his breath hissed out at the contact. Leaking brain matter? No more than usual, despite how hard he'd clocked himself. Just an already rising lump from hell, his usual price for being stupid.

Rising much more carefully, he dressed and hunted down coffee and a sandwich that Betsy was nice enough to make for him because that was clearly beyond his capabilities at the moment.

With his second cup topped off in his travel mug, he tracked Denise down on the flight line.

As he had last night, he simply had to watch her for

a moment. She and Malcolm had pulled the decking on his Firehawk's cargo bay, leaning in to inspect the wiring and whatever else it was that ran under there. One thing his libido was deeply aware of was that the woman looked equally delicious from front, side, or back. His body definitely remembered being pressed against the back of her, and his hands tingled with memory of the splendid curves of her front.

And at the rate things were going, a great view was the only enjoyment he was going to get for quite some time to come.

She turned from giving instructions and spotted him. Weaving between parts and carts and bits of melted helicopter, Denise came over, moving fast and easy. Jeans, denim shirt, and that standard sexy-gunslinger tool belt wrapped around swaying hips. Pure murder.

"Hi." The caffeine had finally reached his speech centers allowing him to greet her with at least one level better than a grunt.

"Morning, Slick." She'd been headed into his arms; he and his libido were pretty happily sure of that. But a single step away she braked to a halt and inspected his forehead. "What happened to you?"

"Nothing." He'd tried putting on his cap to cover it, but there was no way that was going to happen until the pain and the swelling went down.

"Did someone look at that?"

"No need." He shrugged it off. Betsy, who was an EMT in addition to being the MHA cook, had checked it out and told him to be more careful.

"I didn't wake you this morning, did I?"

"No." Looking down at her sunny face and compact body, he wished to hell she had. "Last night, I don't think I woke you."

"You were supposed to."

He closed his eyes. Okay, beyond idiot right over into doofus.

"I mean, I like sleeping with you, Vern. But this is getting ridiculous."

He winced and looked down into those green eyes. On its own, his hand came up and he brushed a thumb over the soft skin of her cheek.

"I won't let it happen again, Wrench."

"You better not, Slick. Or I'm going to think something's wrong with me." There was a momentary darkness. "Or maybe with you." She covered the fleeting shadow with a teasing smile.

"Trust me. It's not you." Vern slid his fingers through her hair, then leaned in to kiss her forehead. "On the other hand, there's plenty wrong with me. Ask my mom."

"I'll do that."

This time it didn't feel so forward, suggesting that Denise and his mother would meet someday. If only he could get some alone time with Denise when they weren't both exhausted. Yeah, welcome to firefighting. He sighed.

"I couldn't agree more." She matched her sigh to his. She rested her hand on his chest, making him impossibly aware of his own heartbeat. "But here comes your ride."

He heard the high-whip sound of his old MD500 descending out of the almost-blue sky. Vanessa, back for refueling. Time to go flying and do some training.

"Crap."

Vanessa did a nice job of setting down her bucket so it kissed the tarmac. Empty, the bucket looked like the lower half of a pumpkin, made of canvas and folded accordion-like. It was big enough for three or four guys to pile into if they had to when it was open, yet it would stow in the back of the tiny chopper if it was collapsed.

She then shifted enough sideways to set the long-line down without landing one of the MD's skids on it. That told him that she'd learned a lot these last few days over rough terrain about exactly where her bucket was. From this point, it would be polish. She had the essentials down.

He could see Mickey's point; Vanessa was fully on display in the MD500's bubble nose. Dark complexion, long dark hair. Even the Nomex and cargo pants couldn't hide the length of her legs.

Vern looked back down at Denise. This was what he wanted. He leaned down to brush his lips over hers, and she opened to his kiss as if they'd been lovers for years rather than, well, never.

"Soon, Slick," she whispered against his lips.

"Real soon, Wrench." They traded smiles and he hurried off to pull on his gear so that he didn't delay Vanessa's return to the fire once she was refueled.

—∿∿—

Denise wondered which god she should curse or make a burnt offering to or something. Yet another night when they'd been too busy and too exhausted to do more than collapse into each other's arms.

As predicted, the high carbon content of the ash in

the air had begun to take its toll, and her crew had spent hours cleaning, tightening, and doing some replacing. It was midnight before the birds other than Vern's had been ready for flight.

Mark's wake-up call had been painful, and she didn't have the energy to tease, promise, or even simply enjoy the moment. Vern was in no better shape. They'd helped each other dress, and it had been about as sexy as helping a friend bind a hurt hand.

At least before he opened the door, he'd sat down on the one chair and pulled her into his lap. They sat for a long five minutes they couldn't really afford that went by impossibly fast. They hadn't traded a word or even a kiss.

He held her close, and she in turn let herself be held as she curled against him. Still not having spoken—for what was there to be said?—they confronted the day.

Denise's team had finished, tested, and certified Firehawk Oh-Three by early afternoon. It was about the same time Mark declared the fire fully contained and handed it off to a Type II Incident Team. The Hoodie smokejumpers had worked their own miracles over the last five days and were even now being trucked back down for the flight out.

The Zulies were still down on the Hard Creek Fire, but the prediction was that they'd be released in another forty-eight hours.

So the MHA Hoodies had decamped from the Zulie base. Now it was an hour to sunset, and they were nearing the MHA base camp in the foothills of Mount Hood.

Denise huddled in the copilot's seat.

A part of her insisted she was making up the whole thing.

No. He held me in his sleep. He held me in his lap just this morning.

But there was an old tape. A stronger, deeper one that lurked deep inside. One that insisted that there was nothing real between her and Vern except a bit of lust and a shared love of helicopters. They didn't even love the same part. He was like a rocket jock and she like a NASA engineer, no common ground.

She tried to hold on to the memories that her body insisted were real, but she was so tired that she no longer believed anything.

Exhausted by it all. Exhausted by her own thoughts and hurt by the pending disappointment of what had seemed so promising, she curled up on her seat and kept quiet. Her life's plan had been right. She was a woman who wasn't built for deep or meaningful relationships, and she shouldn't dream of them, because the pain of losing even that thread of hope cut deep.

Every pilot was talking about the flight Vern had made. He'd been elevated to some godlike-flier status by the MHA core. The flight was even more impressive than she'd thought, and she'd been pretty impressed to begin with.

Then Denise had overheard Bruce and Gordon talking about her and Vern as a couple. They didn't understand how their friend could be such an odd duck when there were all of these normal women who apparently were just waiting for him in some goddamn magical wonderland. Bruce and Gordon envied him all the great women who were apparently holding out for him.

Vern would wake up soon and Denise would be off the pedestal he had her on, real soon. Then he'd be gone and she'd be, well, screwed. Not being a total idiot, she knew how the world worked and that it was better to just let whatever was between her and Vern die now. Fast and quiet. They'd hit base camp. They'd avoid each other until the end of the fire season, which should be any day, and they'd go their separate ways.

"Mark," she heard Vern call out over the radio.

"Here." He was in the MHA formation somewhere. They were returning as a unit, one oh-so-happy team. All for one and all that.

"I'm going to catch up with you later."

"Roger. Fly safe. Out."

Denise didn't think much of the conversation.

Vern curved their route south and began to descend. She looked out the windscreen and saw the other choppers continuing toward the base on the north side of Mount Hood. She and Vern were headed south of it, but they were already below the height of the ridge they'd have to clear to continue westward.

He continued the descent. Circling down until she could see the trees—not the green mat of a hundred thousand spires, but individuals—and then their branches.

"Where are you taking me?"

"Buck Lake."

"And what's there?"

Vern didn't say another word as he continued his descent through the bright afternoon.

Buck Lake was a near-circle of water lost among the trees. It was perhaps five hundred feet across. Nothing else nearby except miles of the Mount Hood National Forest.

"There's a hiking trail through the trees into the south

side of the lake. There are some campsites under the trees just above the rocky shore. It's rarely used this late in the year."

He circled around over the north end and found a spot on a rocky bluff to settle Denise's service container. He landed the chopper close by facing toward the water.

Then he shut down the engines and opened the door.

The silence was immense. It covered the lake and filled the chopper. It washed over her as palpably as the roar of turbine engines coming up to speed. The air smelled so fresh and clean; it might never have been used before. It had the purity of high altitude and deep forest in the early days of fall.

"What's here on the north side of the lake?" Her voice was barely a whisper.

Vern used a brush of his thumb on her cheek to turn her toward him. It was so unexpected after what she'd just been thinking that she would have jolted if she hadn't been so surprised. She shifted over to full-body paralysis when, just as gently, he touched his lips to hers, nudging and coaxing until she could feel herself opening to him despite her certainty that nothing existed between them.

A sound broke the silence, softly at first, coming from somewhere deep inside.

As Vern kissed her, brushed his nose on hers, rubbed a thumb over her lips, and tasted... Oh God! He tasted divine! It rose into a roar, then a pounding that filled her ears, a sound created by the unexpected surge of need within her.

"What's here, Denise?" Vern whispered against her lips. "Just us."

—◦◦◦—

Vern hadn't been prepared for the response. They'd both been so eager to get their hands on each other; he'd expected anything other than what happened.

Denise sat back ever so slowly, pulling away from him until they sat once again in their separate seats of the Firehawk with the vast canyon of the radio console between them.

Was she upset because he hadn't asked her? He'd wanted to surprise her. It was a beautiful lake, one of his favorite spots. Trees ringed almost the whole thing right to the edge of the water. Even this late in the year, the water would be sun-warmed rather than glacier-fed.

"Seriously?" She faced him.

He tried to read her tone, her face, her body language, anything, but he couldn't. She sounded disbelieving, as if he was lying about it. He nodded. "Seriously."

She turned to look out the windscreen. After a long moment, she leaned slightly forward and then slammed herself back against the padding. She repeated it again and again.

After the fourth time, he reached out a hand to touch her arm, and she went immediately still.

"You can't want to be with me." Her voice was even flatter than the silent lake on the still day.

"What makes you say that, Wrench?" He wanted to be with her so much that his body ached with it, and not only his loins. His fingers wanted to brush her cheek. His arm whimpered with a need to encircle her waist and tug her tight against his chest. He longed to taste—

"Because there is no way you want to be with some-one as stupid as me."

He burst out laughing, couldn't stop it. He laughed right in her face.

"Yeah." She smiled wanly. "Dumb as a thumb, I know."

"Stupid? How can a woman as smart as you even think something like that?"

She grimaced, then shrugged. "You have no idea. About the time you were planning this nefarious kidnap-ping so that you could have your evil way with me—"

"That wasn't quite—" He tried to backpedal.

"Which believe me, I want to be a party to."

That stopped his sputtering attempt to build an apol-ogy and left him totally adrift.

"At that same time, I was busy convincing myself that you didn't really want me because otherwise you would have... I don't know. Something."

"Made love to you when we were both too tired to remember it afterward?"

This time a smile helped him read her expression. "Yeah, something like that. So, you want your evil way with me?"

"Oh my God, yes!" Vern couldn't believe they were having this conversation. They were sitting a foot apart, separated by fifty thousand dollars of electronics, talk-ing about how much they wanted each other.

"Oh."

"Oh? That's it? Just 'oh'?"

She nodded, hesitated, then nodded again. Without looking at him again, she slipped out the door on her side of the helicopter. Too dumbfounded to move, he watched her circling around the nose of the Firehawk, coming around to his side.

But she didn't.

She stopped right in front of his position and stared at him for a long moment through the windscreen. Then, ever so slowly, she turned her back on him until she was facing the lake. She may have smiled the moment before she fully turned her back on him.

There, in full view, Denise Conroy began to undress. Boots, vest, pants, bra, underwear. In moments, they were folded and piled neatly on the hard stone that made up this part of the lakeshore.

The sun was off to their right, low in the west. It shone off her mane of hair and her skin as if sunlight had been created for no other purpose. The tan on her face wasn't from living and working outdoors; its gentle golden-butter tone covered her from head to toe.

With an easy motion, she reached over her shoulder and swept her hair forward. Finally seeing her full shape for the first time was a revelation that made him wish that his mother's art lessons had found a more adept student. Denise's shoulders had the strength of her vocation; her waist, hips, and legs had been custom designed for Eve to help her launch the race of humankind— pure woman.

She again twisted her hair into a thick French braid, bent down—which was an astonishing sight in itself— and fetched a clip from a jeans pocket, and tossed her hair once more over her back.

"So, are you just going to sit there?" She didn't even bother to turn as she asked, her voice clear in the perfect silence. Then she walked away from him toward the water.

His paralysis broke the moment she reached the water's edge.

He jerked sideways to get out of the chopper and was brutally slammed back into place by the harness he had yet to release.

She was in up to her knees by the time he fought his way loose.

Her waist by the time he managed to remember how to unlace his boots.

Her neck and swimming before he too was naked.

He ran across the sun-heated rock and did a racing dive out into the water. He emerged in time to see her disappear beneath the surface in an elegant move.

And perhaps the echo of a laugh played in the ripples from her dive.

———

Denise had left Denise back on the shoreline. It was the only way she could think to explain herself to herself.

She'd never stripped naked in front of a man strictly to make him crazy. Actually, she always undressed in the dark or slipped off the last items after she was under the covers. She'd never been naked out of doors. And she'd certainly never been skinny-dipping.

The sensation was intense. She loved to swim, but the water, the sense of motion through it, was always held at a distance by the swimsuit. Even the few times she'd worn a bikini—she was more of a one-piece gal— it hadn't felt like this.

The warm lake water embraced her. When she swam, it stroked her entire body from face to toes in a single long slide that set her nerves alight, all at once.

As if she were a helicopter's main data bus suddenly overwhelmed with information, the sensations poured through her, too vast and wonderful to comprehend.

Then she heard the sharp splash of a dive.

A glance over her shoulder told her that Vern would be coming up on her and fast. She laughed for the sheer joy of it and dove.

She went deep and doubled back to meet him, but he swam right over her, racing to her former position.

He shifted to tread water.

Rising silently to surface behind him, she took a deep breath and tapped him on the shoulder. When he turned to face her, she drove a great palm-blast of water into his face and dove back under.

His hand brushed down her thigh, grabbed her calf, but slid off her ankle as she kicked down and away.

This time she went for distance.

When she surfaced, he was looking right at her across a hundred feet or more of water, two rotors he'd call it. Vern bellowed like an enraged bull, alarming several ducks into flight, and drove toward her.

He was as magnificent a swimmer as he was a pilot. She lost crucial seconds admiring his form, the way his shoulders rippled with muscle as he shot toward her.

Her squeak of alarm was too late in breaking her momentary hypnosis.

One of those long arms managed to snare her about the waist, and in moments his kiss crushed down on her mouth.

Flesh to flesh, nothing between them, not even water. How she had craved this, dreamed of it over these last days. But it had never felt this good, not even in her imagination. They each kicked their legs to stay afloat, but that was the only concession.

Denise gave back every bit as good as she got. With their mouths locked and their tongues exploring, she raked her hands over his back and shoulder muscles, wanting to learn every curve, every nuance as fast as she could.

Vern had one hand dug up into her hair and the other cupping her behind to keep them close. He was so powerful; it felt as if he could hold up the world to keep her close.

They both became so lost in the sensations that their legs stilled and they slid beneath the surface.

In moments they were apart, back on the surface, and both sputtering and choking.

"Hell of a place to be making love to someone," Vern observed, clearing his throat once more.

Denise let herself slip momentarily back below the surface to cool her flaming cheeks. "Make love to someone." The few guys who ever said something like that actually just meant sex, not understanding the difference between sex and love. Not that she'd ever experienced the latter, but she had a good imagination.

Vern's voice sounded as if it knew exactly what it meant, which made the blood roar in her ears once more.

Back on the surface, she wanted to tease him. Teasing was an unheard-of practice in Denise's experience, but she still wanted to try.

"If you want to make love to me, you'll have to beat me to shore." They'd crossed most of the lake.

He grinned and opened his mouth to reply, exactly as she'd expected. She drove another faceful of water at

him and set off at a racing crawl toward the distant bank
while he choked and spluttered.

Again, that roar of need resounded from behind her,
and she used its energy to drive herself ahead even
faster. She'd never had such an effect on a man. Not
Denise Conroy.

Don't think. Swim!

He caught her twenty feet from the rocky shore. A
big hand came down and grabbed her ankle; her forward
progress was abruptly halted. He dragged her back to
him. As he turned to stand in the chest-deep water, she
had an idea.

She let herself be dragged in until he tried to shift his
hold from her ankles to her wrists.

With a quick tuck and twist, she lay on her back
with her feet placed squarely on his chest. She pushed
off, hard.

He tumbled backward into the water.

She shot for shore.

But he was quick! He snared her ankle again before
she got clear.

This time when he grabbed her, she had no interest in
escaping. Being a cautious man, though, he didn't give
her another chance. He pulled her in, one leg to either
side of him, and in moments she was still floating on her
back with her knees over his shoulders and her ankles
crossed behind his neck. She was helpless to retaliate,
needing her hands to keep her head afloat.

He nuzzled the inside of her thigh, a sensation so
intense that it rocketed up into her and stopped the last
of her struggles.

With a big hand supporting her shoulders so that her

head didn't go underwater, he placed his other hand beneath her hips, then lowered his mouth to her.

All Denise could do was watch the shining blue sky, rimmed by green conifers, as she floated. Her cries gave voice to some infinitesimal percentage of the pleasure he sent coursing through her body.

―∿∿―

They'd finally come ashore at full dark.

Vern had only addressed the very beginning of the list he'd been assembling of things he wanted to do for Denise. But while the lake had offered a lot of room for play, it also had its limitations—liking having to constantly avoid drowning.

And how easily the woman slipped away underwater; she swam like a mermaid. Which gave him a few ideas for later.

Ashore, a suddenly shy Denise pulled her clothes back on as he fixed them a scrounged meal from the odds and ends in the cooler and a few of the MREs that sustained firefighters when they had no time to eat.

One advantage of Denise getting dressed was that after dinner he had the joy of undressing her again. It was under the cover of darkness, but it was an experience he'd never forget.

The moon had retreated from the early night sky while they'd been in Montana. Here in the woods, well clear of civilization, the darkness was near complete. Only starlight graced her body as he slowly unwrapped it like the most precious Christmas gift.

What was lacking in sight was more than made up for in shape, texture, taste, and smell. Unraveling her braid and brushing out her hair with his fingers to dry had been an intensely sensual experience all its own.

On a pile of rescue blankets for padding, and beneath an unzipped sleeping bag that they kept having to pull back into place until they gave it up as a lost cause, they explored.

She zeroed in on the ticklish spot beneath his ribs that made him squirm.

He discovered that she possessed many places, which, if nibbled, sent her into a hail of giggles. The wonder of Denise Conroy giggling sidetracked him quite thoroughly.

They had spent days together, but not.

Nights sleeping together, yet nothing else.

He wanted her so badly, but he also wanted it to last. Wanted to take his time, not scare her back into some shy place with his desperate need for her.

She finally stopped him with a searing kiss that he could feel right past his loins and into his toes. When at last she broke from the kiss, she whispered a single word into the darkness.

"Now."

It might just be the sweetest sound he'd ever heard.

She was the one who'd thought ahead and made a side trip to a pharmacy in Missoula, for which he was deeply appreciative. When she rolled the protection over him, he was even more so.

It took no coaxing on either part; they simply moved together as if locked onto the same flight path. When he finally entered her, it wasn't the frantic conquest his body begged for. Instead, it was a process as slow and silky as unraveling her hair. They built slowly on

discovery, moved to exploration, and when he entered
her, he found joy.

The sensations were so overwhelming, so intense,
that no frantic motion was required; the slightest shift
had them both gasping with amazement. No woman had
ever felt so good, so right.

Their first time together wasn't about speed or heat. It
was about how perfect every tiny motion felt. He drove
her upward, one slow stroke at a time, until she arched
like a strung bow for an impossibly long moment.

And then her release hammered her.

He wished he could see her. He wished there was
light while he drank in her desperate moans. But even
broad daylight would have done him no good because
the fire in his body flooded outward until he felt brighter
on the inside than any mere solar radiance.

He peaked into her and rode down the other side as
she wrapped arms and legs around him, and dragged
him so close that he'd never escape the heat of the shining fire that was Denise Conroy.

———

Vern woke, as he usually did, shortly before dawn. This
time there was no question. He knew exactly where
they were.

"They." No thought or consideration. It was simply
there in his first thought of the day. It was wholly unexpected and wholly wonderful. He could get very used to
thinking of "they" if Denise Conroy was the other part
of that.

The last of the stars still struggled against the impend-
ing day in a blue-black sky. Perched above them, the

Firehawk had watched over their sleep, reaching its rotor blades over them like a protecting hand.

He wanted to close his eyes and go back to last night. They had occupied themselves for hours before finally collapsing into sleep. Not because he was in any way sated. Usually after a good bout of hot sex, he was happily content to sleep it off. After a good bout of hot sex with Denise, he wanted more. There was a richness and depth to their lovemaking he'd never experienced before, like a painting that needed coat upon coat to build up and discover the true image.

First coat had been when he took her the first time.

Second, he had explored her body with his mouth and his hands until he had her writhing once more. Her cries echoed across the lake as she thrust against his hand and mouth. His own release had followed not long after hers.

Third, a midnight swim, her hair pinned atop her head and dunking forbidden. They'd slid across the lake and back with long, lazy strokes and emerged into the cool night air.

Afterward, curled tightly together for warmth and then comfort as the moon finally crept into the circle of stars made by the tall stands of timber surrounding the lake, they talked. They'd talked about nothing: favorite movies, least favorite foods, worst dates. And in some ways, that had been his favorite part of the night.

Finally, they had simply held each other and listened to the night as the stars spun and the moon shadows moved.

He rubbed his nose in her now-dry hair. Once again she was curled into his chest in her sleep. He'd never been much of a one for tally sheets, but he could easily count each touch, each kiss, each…

Somewhere around first light she shifted and slowly stretched without making any move to escape his arms. It was a long, languid process that he wanted to catalog in every detail. The way her instep slid down the inside of his calf. The way her hand slid from where it had been tucked by her chin, slowly outward to explore across his chest.

The pattern shifted when she hooked a leg over his hips. He'd been rock hard since her first sigh of awakening, but now with the coming dawn, she was aware of it as well.

"Hmm." She made a small hum of pleasure as she kissed the center of his chest. He could feel the tiny vibrations from her lips.

Then she shifted to kneel over him. Her eyes were still half closed, as if she were sleepwalking. Her hair now flowed about her, halfway between Lady Godiva and Cousin It from *The Addams Family*, her face and upper torso invisible behind a veil made entirely of hair. The ends tickled his bare chest. When she leaned down to kiss him, it felt as if he were disappearing into a golden cave that held only them.

Still moving as if more asleep than awake, she took some protection from the supply that had been seriously dented last night and shifted down to sheathe him.

With a deep sigh, she settled over him.

The slow sunlight was a revelation. When she leaned back, her golden skin and perfect shape were open to inspection. When she leaned forward—hunching against the pleasure, her fingers digging into his chest—then his hands were strictly on instrument flight rules, plunging through the gold-blond shield and exploring passages and curves that were beyond his vision.

He lay there, marveling at the look and feel of her, expanding his universe of appreciation for this woman who was taking him flying. The ground fire of last night was building in a spark here and flare-up there until with no more warning than a whispered "Oh God," they both flashed over into frantic need.

Denise bucked and writhed each time he drove his hips upward into her. She clamped her hands over where his had already been greedily fondling her perfect breasts and used that support as leverage to drive down against him. They writhed and gyrated as if they were the very heart of the firestorm.

Then their groans matched, found a common flow—a shared rhythm as in sync as any music he'd ever found—and finally an explosion that forced hard, gut-wrenching gasps from each of them; it was the only sound he was capable of at that moment. The roaring maelstrom of release had them both shuddering again and again as it rolled over them.

Afterward, after they'd pressed tightly against each other to sustain every last possible moment of release, she slowly collapsed onto him. Still joined, she lay on his chest, her head tucked under his chin.

Her hair now draped as a smooth cascade along his arms and shoulders. He managed to snag a corner of the blanket without disturbing her and pull it over them.

With a deep sigh of contentment, Denise seemed to

go to sleep upon him, every limb so loose, every muscle so relaxed that they flowed together.

"I've never made love outdoors before." Her voice was no more than a murmur.

"Well, I've had sex outdoors before, but never made love like this." He'd meant it as a joke and a compliment.

It should have been a line and nothing more, but it hadn't come out that way.

Not even a little.

Had he actually just said those words? Had he told a woman that he loved her?

Even worse, had he just told himself that he loved a woman?

That was nowhere in his repertoire. The fact that they'd finished body-shuddering sex moments ago wasn't even a factor he could hide behind. It hadn't sounded that way when he said it. He knew the sound of a stray comment after good sex and this wasn't it. And attaching a word as simple as "good" to what they'd just done was wrong as well.

He sort of peeked around inside his brain, inspected dusty corners looking for some deep-rooted panic, but it just wasn't there. What he found was that he was totally gone on this quiet, petite woman who laughed at his jokes and made love as if they were the ones who'd discovered the concept.

His world had shifted, but nothing else had changed. The sky above was still blue and sunlit. The woman beneath the blanket with him was still warm and languid and felt absolutely perfect there. Without disturbing the blanket, he ran his hand down her back, up that marvelous curve of waist, onto hip, then back up the slender thigh where her knees were still tucked up alongside him.

"You're going to have to make me a promise." Denise offered a sigh again.

"Sure. What's that?" Vern was pretty pleased that he'd managed to keep the choke out of his voice. A woman requesting a promise was a really bad sign.

"We're going to have to do this as often possible in the future." Her voice slurred. "I had no idea that's what sex was supposed to be like." Moments later he was sure she was back asleep while lying on his chest.

He allowed his hand to continue to roam, slowly, gently, appreciating every sensation. Maybe he should have tried being a sculptor so that he could re-create such a form, for he'd certainly never felt anything so magnificent.

Meanwhile his brain kept trying to kick into a panic mode as bad as that fire whorl.

When she said "future," did she mean as long as they were going out? Or did she mean…the future?

He lay wide awake throughout her nap, which lasted until the sun was well above the trees. Even then, it still had shed no more light on how he was feeling about her requested promise.

Or about the fact he wasn't trying to take it back.

Chapter 8

DENISE FOUGHT AGAINST HER OWN WORST INSTINCTS AS THEY returned to MHA's base. It was lunchtime and her body was hungry. Breakfast had been…forgotten. She hadn't wanted to waste a second of her time with Vern on something as mundane as food.

With him being of a similar mind, they hadn't. So, except for the empty stomach, her body felt glorious. At some time or other in the last eighteen hours, Vern had paid special attention to every single inch of her. She had been quite overwhelmed by her own desire to do the same with him.

Denise had never explored a man's body before. Oh, she'd enjoyed them, some of them. But she'd never explored how a man's skin shivered when she brushed her hair over it. Or how he sighed when she cupped and held him, nothing much else required until he was writhing beneath her touch. Or the time she'd teased him so much that he threw her down on her back and simply took her hard and fast in broad daylight as she wrapped her legs around his hips to keep him as close as possible.

And laughter. Laughter was not familiar to her, but with Vern it was deeply integrated into the lovemaking, sometimes bursting forth over the sheer glory of how they each felt. Saying this was the best sex of her life was like comparing a Black Hawk to her childhood tricycle.

Saying that she was about to be more embarrassed than ever before in her life was equally true.

It was lunchtime at the airbase, and most of MHA's staff were seated at the picnic tables as Vern flew over the field.

Malcolm spotted them coming and rushed across the airstrip to the flatbed service truck. He grabbed a radio and guided Vern in until Denise's shop-box was once again set back on the truck bed as gently as it had been taken away.

Once Vern set them down in Firehawk Oh-Three's parking spot, Denise found that she was terribly reluctant to step down.

What if the tentative beginnings they'd found unraveled in front of everyone's scrutiny? She shoved that thought aside, kicked it in a footlocker, and flipped the lid shut.

What if it had been nothing but a facade? What if they'd both been fooling themselves? That one she clopped on the head with a hammer, dumped down a manhole, and then slid the massive iron cover back in place. For good measure, she imagined a couple of big bolts and torqued them down with an air-impact wrench set on maximum.

What if this meant even half as much to Vern as it did to her?

That one finally stopped her. She would take courage from the fact that she hadn't scared him off yet. She'd revealed more of herself to Vern in the last week than she'd revealed to Jasper in a year. And still he was… holding her door open for her to climb down.

"You're done?"

He reached in and undid her harness. Took her hand to help her down, not that it was a big step. Their packs were set side by side on the ground. She hadn't even heard the heavy cargo door open and close.

"How do you want to play this to the public, Denise?" He cocked his head sideways, and she turned to look.

Through the glass of the still-open helicopter's door, she could see the picnic tables with most of the crews gathered about them. She was in a small, shadowed triangular box of safety at the moment: the chopper behind her, the helicopter door between her and the rest of the MHA team, and Vern.

"We can play casual and circumspect. Or we can be public and to hell with them."

This time she didn't look out at the people. She looked up at Vern Taylor. His sunglasses were dangling from a shirt pocket by the earpiece so that she could see the softness of his dark eyes. Waiting for her. Giving the choice to her.

"Which would you prefer?" she asked but felt something shifting inside her. Felt the layers of the dutiful, careful, overly self-conscious Denise Conroy slipping away even as she asked.

Vern shook his head slightly. "Lady's choice. Though I'm sure they're speculating even more the longer we linger here."

Denise didn't look away from his eyes. She could feel that wildness come over her. The wildness that had made her go to dinner with him, slide into his bed, and finally strip down right in front of him at the water's edge in broad daylight.

Not looking away, she drew courage from him that

maybe, just maybe, she was okay. And maybe, just maybe she might be worthy of someone who really cared about her. Someone like Vern Taylor.

Once she followed that logic…

She shifted sideways out of the triangular box of "good girl" and helicopter door. She closed it firmly and leaned back against the massive helicopter of her past.

Then she reached out, in plain view of anyone who cared to watch, and pulled Vern Taylor down to kiss her.

He tried to make it small, quick, polite.

She wrapped her arms around his neck and pulled him hard into the kiss.

As always, he didn't hesitate more than a moment until she was crushed back against the chopper's smooth metal skin, his hands raking up into her hair.

Whether it lasted a day or a lifetime, Denise knew she had, for perhaps the first time ever, embraced the future without being trapped by the past.

It was one of the headiest moments of her life. And it was punctuated by friendly cheers and applause softened by their trip across the width of the airfield and warmed by her lover's kiss.

~~~

Vern tried to recall the last time he'd felt so damned pleased with the world and came up blank.

All of the service tasks had been taken care of through the bright afternoon, from repacking parachutes to restocking Denise's service inventory—she'd placed an overnight order from Missoula.

They even had time to finish the repaint job on Vern's

bird. He'd enjoyed doing that. He, Mickey, and Cal—Jeannie's photographer husband.

Denise's team had laid down the gloss black undercoat in Missoula as part of the repairs.

Now the three of them had worked in silence for some time, amid the bright smell of fresh paint, discussing only where to draw the outlines of the flames to complement the still-intact side.

"Hell of a kiss, dude," Mickey said without looking over at Vern as he began filling in the outlines of the yellow flame edges.

"Felt good." Kissing Denise felt way more than good, but there was no way to say that.

They painted a while.

"Where'd you guys go?" Cal asked from deep in the orange.

"Place called Buck Lake."

"Damn!" Mickey cursed. Vern and Mickey had had a couple of double-date-by-helicopter parties out there. Though they'd never had the whole lake to themselves the way he and Denise had.

"Where's Buck Lake?"

Vern focused on the line of the red flame's heart. "I'll tell Jeannie. You'll like it."

"Yeah?"

"Oh yeah!" Mickey assured Cal.

Vern tried to recall who they'd taken out there with them on the double date. The two UC Berkeley brunettes? Or maybe the Boston blondes? Mickey could always catalog every conquest they'd made as a team.

Conquests weren't hard. "Hi, babe. Want to go make

love in the wilderness? I'll take you there in my fire-fighting helicopter." Never failed.

Mickey would remember who they'd taken, but Vern didn't want to ask. Those memories didn't matter after last night and this morning.

It was weird to think about. He wasn't sending Cal and Jeannie out there for a hot date; they were already married. A place he'd always thought of as "great place to take single women" was now "great place to send a couple in love."

There was that damned phrase again.

That he knew exactly when that change had taken place didn't make it any more comfortable. Rather than it making him uneasy, he was thinking of taking Denise back there in the spring. There was a patch of wildflowers, mostly daisies and buttercups, a couple of hundred yards north of the lake that he could easily imagine her lying in.

"You gonna paint or daydream, buddy?" Mickey warned him. "Shit! I know that look. How can you have that look? The Lady of Steel was actually good?"

Vern considered punching his closest friend in the face. But he'd have been equally shocked himself a week before. The Lady of Steel was perhaps the warmest human being he'd ever met.

So he kept his mouth shut and went back to painting.

—◦◦◦—

Mark rapped a knife sharply against his beer bottle at the end of the dinner service, and everyone slowly quieted. The twilight evening had spread a festive air over the outdoor tables of the MHA mess area.

The air was warm, but snow had fallen on the higher

slopes of Mount Hood while they were out of town. That massive prominence of the eleven-thousand-foot dormant volcano shone in the last of the evening sunlight. Another month and the snow would be down at their level, but this fall evening was exceptionally fine.

Betty had served up great stacks of nachos, grilled enough ribs to satisfy even the hungry maws of the MHA crews, and provided plenty of beer. The music was light and cheerful.

Of course, Vern was in a mood to be pleased by anything, with Denise sitting across from him and making him feel totally teenage goofy. Their ankles were locked together under the picnic table.

Malcolm, Brenna, Mickey, and Bruce had spent much of the meal giving them shit. Vern had handed it right back, and Denise hadn't blushed but once or twice. Vanessa was down beyond Mickey and only occasionally joined in. She was still suffering from first-season shyness, even though she was doing really well.

Denise shot him a grin and ran a bare foot up his leg. She was dressed in an emerald green T-shirt from the Eureka fire they'd fought back in the spring. She was also wearing cutoff shorts that had sent his imagination soaring when she'd walked up to the table. He tried to remember if he'd ever seen Denise Conroy in shorts and flip-flops. By the height of Mickey and Bruce's eyebrows, the answer was probably not.

Clearly, she was doing it to tease him. Vern could really, really get to enjoy being with this woman.

"Shaddup, everyone." Mark's big voice, though cheerful, had a ring of military command that shut down the last conversations like a load of retardant.

"The good news is that the fire season is officially over for MHA. The U.S. Forest Service released us from contract today under the sole condition that we would renew for next season, which we agreed to." He raised his beer high and shouted over the applause, "To the MHA team!"

Bottles were raised, clinked together, and drunk from.

"So, all you seasonals, see me for your bonuses before you go. Unless…"

Malcolm winced, then shook his head no—as much to himself as those around him. Denise had told Vern that Malcolm had been torn between staying local and staying on the contract year-round.

"MHA has two simultaneous winter contracts this year. We'll be splitting forces to fulfill those."

A buzz of conversation erupted throughout the tables. Everyone, including Vern, had assumed they'd be back in Australia like last year. He and Denise had even discussed some of the places they'd like to visit together if there was time.

Making long-term plans already. Wow! He'd missed that one when it went by. It had felt so…normal. Despite the fact that they'd been sprawled naked and spent beneath a warm sun beside a mountain lake at the time. Otherwise normal. Weird.

Nobody looked upset by the team split, but the vocal surprise was universal.

No…it wasn't.

Jeannie, Carly, and their husbands, Steve and Cal, were at the next table over. They showed no surprise at all. If he had to peg them, he'd go more for thoughtful.

He nodded for Denise to turn and check them out. She

did this coy, look-without-looking through the sheath of her hair. It was so damn cute to watch. And then he realized that he'd never noticed it before. Just how observant was she? "Very" was the answer now that he knew her.

She turned back to look at him and offered the smallest nod. Whatever had happened last year in Australia—when the Firehawks had split off and they'd done the switcheroo on Oh-Two—was happening again.

Mark was making patting motions and the crowd eventually quieted.

"The MD500s and Twin 212s *are* bound for Australia. TJ and Chutes will lead that group. Your choppers will be going out of Portland via FedEx cargo in five days. Enjoy your time off, because the Aussies will keep you hopping once you're down under. Firehawk One and Two will be shipping out in six days. Vern and Denise, where are you?"

When he raised his hand, Vern felt like the bad boy, which he'd been enough times in high school that even the motion gave him shivers. Denise's hand went right up, just like the star pupil she'd probably been since preschool and kindergarten.

"We'll talk later about which way you're each going."

The other tables were again abuzz about what the split could possibly mean—except for their table. Everyone was eyeing Vern and Denise speculatively, except for the other Firehawk crews at the next table over.

He ignored Mickey's questions and looked at Denise. Winter contract was typically November through March. Five months.

There was a chance that after less than five days together they'd be going separate ways for months?

He started shaking his head no, only realizing he was doing it when he saw that Denise was doing the same.

Mickey was asking what the hell was going on.

"Excuse us." They rose to their feet in unison and headed for Mark's table.

Mark, of course, saw them coming. With a casual nod of his head, he indicated that he'd meet them down on the grass airstrip.

Denise didn't have the nerve to speak. Her old tapes were telling her that she should have known it was too good to last.

She was not in the habit of speaking up for herself. For her aircraft, absolutely, but not for herself.

This time she would. For strength, she held on to Vern's hand and stood out in midfield waiting for Mark. There were some things worth fighting for, and being with Vern right now was way high on her list. She didn't question that he'd become so important to her in such a short time, and not just physically. For the first time in her life, she also understood that there was a woman who she didn't know but who Vern kept thinking was pretty wonderful. She knew if they kept together, she'd start to find that woman as well.

"I don't care which." Vern's voice was soft. "We go together."

She squeezed his hand and leaned against his shoulder for a moment, desperately hoping it was that easy. That it would even be a choice.

Where would they be going? That spooked her.

Australia had been scary enough, though the idea of going back sounded fun.

She'd only traveled outside the Northwest four times in her life before that. Once to the National Museum of the United States Air Force at the Wright-Patterson base in Ohio and once to the U.S. Army Aviation Museum at Fort Rucker in Alabama. Both times with her dad to review some possible exhibits for the Boeing museum. Three years to Connecticut for the Sikorsky plant, which had included the trip to Beijing. And that didn't really count because she'd never left the air show and hadn't been able to see anything while there due to the smog. She'd never even explored New York, though the city was about an hour from the Sikorsky plant.

Australia had left her head spinning for all five months she'd been there. She'd never really gotten used to it.

The sun had finally set enough that the shining beacon of Mount Hood's glaciers was extinguished. Night had come on quickly after that.

"Oh shit!" Vern cursed in the darkness. "Remember what I said Mark and Emily were talking about? It's going to be goddamn Honduras."

Honduras? Denise almost choked. She didn't doubt for a second that he was right, and it was totally freaking her out. Vern had told her about the troubles he'd had there. The coup. The murder rate. They spoke Spanish there, and she'd taken French in high school. It had all sounded so…foreign. She knew that was terribly parochial of her, but that didn't make it feel any less true.

So quietly that she hadn't heard them coming, Mark and Emily were beside them. From slightly different directions, Steve and Carly came up, and then Jeannie and Cal.

At an easy stroll, Mark started leading them down the runway, farther from the lights over the still-boisterous group at the tables.

"You've had questions about some of the, ah, occurrences at MHA." He made it a flat statement and Denise knew he was talking to her.

She nodded, realized it was useless this far from the lights, and acknowledged the fact aloud. He was talking about the new airframe on Oh-Two.

"Vern?"

Denise could feel him shrug through their still-clasped hands.

"You know me, Mark. Tell me the plan and I'm aboard." He squeezed her hand in the dark before she could protest. He hadn't forgotten that they were going to decide together. "But did it have to be Honduras?"

"How the... Shit!" Mark stopped himself. "Well, so much for being circumspect. You both signed non-disclosure agreements when we redid the paperwork last year."

"I knew it!" Denise clamped her lips together, but she'd known it.

"Knew what?" Vern hadn't put it together. "What paperwork?" he asked Mark in turn.

Mark stopped and did his folded-arms thing. The group gathered in a circle about him.

"Mount Hood Aviation flies under a second contract, about which you've signed an NDA—a nondisclosure agreement—as part of last year's re-up of your contracts. The people standing here with us know what's behind the wall of that NDA, as does the company's owner. No one else. Absolutely no one else. If you decide to step up on the second contract, you will perjure yourself to the police, the military, the Supreme Court, and the President before you mention anything done under the scope of that contract."

"Is it legal?"

"It is authorized."

Denise harrumphed. That wasn't an answer, but she knew it was all she was going to get.

"You will never be intentionally placed in harm's way." The fact that Mark felt it was necessary to say that wasn't a good sign.

"What happened to the original Firehawk Oh-Two?"

Jeannie started to speak, but Mark cut her off.

"Need to know."

Denise felt a shiver go up her spine as the pieces fit together. "I know that the bird I sent to Australia with Jeannie last year is not the one she came back with. Cosmetically the same, and someone went to a lot of trouble to fake the service logs." She smacked her forehead as the next piece slid in neatly beside the others. "You said 'harm's way.' I get it now. Firehawk Oh-Two didn't manage to stay out of harm's way. And that fire-whorl photo that Cal shot last year of firefighters going into shelters at 'an unspecified fire' was you guys."

"Me, anyway," Jeannie whispered.

"Jeannie!" Mark cut her off.

"By the way, great photo, Cal." Vern spoke up from the darkness beside her. "That wasn't Australia. No forests like that."

"Thanks. East Timor."

"Will you people stop it!" Mark sounded pissed.

Steve spoke up. "They already know most of it. And, as you said, they're on the inside of the NDAs."

"But not the contract." Mark's voice took on the edge that silenced everyone.

"How could you dare to fake the service logs?" Denise felt sick that anyone would do such a thing.

Mark groaned. "I'm not a complete idiot just because I'm a pilot. Why do mechanics always think that?" he asked no one in particular.

Denise could list several dozen reasons not to trust a pilot about anything mechanical.

He didn't give her a chance to answer but continued right on. "Our sponsors tracked down a bird in storage that was manufactured within a hundred units of the original Firehawk Oh-Two. They then went through your entire electronic service record and made sure each of those services were done. So, it was a safe and accurate record for this craft. How did you know?" He motioned down the field toward where the Firehawks were parked.

"A mechanic recognizes her own repairs. Besides, there were differences inside the machinery as well," she informed him, trying to decide if she was livid that she'd finally confirmed the falsification of the record or impressed at how thorough the cover-up had been.

"Shit," was Mark's comment. "Well, we tried. Should have known you were too damn skilled to fool. That's my bad."

As compliments went, Denise decided that was a pretty good one. "Are you going to tell me what really happened to the original?"

"Not yet."

"Stalemate," she told him. She wasn't going to get crossed up again.

The other five in the party were just shadows, silent silhouettes in the night.

"Do you need us both?" Vern asked the darkness.

"Ideally, yes. Vern, you're the best pilot I've seen outside of SOAR. Sorry, Jeannie, but he is."

"You wouldn't catch me trying to survive what he flew through in Missoula."

Denise was surprised by the awe in Jeannie's voice. She'd seen the damage to the chopper and had guessed enough from that to know Vern was good, but she hadn't known that he was that kind of good.

"And you"—Mark's silhouette turned more toward her—"there's a mechanic named Connie who I'd like you to do some training with someday, but that can only happen inside the second contract. You two were made for each other in many ways."

"I've heard of her. She's a legend at the Sikorsky plant. I always tried to live up to that standard."

"Well, you're doing pretty well so far."

Denise was glad for the darkness. Connie Davis was a complete legend at Sikorsky. When her notes had come in from the field, changes had been implemented in production standards, inspection cycles, even wiring layouts. It had gotten to the point where Denise wondered if the woman was mythical. To be compared to her quite took Denise's breath away.

Silence settled over them. Clearly the decision point had arrived.

Through their connection, she could feel Vern turn to

face her. He kissed her on top of the head and whispered too softly for the others to hear, "Lady's choice."

Last time he'd said that, she kissed the living daylights out of him.

"Nothing further until we agree?" she asked Mark. "Honduras and secretly swapped helicopters and a mysterious second contract?"

"That's it." His tone made it clear that was his last word on the subject on this side of the line.

Being together with Vern wasn't enough of a reason by the sound of it. Denise weighed factors as quickly as she could. Two of the finest pilots ever, now retired from SOAR. Carly was rumored to be the best Fire Behavior Analyst out there, and her husband helped her with his spotting drone and had also been the lead smokejumper in southern California before an injury. To make lead really meant something; to make it in California meant he was one of the very best in the world.

Jeannie, she knew, was a damn fine pilot. Most people thought her husband, Cal, was simply an award-winning photographer and former hotshot fire crew member. Yet last year in Australia, when the MHA crew had split up, Cal had traveled with these people rather than joining her and the rest of the choppers.

They must have been traveling under this "second contract." And it was Cal's leadership that had saved the town of Alice Springs from a rolling bushfire. A man with many hidden talents.

Denise tightened her grip on Vern's hand and he responded in kind, maintaining the comforting pressure. She really hoped that she wasn't about to totally screw everything up.

"I think that the chance to fly with a team as good as this one is a once-in-a-lifetime moment. We're in."

A wave of relief rippled around the circle.

"Good!" That simple and it was done.

She heard someone slap Vern solidly on the shoulder. Such guys.

Now Mark raised his voice to make it clear he was addressing the whole group. "In six days we leave from here and fly to Joint Base Lewis-McChord where we'll be loaded aboard a C-17 for transit to Honduras. Denise, I need you to split your service shop container, one for the three Firehawks, one for the rest of the group to take with them. You told me Brenna was up for it on the smaller birds, so she will travel as chief mechanic for them, hiring assistance as she needs it. Get it done and get off base for a break. We're going to be busy when we get there. Any questions?" Mark delivered the whole thing in a single breath, or close enough.

Denise was still trying to digest it and think about how to split the gear when Vern spoke up.

"What are we going to be doing when we get there?"

Mark chuckled. "Fighting fire."

Chapter 9

"This *is* kind of fun. Though the automatic really is a crime. I can't imagine a single situation in which you'd think an automatic is better than a standard."

Vern had foolishly assumed that riding in his Corvette would feel less life-threatening than in her Fiat Spider.

Giving Denise a five-hundred-horsepower engine in a car capable of a sub-four-second zero-to-sixty was not a wise choice. How she didn't get a ticket, he'd never know. Maybe it was because they were little more than a bronze-colored streak as they soared along the roads. Whether he'd live to tell about it was still in question.

The quiet country roads of Vashon Island would never be the same. They'd reached the Tahlequah ferry at Tacoma in record time. The fifteen-minute crossing to Vashon gave his heart a few moments to recover. But any recovery was wasted as soon as Denise launched off the boat. They should never have let her be first off— she'd treated the raising of the red-and-white traffic bar at the head of the ferry ramp like a green flag at the Indy 500.

He hoped that Mike had his cruiser in for service or was working his speed trap up by the Fauntleroy-Southworth ferry at the far end of the island, a dozen miles away. Hopefully that would be far enough away that Mike couldn't hear six liters of engine begging for an open stretch of road.

The number of times Vern had cruised these roads was beyond counting. Headed down to the Tacoma Dome for a Bruce "The Boss" or Britney concert, his old Chevy Blazer packed to the gills. Fetching some boat hardware for his dad. Headed off to find a quiet corner of the island for a round or two of female adventuring.

He guided Denise down narrow two-lanes almost lost in the towering trees, at first to slow her down, and then because he wanted to show her the views and some of his favorite hangouts. The view from Neill Point out by Kevin's construction shop. Camp Sealth perched over Paradise Cove on the West Passage. Up to the Wax Orchards airport.

The last was a small, private grass strip with apple trees planted down either side of the runway and for a fair way around. At this time of year, hundreds of small planes flew in because they could pull up right beside the cider press, buy a couple gallons of the best apple cider on the planet, grab a caramel apple, and zip aloft once more.

They parked and drank glasses of cider that were less than a minute old, so thick you couldn't see the shadow of your fingers through the glass, and snacked on local Dinah's cheese that put paid on any Camembert he'd ever had. Those were two of the tastes of the island. For all the traveling he'd done, he was surprised each time he came home how much he'd missed it.

"I love this place."

Denise nodded her agreement. She seemed to down-shift gears herself as he showed her the island. It wasn't that she was frenetic; quite the opposite. She was…

"Why are you so driven?"

She brushed aside enough hair to look over at him as they sat side by side under an apple tree and watched a small Cessna land on the grass. "Am I?"

"Let me guess: straight-A student, never traveled except for work, never thinks of sleep when there's something to be fixed or a system to be improved. You drive better than probably half of the NASCAR field, and I'll bet you haven't met a machine you couldn't fix."

"Yeah. Maybe." She let the hair fall back in place.

He caught it and tucked it behind her ear. "Didn't miss a single one, did I?"

"No." This time she turned to him. Her face was set hard, as if she was trying to pull up the steel shields, but they didn't scare him any longer. "What about it?"

"Denise, my beautiful, crazy mechanic, I'm blown away by you is what. I'd wager you don't know how to relax much. That's all I'm saying."

"While you do?"

He cracked open the gallon jug he'd bought to take to Mom and Dad and took a slug off it before passing it to Denise. "Professional slacker Taylor. That's me."

"Now let me guess: didn't like school, probably one of the troublemakers." She began counting on the fingers of one of those delicate but strong hands he'd learned to really appreciate. "Six years U.S. Coast Guard."

"Chief Petty Officer Taylor, at your service." He saluted as well as he could while leaning back against an apple tree in the warm fall sunshine.

"Is that good?"

"In six years, without college? Hell, yeah."

"So, damn good in the Coast Guard, maybe even a couple of medals that you aren't admitting to."

He shrugged nonchalantly. Three. "Yeah, maybe. If you don't count the Good Conduct Medal for a protracted bout of behaving against my natural tendencies."

"Four years flying fire for MHA," Denise continued. "Has the respect of two of the best military pilots on the planet. And loves his parents. Did I miss one?"

"Nope. Wait, yes. Totally crazy about an overwound Wrench who really needs to learn to relax."

"I need to relax?" She ground out each word separately.

"Couldn't hurt to try."

She snarled at him, rolled from sitting beside him, and landed kneeling across his lap. Hands on his shoulders, she pinned him back against the tree he'd been leaning against. "I. Don't. Need. To. Relax." Then she cursed under her breath. "Okay"—she unfisted his T-shirt—"maybe a little."

He ran his hands onto her waist and up along her back. When he gently tried to pull her into a hug, she kept her arms stiff. "Relaxing right now might make this a good moment."

"Damn you, Taylor." But she was smiling as she cursed him and didn't complain as he pulled her into his embrace and kissed her.

―∿∿―

The way Vern kissed her beneath that apple tree sent waves of heat coursing through Denise's body. It didn't matter where or when...or what they'd finished doing only moments before. She didn't want to have an insatiable need for anyone.

But she did. For him.

He took his time kissing her. As if doing so was the most important thing in the world.

And every time he did that, her lists and agendas faded from her brain, scattered as effectively as a rotor's downwash over autumn leaves until there was only the present—this moment, this place, his embrace.

How in hell was she supposed to relax? Brenna was headed off for her first time as lead mechanic. She and Vern were flying into a total unknown—the elusive "second contract" job flown for...who knew. Honduras. It was in Central America. The people wouldn't even speak English there. Not just foreign, scary foreign. That she was going to meet Vern's parents only added to the load.

And the biggest stressor at the moment was that, god-damn it, she was in love with him.

She definitely didn't know what to do with that.

She'd never told Jasper she loved him because she hadn't. Never told anyone except her dad. And that had only been when she was a little kid. After Mom died, it was like that part of them was killed along with her. She and Dad were careful with each other, taking care to not brush against sore places. A bullet had taken the words "I love you" out of her life and they'd never come back.

Until now. Here they were.

Vern was no longer kissing her.

"Where did you go, Wrench?"

She sat back on his thighs and brushed her hands down his chest in apology.

"Somewhere not good." He didn't even have to guess.

She nodded but didn't look up to meet those dark, caring eyes. She didn't want pity for her pain. She just wanted… There was the question that had always eluded her. Wanted what?

Vern slowly pulled her in until she could bury her face against his shoulder and just hold on. Just stop for a moment and be held; another part of her father that had died and left a hollow ache in them both.

Denise considered crying, considered having a good weep and letting it out. Against Vern's shoulder she felt safe enough to, but nothing came. She was—

"I thought that was your car in the lot." A terribly cheerful female voice that Denise half recognized spoke from somewhere nearby.

"Mom!" Vern struggled to shift Denise while getting to his feet, while knocking over the uncapped cider jug, then reaching to rescue it, while… He collapsed back against the stout tree hard enough under the burden of Denise's weight in his lap that she could hear the *thonk* as his head hit.

"Ow! Shit!" His hands were gone from around her and were now wrapped behind his head. If she hadn't jerked back in time, he'd have rapped her sharply in the nose with the top of his head as he bent forward to cradle it.

Denise rescued the jug and capped it. Then she was left, still sitting on Vern's thighs, with no choice but to look up at the woman standing a few feet away.

"Good thing I bought another jug. Knew you'd be wanting some, but I thought you'd come see your mother first."

This time Denise was able to place the voice, rich

and melodic even in speech. Margi Taylor—Denise had hours of the woman's music on her main playlist.

She was tall, nearly her son's height. Her hair, rather than dark with a hint of curls like Vern's, was a cascading flutter of rippling coppery red that brushed her shoulders and framed her freckled face.

Her blouse, a flowing gypsy cut in darkest blue, revealed a freckled cleavage, and tight jeans showed where Vern had inherited his lean form. She had a smile for her son that radiated good humor as she bent to kiss the top of his head and say in that wonderfully rich voice, "You are so damn cute, Vern. All better now?"

"Yeah, sure. That helps a concussion a whole bunch."

"You're beautiful." Denise hadn't meant to say it aloud, hadn't even thought it clearly before speaking, but it was true. Margi Taylor radiated "mom" in a way that Denise had no other appropriate words for.

"Thanks." Margi accepted the comment cheerfully. "What's a beauty like you doing with someone who can't even stand up to greet his mother without banging his head?"

"Uh… falling in love with him, I guess."

Margi raised a single eyebrow.

Denise's words registered in her own brain at about the same moment as Vern's.

"You what?" He jerked his head up fast enough to bang it on the tree again. "Ow!"

Denise took the simple expedient of slapping her hand over her mouth. She was going to keep it there forever, never speak again because who knew what would come out next.

Margi's laugh rang through the orchard. This time she pulled Denise over to kiss the top of her head.

The great laugh was another thing Vern had gotten from his mother.

Vern spent the rest of the afternoon trying to get Denise aside, but he was stymied at every turn. First, Mom insisted Denise join her for the drive to the house, leaving Vern to follow in his Vette. Dad was out of town, moving a boat for someone from Tacoma up to Tofino, at least a three-day trip. They were going to totally miss him.

Then at the house, the two women had gone for a walk together down to the Point Robinson lighthouse. He'd tagged along, more than a little miffed. Had Denise really said that she loved him? Man, if ever there was a conversation he did *not* expect to be having…but his mother wasn't even giving him a chance to try.

Point Robinson reached halfway across the east channel of Puget Sound. The low, sandy beach had two keeper's cottages, a radio tower, and a lighthouse so automated that it no longer needed its keepers. The red-roofed white structure and its three-story tower guarded the dangerous shoals along this side of the main shipping channel to Tacoma's busy port.

It guarded the shoals as carefully as his mother appeared to be guarding Denise from his questions about what the hell had just happened.

He finally clued in to what was going on, found a nice driftwood log, and sat down to wait. On further consideration, Denise had looked as shocked as he felt.

So Mom was giving Denise some time and space to deal with it. As long as Vern was hovering over her shoulder, that wasn't going to happen.

So, they wandered off, and he stayed perched on his driftwood bench and studied the far shore. The rising hills of Des Moines were thick with houses. Beyond, looking four miles away rather than forty, Mount Rainier punched its volcanic cone up into the blue sky. Fourteen thousand feet, with nothing around it.

He'd flown Colorado fires. There, the peaks, the Colorado Fourteeners, started at six or even eight thousand feet. Mount Rainier was just as tall but the upslope turn started at around five hundred feet. Even Mount Hood was snarled up in low foothills, whereas Rainier punched upward out of nothing, ruling the land far and wide. Today it looked as if it had been painted against the sky.

Denise loved him.

What the hell was he supposed to do with that?

Mom was as unflappable as ever, so who knew what she was really thinking. Actually, it wasn't hard to know. The two of them might have been mother and daughter, the way they were acting.

He glanced down the beach. They'd walked out to the very end of the point and were strolling back toward his position near the lighthouse.

He knew Mom was actually an amazing judge of character. And he could read her. Margi was not being polite to her son's girlfriend; she genuinely liked Denise. If she didn't, it would show. He'd see it. So his first guess had been right. They should meet and would like each other.

Vern had also learned to read Denise. A little. It was as if her cloak of invisibility was becoming tattered at the edges. Or maybe she didn't need it as much as she had before.

Normally when she spoke to someone, she was doing her intense, "how much can I communicate in how few words" thing. He'd always thought it was an efficiency monomania, but he was starting to suspect the reason had more to do with shyness that she kept hidden behind that efficient facade.

At the moment she looked…happy.

He turned back to inspect Rainier. The day was calm and the sky clear, but it was early October and the top of the mountain didn't know that it was a nice day below. A massive lenticular cloud, the shape of two contact lenses back to back, loomed ominously above the peak. He'd grown up able to see the mountain creating its own weather systems out the living room window.

Some part of him suspected that the lenticulars were a special warning. High winds, high danger coming. But what portent were they warning him about?

"Do you think he's calmed down enough?" His mother was now close enough behind him for her voice to carry easily over the low rumble of a rusty, blue container ship rounding the point toward Tacoma.

Denise's voice was softer and he had to strain to hear her. "It's not him I'm worried about. It's me."

"Don't be." Mom made that comforting "Oooo!" noise she always did while giving someone an especially fierce hug. "Now go talk. I know my own way home."

— ᵐ —

Denise still hesitated. She could feel Vern waiting. He didn't appear angry, though there was only so much you could read from someone's back. She wasn't feeling brave, but she forced her feet across the packed sand and circled the log to sit beside Vern and watch the passing ship.

The silence stretched. At first she felt uncomfortable with it. It took her a while to figure out that Vern was leaving her the space to talk when she was ready. He melted her heart. She leaned over and kissed him on the shoulder. "She's wonderful."

He nodded his agreement and kept watching the ship heading south, slowly turning his gaze further and further from her.

"Something she passed on to her son."

"What did you two talk about?"

Denise tried to remember but couldn't. "I'm not sure, really. We talked about my job, her music, my family, yours, the weather. Nothing, really. But it all felt important despite that. I don't know why, but it did."

That finally broke his attention from the ship and returned it to her. Now that he was facing her, she could see the question that he was holding so carefully inside. Well, so was she.

"Yes. I did say that." No need to define "that."

"And?"

"You don't make it easy, do you?"

He offered the slow smile, the goofy one that tugged on one side of his mouth long before the other, but started in his eyes. "I think it would cost me major demerits to speak first. I have to check my manly club ratings-guide under the 'macho reticence' heading, but I'm sure it's bad."

"How about doing it for me anyway?" It was a low move, making the guy speak first, but she didn't know what else to do.

"Do I love you?"

She shivered despite the warm sun and her light jacket.

"I'm thinking that I do. Our bodies love each other. There's no question of that."

"None," she agreed.

"Every time you come around or even walk by, my mind goes blank and all I can think of is you."

"Mine goes quiet."

"Same thing."

"No, I don't think it is." She tried to puzzle out how to describe the feeling. "I've spent my whole life trying to be the perfect child. Take care of Dad. Be a person he could be so proud of because I never made a single misstep or mistake. Trying to make up for Mom's death, I guess." She'd never put it in quite those words, but it rang true.

"Sounds like a lot of work."

"It is. I never noticed it until you." She reached out and their hands slid together as naturally as if they'd always been that way. "Because my mind was never quiet until I was with you. No guy ever did that for me."

"Is it a good thing?" There was worry in his voice. Worry because he cared for her?

She looked around her at the water, the mountain, and a seagull soaring silently above them on the light breeze. The setting was idyllic, yet it had probably looked no different in the last decade, or the one before that. Could there be something this stable between them? Beyond that, could *she* be a part of anything that stable? "It's *not* a good thing, Vern. It's the best. I don't know what it means, what I said, but I think you're the first man who can help me figure it out."

"What you said? You mean that you love me?"

"Yes, you turkey."

"Good, that's settled." He stood and pulled her to her feet by their joined hands.

"What's settled?" She stumbled in the sand as he turned and slowly led her back up the beach.

"That we're in love with each other and it's confusing the hell out of both of us."

"Oh, that?" She sassed him just as he'd been teasing her.

"Yeah, that."

It thrilled her that she kept finding jokes around Vern, another previously undiscovered piece of herself brought to light by his presence in her life. Even in the span of this supremely strange conversation, the truth had become clearer—as it did whenever they were together.

"I love you, Vern Taylor."

That ground him to a halt. He turned slowly without releasing her hand.

"Wow." She hadn't expected the reaction that coursed through her and made her feel as if her feet weren't quite in contact with the earth. "It's quite something to say that out loud."

"It's quite something to hear it," he agreed.

"So?"

He didn't sigh. He didn't evade. He leaned down to brush his lips over hers before shifting his mouth to whisper in her ear. "I love you, Denise Conroy."

It really was quite something to hear.

Chapter 10

"I REMEMBER IT." DENISE HAD DUCKED INSIDE THE COOL dimness of the hangar as soon as Vern had the door cracked open.

Yuri's Bell 47 helicopter was right where he'd left it, huddled in the back of a hangar at Vashon Municipal Airport. It had a large, transparent-plastic bulbous nose and no doors. The bench could seat three in a pinch. The instrument console sported a bare dozen gauges on a stubby pillar between the two pilot positions. It was such a simple machine that nothing more was needed.

The engine was mounted vertically on the back of the cockpit, its driveshaft attached to the rotor blades through a simple centrifugal clutch. The back was an open frame metalwork truss stretching rearward to a tiny two-bladed tail rotor.

If you painted it dull green instead of shining white and attached a pair of stretchers, it would be right out of the *M*A*S*H* television show.

"What did you do to my poor bird?" Denise walked up to pat it on the nose.

Vern laughed. Those were exactly the words that had begun their relationship. "The few, the proud, the heli-aviation firefighter pilots of MHA. We're all in the crapper with you, Wrench."

"Leave me alone, Slick." She stuck her tongue out at him. "Go find me some fuel and oil."

He really was gone on this woman. By the time he tracked down the fuel truck—thankfully Gary kept the keys behind the passenger-side sun visor for locals, she'd popped the small chopper up off its skids onto a set of wheels and scooted the bird out of the hangar where it had been quietly sitting for the year since Yuri died.

Well, he liked her confidence that she'd get it running.

"At least you drained it before storing it. Fill it up." She was inspecting the logbook. "Another year until the next airframe inspection is due, but I'll go over it anyway before we take it up."

"As simple as that?"

"It's a Bell 47 with a Lycoming O-435-D, what's to know?"

"Okay, goddess-incarnate mechanic, let's see you do your stuff."

And she did. Suddenly he was watching Denise the Machine. She of the massive steel barricades had reappeared. But she didn't scare him anymore.

Now he could see that they weren't barricades meant to ward off any who dared approach. They were formed by a focus so intense that there was no way in from the outside. Nothing to do except to wait until she came out from behind there.

So, Vern filled the gas tanks, added oil, and then sat back to watch the show.

She circled the craft, starting at the pilot's door. Somewhere she'd scared up three simple tools: a hammer, a wrench, and a screwdriver. It took her most of an hour to do a full inspection. Then she circled a second time taking mere minutes to perform the preflight inspection.

It was a ballet of grace and brains. No wasted motion, no wasted thought, and not a single detail missed. A tap with a hammer to test soundness of the metal and the welds. They rang true to his ear; they probably sang a symphony to her. A twist of the wrench, and he'd bet she could tell him the tightness of each bolt down to the closest five foot-pounds of torque.

Denise took his breath away. He was a good pilot. But this mechanic-woman was something other, up at a level that he could only imagine. He knew enough to truly appreciate what she was. Not enough to know how or why, but that didn't matter.

"I love you, Denise." He had to whisper it so that at least he could hear it. He might have said it when they'd curled up in his old bed last night and again when they woke up in each other's arms. But he had to say it.

"Shut up, Slick. You're distracting me."

"Yes, ma'am. Wrench, sir." He saluted.

She didn't turn to look, but her giggle reminded him of a lunatic elf.

Then she clambered into the cockpit, opened the throttle, and cranked the engine.

Nothing except the slow, reluctant whoosh of the two long, wooden blades of the rotor turning around once, twice, and then nothing.

She shut off the ignition.

"Same problem I was having."

Without a comment, she poked around the engine for a few moments. "Crank it."

He climbed aboard, set the choke and the throttle, and hit the starter.

Nothing. One end of the rotor lumbered by outside the bubble.

More nothing. The other end put in a reluctant appearance.

Then a rough bang of the engine misfiring. On the next lumbering rotation of the blades it caught, fired, and finally ran. He eased the choke as the engine warmed and the rotor began really working its way around with that slow *whoop-whoop* he remembered so well.

She was still fussing with something while the engine smoothed out, and finally it found that solid rumble he knew from hundreds of hours flying this craft when he was still a teenager.

By the time everything had stabilized and warmed up, Denise had clambered into the copilot's seat. She pulled out the log and began making notes about her inspection.

"What did you do?"

"The timing was off. Way off. There's a new rule for as long as we're in a relationship together."

"I never thought rules were a good way to go." His parents always simply worked things out as they came up. It had worked for them, and he didn't want to start burdening down this relationship with—

"This rule is a good one. Trust me when I say our future depends on it. Nonnegotiable."

He clamped down on his tongue, not wanting to snap at her.

"You are hereby forbidden, under any circumstances, to try to fix a helicopter engine, for as long as we're together. That probably goes for a car engine as well, but we'll have to see. Understood? Or else I'm out of here."

The laugh burst out of him. He hauled her against

him, dragged her across the bench seat, and kissed her for as long as he could until their laughter drove them apart.

They buckled in, though he was tempted to shut down the engine and take her right here and right now. The field was empty except for them. He'd tear her clothes off and throw her down on the long cushion and have his way with her.

As a matter of fact…

———~~~———

Vern pulled the throttle just moments before the rotors reached takeoff speed and killed the dual magnetos.

"What's wrong?" Denise double-checked the gauges, but it all looked good. Or it had. Now everything was winding back down.

She glanced up at Vern's face, but he wasn't looking worried. He was looking right at her—with a heat rising in his eyes that had become gloriously familiar.

She looked out the front plexiglass bubble of the tiny helicopter. The runway stretched out ahead of them; the sky was bright blue and open above.

He wasn't really thinking about…

"No, Vern. No way in—" She mumbled the last word into his mouth when he kissed her.

This was no gentle kiss. It started hot and lustful and went for full burn faster than her heart could skip a beat.

"No." She couldn't get the breath to even manage his name as he slid her T-shirt off and unsnapped her bra. As protests went, it was a pretty feeble one, totally belied by her body responding to him.

As he tipped her back on the seat, she could see

the field was empty, no traffic in the pattern or on short final.

Words were completely beyond her as he attacked her breasts with a need that drew an answer from deep inside her until she could only wrap her arms behind his head and pull him ever harder against her.

Riding the edge that would have turned pleasure to pain, she missed when her pants and underwear went missing.

Naked.

It was her only coherent thought as she looked out at the airport through the broad windshield and spread wide for him on the bench seat. The Bell 47 did not offer a spacious cockpit. Her head was half out one door, barely supported by the edge of the bench; her feet were out the other.

Denise could feel his greedy grin against her even as she rose to him. When he made to move, she reached down and dug her hands into his hair to encourage him to remain precisely where he was.

One leg hooked up along the back of the seat, while the other foot pressed hard against the windshield.

Vern Taylor knocked propriety right out the non-existent helicopter door. He drove the lists out of her head. He left her no ability to think, no awareness of the outside world. All that he left her was the ability to feel.

It was not a sensation she was used to.

Ever.

When he finally stripped off his own pants and entered her, it was with the perfect timing of a clean engine at the very peak of performance. It wound her higher and higher until his release slammed into her and the only sensations were beyond the physical. All that remained in her awareness was how much she loved this man.

———∿∿∿———

"Where should we go?"

Denise couldn't form a cogent thought. All she could think of what was what they'd just done. They'd made love beneath a clear bubble of plexiglass on the edge of the runway at a municipal airport, although thankfully not a busy one.

No, this hadn't been making love. This had been hot, mad, brainless sex. This had been skyrockets at night and tidal waves at high noon. This had been two bodies groping, clinging, and consuming until they each cried out in frustration that they couldn't get more.

It was something she'd never had in her life—pure sex with a man she really, really wanted it from. It had been glorious!

Her bones had turned to liquid. Her breasts were sore from where she'd hauled his mouth so hard against them, and her jaw ached from her need to kiss him as deeply as possible again and again and again.

"Hey, Wrench. Straighten out your clothes. It's time to go."

Straighten out her clothes? She wasn't wearing any. Except one lone sock.

Vern was already dressed and looking awesome, totally cat-who-ate-the-canary. Men had it so easy: jeans, T-shirt, shove a hand through his short hair, and put on a smile. Done.

While she was still here with her one lone sock,

sprawled like a wanton in the impossibly small cockpit. There was no way there'd been room here to make
love, yet they had. Sweaty palm prints and a couple of
footprints on the inside of the plexiglass bubble stood
testament to the fact that, oh man, they'd managed it
big-time.

Clothes. Right. She shimmied her pants back on and
shoved her feet into her sneakers, once she found her
second sock. Her panties had gone missing in action.
As Vern was already cranking the engine, she snapped
the seat belt around her waist before reaching down to
retrieve her bra and shirt from the floor.

Vern had the chopper aloft before she'd arranged
either one.

"Vern! I'm still naked over here."

"Half-naked. Looks great on you. Have I mentioned
what amazing breasts you have, Wrench?"

She was half-naked, flying through the midmorning
sky over Vashon Island in a giant glass bubble, and he
was teasing her. Well, she certainly hadn't signed up for
boring or expected to get it with Vern. Instead she felt
full of smiles.

Once she was dressed reasonably well, she wondered what state her hair was in and decided it was
better not to know. She stuck her head out the open
doorway into the edge of the slipstream, letting it flutter her hair into some semblance of order, and then
grabbed it at the base of her skull and went for a plain
but messy ponytail.

"How about Boeing Field?"

"What about Boeing Field?"

"Your dad works there, doesn't he?"

"Over at the museum. He's the curator."

"Curator? Wow! Well, I have a question to ask him." And he got on the radio to Boeing Field tower before she had a chance to protest. It was only a five-minute flight from Vashon Island.

She rubbed at her lips, sure they were swollen. And tried to finger-comb her ponytail, but it was a lost cause. She would look exactly as she was, a woman who had just been immensely satisfied by her lover.

That left her to consider what question he might be asking of her father. She was still trying to wrestle with the concepts of relationship and love.

If Vern hit her dad with the *M*-word question, she'd hit Vern with a wrench for real.

A brief flash of pink caught her eye. She was too slow to grab her panties. They blew out the open doorway and began fluttering down toward the houses below.

―――

"So, Mr. Conroy." He, Denise, and her father had met at the glass-door entrance to the museum. The old chopper, now parked out front, would fit right in the collection here.

"Dale." He was a graying man in his fifties, though he looked older. Still in pretty good shape though.

"Thanks." Vern tried not to feel daunted by the combination of him being Denise's father and the museum's curator. What a cool job! "So, Dale, I've got a question for you."

"Fire away." He guided them in and waved them past the ticket counter.

Vern could see Denise's face flash through an

impressive series of colors. First sheet white from terror about what he was going to ask.

"Denise was telling me how she practically grew up here at the museum."

"After her mother passed, yes. The school bus would drop her off right out front. The museum staff and I sort of raised her together."

"Well, I think she came out amazingly wonderful."

Denise's face was now shifting to a shade of red that warned of approaching fury. It wasn't something he'd known she was capable of. He'd rather not find out what that was like. She was so sweet to the core that she might blow a gasket or something if she became truly angry.

"The way I figure it..." He waved his hand at the main exhibit hall of airplanes for the Museum of Flight but kept his eye on Denise. She was sliding back toward sheet white. "I figure..." Vern decided if he dragged it out much more, she probably would do him bodily harm. "There have to be some great stories about a little girl who grew up to be the best mechanic I've ever met. I'd love to hear some of them."

Denise went through huffing out a breath of relief and then blushing bright red. Oh, he really had to find out the story behind that particular look.

"Might be a few." Dale's laugh was as soft as his daughter's.

Denise stared at her father's back in clear shock. She was a step behind him, so only Vern noticed. Apparently her father's laugh was as rare and elusive as her own.

Dale led them forward into the main hall.

Vern hadn't been here in a decade and wished he had a month instead of an afternoon to explore. He'd spent a couple of days in his teens over in the World War I and II Galleries. He'd imagined flying with aces, sliding a Sopwith Camel or Curtiss Jenny biplane out of the sun to stoop on a Fokker triplane. Or taking a Messerschmitt 109 aloft to see what one of the last great prop-driven fighters could really do. Even if he'd never been much of a fixed-wing guy.

But the main gallery was the heart and soul of the museum. Over the lobby were reproductions of da Vinci's rotorcraft, the Montgolfier balloon that made the first flight and first manned flight, and the Wright Brothers *Flyer*. Beyond that stood the early airmail planes—the need to move the mail had been the major driving force behind the beginning of flight innovation.

For contrast, up and to the left was a collection of drones including one like Steve's that he flew for MHA. They progressed to the balcony edge and from there the room was dominated by the M-21 Blackbird, the fastest production aircraft ever built.

Three times the speed of sound. It made his palms sweat just to look at it; it was a dozen times faster than his beautiful Firehawk. It was a hundred feet of pitch-black, evil reconnaissance plane.

"There's one story for you." Dale was pointing up at a DC-3. The same plane MHA still used for its smokejumpers. It might be a museum piece, but it was an immensely reliable museum piece particularly well suited to smokejumping.

"The bunny rabbit." Denise was standing at the hand-rail between them.

"The bunny rabbit," Dale confirmed.

It was odd. Their words were close, companionable

sounds as he'd expect from family. But their greeting at the front door had been stiff, a sideways one-armed hug so brief that he'd have missed it if he blinked. Dale was nearly Vern's height, but there'd been no gentle kiss atop his daughter's head.

"When we first hung the DC-3, it was a standard cargo paint job, blah-gray. As part of an acknowledgment for some major financial assistance, we wanted to repaint her in Alaska Airlines colors. So, we lowered her to a few feet off the floor and built a plastic tent over her to catch the fumes. You were what, six?"

"Seven," Denise said quietly.

What had she been like at seven? Vern wondered if he could ask, but there was a reserve to her father that made him suspect it would not be a welcome inquiry.

"Then we vented the tent out that door over there with a big tube."

"A bunny got in through the vent."

"So there we were, running around the museum trying to catch the rabbit."

"And I was begging them not to hurt it."

"And I was telling her not to go near it because it was wild and who knew what contagions it carried."

"It was so cute. I wanted to adopt it."

Their words were overlapping. How could they be so close yet stand a foot apart as if they weren't related? Vern liked picturing the little girl—he imagined her with long, blond hair even then, floating along behind her—as they chased the rabbit under this plane and around that one. A pound of scampering furball creating complete mayhem for a dozen adults and one child.

"We finally herded it back to the door."

"And it was free." Denise sighed happily as if somehow a part of her had gone free with it to romp over—what? Were there fields around the museum twenty years ago? One of the thirty busiest airports in the country to one side and a congested six-lane thoroughfare to the other. Where had the rabbit come from and gone to? Or had it somehow been manifested in that place and moment of time so that the child Denise could dream of it running free through meadow grass and wildflowers?

Oddly, the story did tell him something of the woman beside him. Behind that careful exterior was a dreamer. *What dreams do you have, Wrench?* He expected that they'd been so long buried that to even ask would send them skittering aside as fast as the legendary rabbit.

They strolled through the museum. Except when nudged, Dale spoke of the planes, not the girl standing beside him. Date of acquisition of this one, why that one was of special historical interest.

"What's with the dog?"

They were looking up at an HH-52 SeaGuard Coast Guard helicopter, one of the few choppers in the collection. The SeaGuard had predated his own service, but it was a classic—the mainstay of the fleet for decades. With its shallow, boat-hull bottom, it could make water landings if conditions allowed. This one hung twenty feet above them. And in the pilot's lower right window, the curved pane that would be down by his feet and offer a view of the sea as he hovered to a rescue, sat a large stuffed dog. He was brown and white and grinned down at them.

"He's mine."

Vern checked. Still no blush. He hadn't hit the blushing story yet. It had to be around here somewhere.

"When we were hanging it"—Dale had stuffed his hands in his pockets as if he didn't know what to do with them—"Denise asked what happened when they rescued people. Were they scared? When I said they probably were, but they would also be glad to be rescued, she asked if they ever rescued kids."

Dale appeared to become less comfortable with him, rather than more, as they went. It puzzled Vern. Most people liked him. Of course the fact that he was sleeping with Dale's daughter probably had something to do with it.

"She disappeared for a few minutes, apparently up to my office. When she came back, we had the chopper halfway up into position. She insisted that we lower it back down, then she put her favorite stuffed animal there. Said any pilot who was a good one would have a stuffed animal to give to a scared child."

Denise eyed Vern speculatively.

He couldn't help himself. Right in front of her father, he pulled her into a hug and kissed her on the head. She had the best heart. "Yes," he told her. "I was usually too busy flying, but I made sure that the crew chief always had a couple of stuffers tucked away somewhere. Nothing as magnificent as your dog up there, but it is an old Coast Guard tradition."

She stayed in his arms a moment longer.

Dale's face held an odd expression. He wasn't glaring at Vern. Instead he was looking at his daughter and appeared to be terribly sad. With a shock, Vern realized that it wasn't him that Dale was uncomfortable around; it was his own daughter.

Solving that mystery suddenly felt far more important than finding whatever story had made Denise blush.

—∿∿—

Denise was glad when Dad joined them for lunch down the street at Randy's. She knew that it was hard for him, but she could tell that he was glad to see her.

"It's tradition," she explained to Vern. "The café at the museum opened only shortly before Mom died. Our place to eat together was always Randy's. The owner is ex-Air Force, and his wife is Italian."

The restaurant was far cozier than the museum's utilitarian café. It had deep, red-leather seats and more flight memorabilia per square foot than anywhere else she'd ever been. From postcards to pitot tubes to airplanes hanging from the ceiling. Even as a young girl, she'd always had permission to come here alone. Lucia would keep an eye on her and slip her the occasional piece of pie. She'd spent endless hours studying each piece of memorabilia…and occasionally doing her homework as well.

She'd been on pins and needles throughout morning. At first because she'd arrived in front of her dad in complete disarray from Vern's earnest attentions to her body. But more so because of the conversations. The past was always there, but rarely spoken of. Vern's questions had brought back so many good memories, but she knew from long experience that you couldn't have the good without soon remembering the bad. Dad was doing his best, but it hurt watching how hard it was for him.

He'd suggested that they visit the Restoration Center together. It would take an hour, maybe two with traffic to drive there. The Boeing museum's restoration hangar was up at Paine Field in Everett.

Vern had solved that by loading them into Yuri's Bell chopper. Denise had squeezed into the middle of the bench seat, trying not to be too obvious about leaning against Vern so that she didn't have to lean against her dad. Physical contact had never been comfortable with him, but the cockpit was so small that it was hard to give him the space he always seemed to need.

Thankfully, the flight was no more than thirty minutes. A special request to the tower and they were able to land on the grass close beside the center's two hangars. Outside she showed Vern one of the first Learjets and the very first Boeing 727, and he poked around an old Air Force Piasecki CH-21 Shawnee helicopter.

"This was always my favorite place," she told Vern as they headed inside. Somewhere along the way, she'd taken his hand to lead him ahead. She'd never been with a man who wanted to hold her hand in public. Every man she'd ever been with was like her father—no PDA. Public displays of affection were for other women, not her. As if she wasn't worth it, something she now understood to be an evil lie that she'd completely bought into. Vern was practically attached to her, and she was discovering how much she could enjoy that.

"We came here every Saturday. You have to start up here on the mezzanine level." She led him up the steel-grate stairs to the small group of weary Formica tables where most of the staff and volunteers ate and took breaks.

In a space that would normally hold four or five small jets or other working craft, there were crammed more than thirty planes—each in various stages of restoration. They were spread out down the hangar in either direction. The massive de Havilland Comet 4 jet had become a fixture. They'd cut out a section of the hangar's wall, made a large circular opening, and stuck the plane's entire nose section inside the hangar. From the outside, it looked as if the plane had crashed into the building.

There was a Russian fighter and a Japanese Zero. A couple of gliders and even a Boeing Apache attack helicopter hanging from the ceiling in the crowded space. The cavernous area was a massive jumble of airframes in varying stages of repair that took even the practiced eye a while to sort out.

The huge space echoed with numerous discussions among the forty workers on the floor, covered by the punch of air hammers knocking loose rust, the high whine of drills cutting out old rivets, and even the sharp snap-and-hiss of welding torches.

She breathed it in as Vern admired the view. Denise let the smell of old planes and new paint wash over her. This was as close to home as she had. More than the echoingly quiet house at Fauntleroy, more than the museum. This was where she belonged.

Denise shared a look with her dad and they both glanced down, as they always did, at a space currently filled with a WWII Grumman FM-2 Wildcat carrier-based fighter plane. Mom and Dad had met right there, working on restoring a Lockheed Model 10-E Electra. She'd been a friend of Linda Finch who had restored it to look exactly like Amelia Earhart's final, fatal plane. Dad had been doing some volunteer work, trying to get on as a docent at the time.

He'd proposed in the finished cockpit. Denise had

never before wondered if they'd made love there, but after this morning's experience in Vern's helicopter, she rather suspected they had. She could feel the heat rising to her cheeks. Parents didn't do things like that. Though she half hoped for her dad's sake that he had.

Vern inspected her curiously, and Denise did her best to ignore him, but it wasn't working. Standing here, looking down at the shop floor of her favorite place on the planet, she felt far more naked than stripped to the skin but for one sock.

"Denise!" The shout from the floor could only come from one man. Sure enough, Huey Kemble heaved his powerful bulk out of the belly of a Vought Cutlass jet and headed in their direction. He was puffing as he reached the top of the stairs, his long, gray ponytail even longer now.

She returned his bear hug, wrapping her arms as far around him as she could. He thumped her on the back several times before letting her go.

"And who is this young man come sniffing around my girl?"

"Am I that obvious?" Vern grimaced in that friendly way of his. "Vern Taylor." And he extended his hand.

Denise had to smile. How like him to play none of the cards that would automatically get him in good here. So she did it for him. "Chopper pilot. Ex-Coast Guard and now he flies one of the Firehawks I service for MHA."

"MHA? That's solid." Huey, typically, had forgotten that he hadn't yet introduced himself.

"This is Huey, uh, only I get to call him that. Hubert"—she gave it the proper French roll—"Kemble. He's the curator here at the Restoration Center."

"Curator, chief mechanic, and I can fix a toilet when

it's plugged. When Denise was even shorter than she is now, she couldn't pronounce my name, so I told her to call me Huey. She said that if I was named for a duck—Huey, Dewey, and Louie—then where was my ducktail? So"— he pulled on his gray ponytail for show—"I grew one."

"That was because of me?" She hadn't remembered that.

"Of course, sweetheart. Anything for our Denise."

She felt suddenly smaller, even more so than normal. Vern's height, her father's massive silence, and Huey's equally massive frame and personality were all shrinking her by comparison.

"I remember many things." Huey winked at her as he waved for them to sit at a small table overlooking the floor. "I remember the day that you—"

"No!" She tried to stop him, but once Huey was on a roll, such efforts were pointless. He turned to Vern and ignored her.

"—the day she threw over Tom Cruise." He waggled his bushy, gray eyebrows at Vern.

"She didn't!" The men were grinning at each other. Denise wanted to bury her head in shame.

"When she was eleven or twelve, I'd find her sitting in the cockpit of whatever our hottest jet was on the floor. A picture of Tom from *Top Gun* would be in the copilot's seat, and they'd fly together for hours."

Maybe if she pulled a fire alarm, she'd be able to get out of this conversation.

But Huey was implacable. "Then it happened!" He slapped his hands together with a boom as loud as the hammer on steel of someone below presently driving a shaft punch into the French Fouga Magister training jet.

"What?" Vern sounded way too eager.

"Why, *The Aviator* came out. Whatever else Howard Hughes was, he was a crazy-good mechanic. Overnight, Cruise disappeared, and Leonardo DiCaprio was her only copilot after that."

All of the men laughed. It was good-natured and totally embarrassing. All of the men… She glanced at her father. She hadn't heard him laugh in so many years that it was alarming when he did. Was it something Vern had done?

"Though I must say it looks like poor Leo has finally been thrown over after so many years." He offered a broad wink at Vern.

Denise wanted to shake her head, but it was too confusing to explain. She wasn't casting aside Leonardo. It was that she'd never let a real man in. She'd set aside teenage fantasies, and no one had stepped up in their place until she'd begun to think no one would.

Vern was in her heart, further than anyone had ever been, but that didn't mean she was in love with him…

But she had said that she was, hadn't she? That meant…that she was an unholy mess.

She really needed some fresh air. Some quiet time working on an engine and giving her head time to clear. People were too confusing. They kept—

"Got something serious to talk to you about, girlie." Huey sobered as much as he ever did. "Reason your dad brought you here. I asked him to next time you were home."

Not trusting her voice yet, she nodded for him to continue.

"I'm retiring in six months."

"No, you can't!" It burst out of her. Denise couldn't

imagine the Restoration Center without Huey. He'd been a fixture here since her first memory.

"I'm past seventy now, and I can. Promised the wife I would so that we could do some traveling while we're still healthy. Don't worry your head, girl. I'll still be around to bother you as a pesky volunteer whenever we're in town. I'd miss the planes too much."

"My head?" It was spinning. What would it be like without him here? This is where she'd learned more about airframes and engines than any class or certification course she'd gathered along the way. By the time she'd signed on with MHA, she'd known the heart and soul of every aircraft on the lot from the 727 out back down to the small Letov LF-107 Lunák glider she could see still hanging from the rafters.

"Your head. I've talked to your dad and the board. They'd like to offer you the job. Restoration Center curator. It's what you always wanted."

It was. It had been. It was. Wasn't it?

Dad and Huey were beaming at her.

She looked to Vern. His face was very carefully neutral.

She tried to swallow but couldn't. Her throat was too tight. Her stomach too clenched. "I—" Her first attempt to speak was a total failure.

"Stunned her speechless with that one, didn't I?" Huey sounded pretty pleased with himself.

Denise tried to speak again, but was afraid to unclench her jaw for fear she might be sick. No one to help her. Unless… She knew it was horribly unfair. It would tear them apart if she accepted. But she couldn't turn it down. But—

She turned a pleading look on Vern.

He met her gaze.

She couldn't read a thing there. Not hope that she'd turn down the offer. Not fear that she'd take it. Nothing. He'd never been shut off to her before, but now he was a million miles away.

Unable to look any longer, Denise closed her eyes.

Then, after she'd given up all hope, she felt an arm slide around her shoulders, one she'd come to know so well in such a short time. She collapsed against him, hiding her face in his chest.

Then she felt him speak, his deep voice vibrating his chest against her cheek. "How long, Hubert? How long before you need an answer?"

She didn't hear his reply but could feel the disappointed tone. The greatest gift anyone had ever given her, and she felt as if she were trapped in a fire whorl as brutal as the one that had almost killed Vern.

Vern nodded at whatever Huey said.

For now that would have to be answer enough.

Chapter 11

VERN HAD DONE HIS BEST TO COVER FOR DENISE. HE'D CHAT-
ted with Hubert. Made small talk with her dad through
the flight back to Boeing Field. Done his best to hide his
own shock, keeping it buried even after they were back
on Vashon.

Still Denise had spoken barely a word.

It was the perfect job for her. Truly a once-in-a-
lifetime offer, proven by the fact that Hubert had held
the position for twenty of his forty years there.

What did he have to offer in return?

Shit! None of it was making any sense. So he shoved
it aside as well as he could. Once they'd stowed the
chopper back at the hangar and he'd left a note for
Gary to drain the oil and the couple gallons of gas
that were left, he tucked her into the passenger seat of
his Vette.

They stopped at ZuZu's and got ice cream cones,
then he drove her down to the lighthouse. He led her
back to the beach log he'd been perched on before.

A fifty-foot sailboat with a bright blue hull and red
sails moseyed along beneath light winds. The crowd
aboard appeared to be enjoying themselves, no hurry to
be anywhere other than where they were.

"This is where I always came to sit when something
was troubling me. It's the best thinking spot I've got,
Denise. Maybe it will help you too."

She still hadn't spoken by the time they finished their cones.

So he broke the silence. "Why didn't you say yes?"

"I don't know."

"Was it because of me, of us?"

She shook her head no, then whispered, "Not only."

It had been the first thought to slam into him. Just that fast, he could lose her. Three little letters, one word, and their service together at MHA would be history. He didn't know how he felt about that. It was the best job he'd ever had, even better than the Coast Guard—very few drug runners shooting at your chopper in MHA. Very few people dying a hundred yards from the beach because they were too dumb to heed the riptide warning signs.

"How soon do I have to decide?"

"Hubert told you."

"Well, I didn't hear him. I was too busy being shocked. Dad laughing, actually laughing. Huey retiring. The job offer. It's been a busy day for me."

"Don't forget some awesome helicopter sex."

She looked up at him for the first time since she'd silently begged for his help at the Restoration Center. Her green eyes were soft, bright with unshed tears, but soft. "That," she said quietly and brushed a hand down his arm, "in your arms in the helo, is the only moment that has made sense today. And even that is overwhelming the daylights out of me."

"Still tracking," he noted.

"What?"

"That's two of us who are overwhelmed by it. The only thing I know for sure is that it was absolutely fantastic. Sex with you is consistently mind-bogglingly and totally fantastic. How you do that to me, I have no idea, but I'm sure not going to file a complaint."

"Who would you file it with?"

He could never tell if she was being really funny or dead serious—and often only realized afterward that she was being funny. "The Relationship Police are out; their mandate doesn't cover carnal matters. The Sex Patrol is usually too busy enjoying itself to interfere. Yet another reason not to file a complaint with them."

She squinted her eyes at his response, perhaps questioning his sanity. So he'd answer her straight.

"I love making love to you, Denise. But I'm hoping that we're not the issue here, at least not the main one."

"How long?"

"Huey said he's retiring in six months. I got him aside, and he said he did have a backup, so he'd need only a month's notice. You don't have to decide until we're done with the Honduras contract."

"Oh thank God." She rubbed at her face with both hands as if waking up.

He had another question he had to ask, and he figured this was as good a time as any. "Can I ask about your dad?"

"What about him?"

"Is there a reason you two don't hug?"

"Most men don't. You're a bit weird that way. Take that as encouragement, not complaint. But have you ever seen Mark and Emily hug?"

He had, a few times, and felt like a voyeur because it completely changed them into much softer people.

"Fathers hug their daughters. Especially when they care about them as much as he obviously does."

"Not my dad."

"But…" His own father hugged him more than that. Slap on the back and all that, but still a good, solid—

"I look like my mother."

"Which means what?"

"You don't get it." Denise looked up at him, pinning him once again with that green gaze. "I look almost exactly like my mother. Right down to…" She lifted a handful of her long hair and flapped it at him. "I've looked at the family albums. We could have been twins. Every time he sees me, he sees her. Probably sees her bleeding out in his arms. It freaks him out."

"Shit." Vern felt like a total heel for asking. He'd grown up with his mom hovering about, offering hugs and healing kisses. And his dad would think nothing of guiding Vern's hands with his own to teach him a new skill in sailing or boat repair. Denise had grown up without being touched by anyone.

He couldn't stand the thought of her so alone, so apart.

Shifting over the few inches that separated them, he pulled her into his embrace. She slid an arm around his waist, and they sat together a long time silently watching the drifting sailboat. The bright conversation from aboard carried gently over the quiet waters, until an evening breeze arrived to whisk the sailors on their way.

—◊—

Vern parked the Corvette along the main drag of the village of Vashon. "Lucky to get a spot so close." Then he took her hand and led her up to Bank Road and turned west.

Denise stumbled to a halt. The main drag on a Saturday morning had been busy, busier than either time they'd driven through it yesterday going to the airport and back.

Bank Road was jam-packed with people.

Vern, also pulled to a halt by their linked hands, stepped back beside her and immediately understood as he always seemed to do. "Cider Fest. Only happens once a year. A lot of tourists will be over from the mainland. Not a good day to get on the ferry, I can tell you. But it's also a locals' party. Starts with the farmers market, hard-cider tasting, tours of the fire station. Later there is a dance and locals' potluck. Mom and some buddies put together an on-again, off-again band for dancing at potlucks, and they're going to play. It'll be great. Let's go!"

Denise tried to keep up; she really did.

A lot of these people knew Vern, and he had to stop and talk to everyone. Some asked him about the Coast Guard. Some were more up to date and asked him about fighting forest fires. Men shook his hand, women hugged him. Some of the younger women eyed Denise coolly and made a real display of laying their flesh on him. She was pleased to see that he politely but quickly stepped back without grabbing a feel, which was blatantly offered—very blatantly in several cases.

As they approached a couple of women in particular, Vern made a point of taking Denise's hand and keeping her especially close. A particularly overbuilt and underdressed woman was deeply irritated when she couldn't brush Denise aside.

"I think she passed through puberty at birth," Vern whispered as soon as they were out of earshot. "Reni has certainly been a man-hound since the crib. She's been gunning for me since third grade. More than once I've thought she should wear one of those warning labels they put on airliner engines, 'Danger! Jet Intake!' She's like that. She didn't get me then, and she's sure not gonna now. Though I did take her sister to the prom. She was equally hot and only about a tenth as psycho."

Denise was jealous of the sister, but glad to know he hadn't stooped to take advantage of Reni's generous assets. Her senior prom hadn't even been a consideration. That had only been for the popular kids, so she kept her mouth shut.

The fire station was having an open house. Kids were everywhere on the engines, and firemen, already showing the wear of the day, spent more time saying "Don't pull on that" than explaining how their engines worked.

Every one of them knew Vern. He was like a long-lost brother come home.

"I was a junior firefighter volunteer until I joined the Coast Guard," he managed to get out before someone else was slapping him on the back hard enough to send him reeling in a new direction.

When Vern introduced her as the best firefighting helicopter mechanic on the planet, she was instantly in good. She was hugged and her hand shaken more times in the next five minutes than in any single year of her life…prior to the last week or so anyway.

They weren't separated out in the bustling crowds, but here in the fire station, he was gone in a moment. The station's chief mechanic wanted to show her an ongoing restoration project he'd been doing on a 1934 Ford pumper truck with a Flathead V8, a monster for its day with almost as much horsepower as her Fiat, but about an eighth of the Vette.

She wouldn't be admitting anytime soon that she loved driving Vern's car. The additional four decades of engineering and deep-rooted power grabbed at her and pulled… She'd stay with Vern just so she could keep driving that machine. But how could she stay with him and take the museum job? And how—

Again, as she'd done after the beach and throughout last night, she avoided the question. Over dinner she'd talked with Vern's mom. She'd been overwhelmed by what she missed by not having a mother of her own.

Margi had suggested that if Denise didn't have the answer, then it wasn't time yet. The answer of what to do would come when it was good and ready and not a moment before. "When the solution is obvious, then you'll know you've found the right one. Until then, honey"—Margi had taken to calling her "honey," and Denise was finding she rather enjoyed it—"try not to worry at it too much."

So, she set aside her worries as well as she could and made suggestions on how the fire truck's original pump linkage would have been run. She could see the obvious signs of the same linkage that had been used to control the flaps in a Ford Trimotor she'd been able to study when it was still at the Evergreen Aviation & Space Museum in Oregon. She drew a sketch based on that system, but adapted for the needs of a ground vehicle.

The poor guy offered to divorce his wife and marry her instead, he was so happy. His wife was standing right beside them as Denise drew. She winked at Denise and kissed her husband on the cheek.

Denise turned to find Vern. It wasn't hard. The department had their pumper truck pulled out into the October sunshine. He'd hooked up a hose and a fireman was running the pumper's controls. The one-and-a-half-inch hose might be small for truck-based firefighters but it was pretty standard for smokejumpers. Still, it had enough force to lift and toss a kid.

Vern stood three feet from the end, keeping the hose firmly anchored as kid after kid came up to try steering the nozzle at the storm drain.

The entire street was sparkling with ten thousand wet reflections of the sun. He'd coaxed some of the younger kids to tackle the challenge in groups of two or three. The ones who'd had their turns hung close beside him, a couple of the little ones clinging to his legs.

Vern and children.

Wow!

She knew nothing about kids. She'd grown up with the museum staff as her peers. They'd tried to coax her into helping in the Challenger Learning Center where school groups could sit at the various stations of mission control and work their way through a simulated shuttle launch. The one time she'd tried had been a total fiasco. She'd had no idea what to do with their chaotic energy even though they'd been her own age.

But Vern and children...he made it look easy.

Natural. She'd never imagined having kids, had actually sworn she wouldn't. Besides, she wouldn't know what to do with one if she did. However, being the mother of Vern's children didn't seem quite so outlandish, despite the fact that it was never going to happen.

Now whose stupid brain was messing with the *M* word? And here she was compounding it with the *K* word! Granted it was only in the depths of her imagination, but the chaos in there appeared to be growing, not diminishing, as the day progressed.

—⁓—

It only got worse that night at the potluck. Very few mainlanders; this was clearly a locals' event.

Denise had prepared herself by imagining dinner at the MHA field when everyone was in from the field, the fires were beaten for the moment, and the mood was high. Those moments tended to overwhelm her and she always tried to get a table on the periphery, but the MHA dinners were fun to watch.

Tonight, it was coming on sunset when they roared up to the hall in Vern's bronze Vette with the top down. She could see what must be some of his old school chums groaning with envy. The crowd around the front door was already thick, and she wanted to stay in the car or retreat back to the beach.

She'd asked Vern what she should wear, and he'd been absolutely useless, claiming that it didn't matter. He'd tried to prove his point by taking off the clothes she'd had on at the time. But despite his pleas, she was not going to attend dressed as Lady Godiva; though his begging had led to other side benefits that afternoon.

Margi had echoed her son's response about her clothes not mattering: "This is the island, honey, not the mainland. We just show up."

Denise had settled on her best jeans with no grease stains, a satiny blouse the same color as her eyes, and the leather vest that always made her feel a little "brave World War I fighting ace." She left her hair down because it increased the options for ways she could casually disappear behind it.

Vern, on the other hand, clearly wanted to be seen with her. He'd made a point of rushing around the hood to open her door for her and giving her a hand out as if she were an arriving Hollywood star.

"You look completely delicious." He'd grinned down at her, and she felt a little better. He reached behind the seat for the couple of bowls of potluck food he'd stashed there, and they each took one.

Everyone was flowing from the parking lot into the grange hall.

They passed a man selling raffle tickets in front of three pickup trucks. Two had chopped firewood to the level of the bed and the third was stacked high with a full cord of firewood.

"Hey," Vern called after her when she'd started to go by. "You gotta buy a ticket."

"What am I going to do with a truckload of wood?"

"Hey, it gets Mom and Dad some extra chances."

She fished out a five-dollar bill and put it on the table.

"Now don't be gettin' too greedy." The man smiled at her but took the bill quickly enough and handed her back five tickets. "The library thanks you. That's who we're fundraising for tonight."

At the door, there was another pile, this one of small, green logs. Then she looked more closely. It was a stack of a couple dozen zucchini, most the size of a very, very stout dachshund. A cardboard sign said, "Take one home, adopt it for free. Take two… Please!" Some wag had scribbled "(Nonreturnable)" along the edge of the sign.

Passing up the offer, they entered the heavy double doors pinned open to allow the cool evening air to circulate. Inside was a blast no smaller than a wildfire explosion.

She didn't know where to look first. Long tables had been lined up throughout the room. The longest ran down the entire side of the hall. Each person who arrived set down a platter, bowl, or something. There were trays of lasagna, several sides of baked salmon, Crock-Pots of what smelled like Swedish meatballs, and another one of chili.

"Hey, Vern," someone greeted them, "are those your eggs? We've been missing them."

He leaned down to whisper in her ear as they set down the bowls they'd been carrying. "Told you I was famous for them."

She and Vern had spent part of the afternoon making his famous "portable" deviled eggs. They'd hard-boiled and peeled dozens of eggs. He'd filled one large bowl with the halved egg whites and then mashed up the yellow yolks with minced shallot, mayo, and an amazing amount of pepper with a dash of hot sauce. They were wonderful! Stick in a couple of serving spoons and set a bottle of paprika to the side, and they were indeed portable.

They joined the line that was already forming to flow down both sides of the food table. There had to be forty feet of food. In a small corner kitchen, several ladies were tending a couple of ovens that smelled of garlic bread. There were also amiable lines at the two massive coffeemakers.

"Vern. That's coffee. Aren't you going for it?"

He leaned in close and whispered, "May, the one on the left wearing clothes her daughter wouldn't be caught dead in, makes the absolute worst coffee on the planet. You have to live on the island full-time to develop a tolerance for it."

The room itself finally registered through the mayhem of other impressions—slowly finding a place or at least a perspective. The hall had an old wooden floor, an open-beam ceiling, and white walls covered in photographs. A tired-looking American flag boasting forty-eight stars hung on one wall, and a brand-new one on a wooden pole had been shoved into a corner out of the way.

Most of the area was filled with rows of tables that sported white paper tablecloths and a scattering of jam jars overflowing with dahlias and asters. In the center of each long table was a steel bucket holding a large cluster of sunflowers, both large and small. A small stage at the far end of the room commanded a small, open space beyond the tables, an area big enough for a half-dozen couples to at least shuffle their feet.

She watched what and how much Vern took as they moved down the food line. She tried to do the same, but with smaller portions. Occasionally a dish would run out as she approached it, but three more of something else would replace it by the time she got there.

When she reached for a brownie from a bright red platter, Vern grabbed her wrist to stop it. "Those are Mabel's magic brownies. Consider yourself warned. Unless you go that way."

"Mabel?" She'd never tried pot in her life.

"In green." He nodded discreetly toward a corner of the room.

She waited a moment, then glanced over. Two over-stuffed, well-worn couches were pushed into a corner of the room, and several folding chairs had been pulled up nearby. The couches were clearly the places of honor; not a soul there could be under seventy. Those in the chairs were obviously their gray-haired children. Mabel wore a pretty green dress and could easily be ninety. A soft smile emanated from her gentle face.

"Probably already stoned. She a great lady. Very mellow. Maybe you should try one."

"That would be...not. Why, do I need to mellow out?"

In answer, he kissed her on the nose and continued down the line.

Infuriating man. She took a massive chocolate-chip cookie that Vern's nod confirmed to be safe. She took a bite because it looked so good. Definitely not safe! Dark chocolate and a serious dose of sugar. She took another bite before she'd finished the first, then set it on her plate and wondered if it would be rude to take two.

Vern took two. So she'd look considerate and only take one...then eat half of his second cookie.

At the tables they were soon surrounded by Vern's friends. There wasn't a chance of her remembering their names, so she didn't even try. Thankfully two of them

were the fire-engine restorer, Emerson, and his wife
Maylene. Or perhaps Marlene; it was hard to hear with
the downpour of ever-shifting conversations going on.

And more kids. Kids were everywhere, stopping
their communal racing up and down only long enough
to grab a bite before racing off once more. A few dogs—
including a Great Dane so tall that he ever so politely
inspected Denise's plate over her shoulder—worked the
tables seeking treats as well.

She wrapped both her ankles around Vern's nearest
ankle so that she had some anchor in the maelstrom.

"Hey, there's Mom."

Margi was up on stage, a grand word for a platform
raised but a single foot off the floor and lit by a couple of
colored floodlights that obviously came from the local
hardware store.

In addition to an acoustic guitar, she wore a T-shirt
that said "READ!" in massive letters over her chest,
with "Vashon Library" below it. She too wore jeans
and sneakers.

They hadn't been kidding. Denise now felt terribly
overdressed. Then she looked around the room. Maylene
or Marlene wore a nice blouse. Some of the men wore
button-down shirts. One man wore a tie, a sailboat tie
that clashed horribly with the green flannel shirt he wore
it with.

Okay, she wasn't too out of place.

A few other musicians joined Margi onstage: a pia-
nist at an upright that looked as if it had been left here by
accident in a prior century (and not the twentieth either),
a second guitar, a flute, and an electric bass.

"Tonight is about book music," Margi announced

over a microphone that squealed until someone adjusted it. "So we're calling this one-night motley crew the Book Band."

When Denise glanced at Vern, he shrugged.

"They jam together a lot out at the house. She must have decided to run with the library fundraiser theme. Mom's the top of the heap this year. Sometimes we get some superstar here. Once the guy from the island who's in Los Lobos brought his entire band. Man, did we dance that year."

"Dance?" She felt a sudden return of abject terror, worse than flying half-naked in a helicopter headed to see her father. "I don't dance."

"Sure you do." He winked at her, and she kicked him under the table. Hopefully hard enough for it to be a serious warning. She considered kicking him even harder so that he wouldn't be able to dance at all.

Chapter 12

DENISE LET VERN DRIVE THEM BACK DOWN FROM VASHON Island to Mount Hood. He was doggedly slow, barely cracking the speed limit, but she wasn't up to the challenge. She simply lay back and watched the cities give way to the lazy hills of southern Washington. Vern took Route 14 down along the shores of the Columbia River.

They climbed Beacon Rock to look down at the river, though her legs still throbbed from last night. On a dance area sufficient for a half-dozen couples, she must have bumped into every resident of the whole island. Twice. Matriarchs had danced with two-foot-tall great-granddaughters. Teens used it as an excuse to slow dance in a tight clench no matter how upbeat the tempo. One couple had somehow managed to find room to waltz, slicing neat lines back and forth through the packed crowd.

Vern had hauled her to her feet for the opening number, the Beatles' "Paperback Writer," kept her dancing to Jefferson Airplane's "White Rabbit," and they'd finished the night tight in each other's arms moving together in a slow-motion shuffle to a softly jazzy version of the love aria from *The Phantom of the Opera*.

This morning, before they'd left, Margi had given her a wrapped gift, "Not to open until you get home," and a hug that Denise would carry with her for a long time. The hug had been open, giving, and boundless. No admonishments about treating her son well or being careful. Margi had simply wrapped her tight in her arms and held her close for an infinitely long moment.

"Remember to hold yourself gently," Margi Taylor had whispered before moving back and ushering Denise into the car.

From atop Beacon Rock's eight hundred and some odd feet—*how casually inaccurate of you*, she told herself—they could see over twenty miles of river, from the Bridge of the Gods beyond the Bonneville Dam in the west down to the bend in the river near Steigerwald Lake National Wildlife Refuge.

She and Vern leaned side by side on the rail from atop the towering precipice.

"I'm going to adopt your mom," she informed him. "It is so unfair that you get to have her to yourself."

"Dad might have some say in it. Sorry you didn't get to meet him."

"Next time," she said hazily, then hoped that Vern had missed it.

His amused smile said that he hadn't.

She continued before he could razz her about that. "Tough. She's mine now."

"She's pretty great, huh?"

Denise nodded. She didn't trust herself to speak, not even once they were back in the car. She leaned back against the seat and turned her face to watch the tall trees sliding by her side of the road. She let the wind whip a tear from her eyes.

For the first time, Denise finally understood how much she and her father had lost that long-ago day.

Vern reached out and took her hand in his. They drove the rest of the way to her place like that.

She'd finally found one reason to have an automatic shift. It was a compelling one.

—~~~—

Vern had never been to Denise's place before. It was a small, two-bedroom town house in a ten-unit row of them that was tucked into the trees not far from MHA's base.

Denise paused at the door.

Vern stopped close beside her.

"It's nothing special."

"My expectations are limitless."

She stuck her tongue out at him, which he decided was a good sign.

He wouldn't have been surprised if her place had been filled with strange mechanical contraptions like the beginning of *Back to the Future*, an endless expanse of Rube Goldberg devices. Or if it showed a shockingly feminine side of Denise carefully hidden away for no one to see. Or if she was a total slob, such as he'd been before the Coast Guard. But he hadn't expected this.

It was utterly plain; the place had not the least hint of personality. The carpet was a light brown and the walls white. The furniture was typical for a rental. A well-used couch with a cheap wooden coffee table that had seen better days. A laptop computer sat on one end. The dining room had a desk, and the walls were wrapped in bookcases.

He sidled up to them—almost entirely reference manuals on different kinds of planes. The only wall art was a few detailed technical diagrams. He recognized the drawing of the GE turbine engine that powered his

Firehawk. Another, he had to look at the legend, was a "UH-60 Black Hawk Wiring Diagram (typical)." It was one of the most terrifyingly complex drawings he'd ever seen. The kitchen boasted no scattering of kitchen machines, nothing but a toaster and a microwave.

Denise hadn't spoken, simply stopped inside the door and watched his inspection. He still held their bags; she held the gift, wrapped in brown paper, that his mother had presented to her this morning.

"These go upstairs?" He held up both of their bags. There was no way he was leaving her alone here. Not in this place. It was clean, comfortable, but totally devoid of any heart.

The back bedroom upstairs was completely barren except for a small stack of empty-and-folded moving boxes. The master bedroom had a dresser and a comfortable-looking queen-sized mattress under a Macy's plain blue comforter. A quick peek revealed not one thing out of place, not even in the bathroom.

He had more personal items in the bunkroom he shared with Mickey on the MHA base. He'd pinned up some art posters, the first page of the sheet music for *Bad Man-Music*, and a bunch of photos. A bunch. A couple of Mom and Dad, some fires, but mostly friends. High school, Coast Guard, helitack school, firefighters at play or on the line.

He dropped the bags on the foot of the bed and headed back down to her. He had about a dozen steps to determine how to react.

Vern figured this place was the epitome of the old Denise, she who kept herself so carefully hidden from those around her. Except it wasn't only that. Right now, she was the woman in hiding. One he hadn't really believed in until now because it was in such complete contrast to the woman who'd slowly revealed herself to him.

Denise's mandate? "Don't leave any impression on the world because you never know how the world will react." It was a lonely, cautious place that only made him appreciate all the more how much and how freely she shared with him.

So, he'd set that aside and be otherwise honest.

She hadn't moved from the cusp of the living room entry. What verdict had Jasper laid down on her head the one time he saw the place? For Vern would bet good money that there had only been one visit, and based on Denise's silence, it hadn't gone well.

He shrugged. "Seen worse. Serves its purpose, right?"

Her nod was tight.

"Something I need to warn you about before we go any further in this relationship."

Again the tight nod.

"I'm way messier than this. Just think you should know that."

She blinked at him as if waking from a dream.

"Really? Nothing else to say?"

He went up to her and pulled the gift from her hands. He could tell through the wrapping that it was one of Mom's paintings. Cool. He leaned it against a wall and took both of her hands in his.

"The way I see it, Wrench, if this place was important to you, you'd have done more with it. It wasn't important, so…" He finished with a nonchalant shrug. "I don't care about your abilities as an interior designer. I care about you."

She nodded once more.

"Let's take a shower, open your present, and then see what we can rustle up in the kitchen."

"Not much. I eat at the base for most meals."

"Hey, in our house, 'not much' was standard operating procedure. I know how to be creative."

———

The shower, rather than being intense, had been almost chaste. They'd kissed, scrubbed each other's backs, and copped a few feels, but little more.

But Denise discovered that she was finally past worrying about Vern. He'd passed some test she hadn't realized she'd given him. If they were simply showering together, her brain didn't automatically assume he wouldn't want to be with her without sex.

Jasper had been disgusted by the way she lived. Had never let her forget that there was nothing feminine about her. She was starting to see past the veil of a relationship that she had thought failed because of her lack.

Vern's parents lived in an immense clutter of overlapping interests. Boats, music, art...every corner of the house reflected some aspect of it. And now that she thought of it, she could see Vern's own flying interests in the mix. A photo on the family wall of a gangly teen with Yuri and the Bell 47 parked by a remote lake, the two of them holding aloft a string of trout they'd caught. His framed first pilot's license on his bedroom wall.

Looking about her own town house, she could see its starkness. Vern was right; it hadn't been important to her. It was where she slept and studied. The place she lived was up at the airfield.

But Jasper hadn't merely disliked it. He'd used it to…manipulate. That's what had locked her in place at the threshold as Vern had made his nonjudgmental tour. Jasper had used it to convince her that because there were no feminine touches, she wasn't much of a woman. That she was lucky he was willing to be with her. That—

She'd done her best to scrub that off in the shower.

Vern had helped. He was in the shower with her because he wanted to be. He was constantly telling her that she was beautiful. And every touch made her feel intensely female.

That was another thing. Jasper had always driven, insisted on it, even though it was obvious to both of them that he was a far less competent driver. Whereas Vern had offered her the keys to his own car when they were leaving Vashon, simply assuming she'd want to drive. He'd been surprised when she'd begged off.

Vern concocted a pretty decent meal out of her meager pantry. A can of chili, some eggs, and rice served over lightly fried corn tortillas. He'd even scared up a plastic tub of guacamole that she hadn't opened because she'd forgotten to buy chips with it. Huevos rancheros eaten while sitting cross-legged on either side of the living room coffee table. Bumping knees and talking about Vashon. Trading forkfuls across the table didn't make sense to her because they had the same food, but he made it fun, as if offering her the choice bits.

Giggling. She was actually giggling. Vern constantly made her feel very female. No, he made her feel feminine, which was somehow more about her and less about how men saw her. Most guys, you could hear their hormones grunt when you walked into a room, "Look. A woman." Vern made her want to act…like she wasn't acting. Like she wasn't trying to fit someone else's image of her.

So to hell with Jasper and his warped past. He wasn't a tenth the lover Vern was, and his gross manipulations had failed. All through dinner she was…happy.

Though not nearly as happy as she was when she finally unwrapped Margi Taylor's gift. No, that was beyond happy; that was speechless.

It was a framed view of the Point Robinson lighthouse, the beach, and Mount Rainier beyond. It was an oil painting and the lines were soft, suggesting the blending and connection of the landscape—one element to the next. And there—in a state of absolute belonging—a lone woman stood on the beach, her long, light hair caught in a swirl of air.

But she wasn't lonely.

Not at all.

She was at peace. "How did she do this?"

Vern shrugged. "Got me, but it's amazing. I've never seen her do anything like this one before. You must have really touched her. Joke is, Mom wanted me to be an artist. Says she started me with finger paints and a guitar while still in the crib. I guess that I ate the crayons and napped on the guitar. Any string marks?" He turned one cheek, then the other for her inspection, actually had her looking for a moment at the face she was coming to know so well.

"Is that why you're such a colorful character?"

He grinned at her, then asked, "Did you notice the signature?"

"For Denise, from your friend Margi." She read it

aloud and again silently to herself. She'd dated it yesterday. "She made this for me?"

"Apparently."

"I've got to hang it. I don't have any picture hooks."
It was an almost panicky feeling. She had to get this
painting on the wall. Had to make this image a part of
her life.

"Mom usually tapes one to the back."

She was going to put it in the living room until
Vern suggested the bedroom. They carried it upstairs,
and he was right. The blank wall opposite the foot of
the bed would make it the first and last thing she saw
each day.

She sat on the foot of the bed and admired it. It was
so perfect. She really was going to steal Vern's mother
from him.

"Do you have any candles?"

"Sure. Under the bathroom sink in case the power
goes out. Why?"

"Because the only lighting you have in here is a halo-
gen reading lamp and the sun is going down."

Indeed, she could see by the view out her window
that the sun had already gone behind the mountain,
plunging the western reaches into deep shadow. In fact,
it was late enough that the colors of the painting were
blending together.

"The painting will look better by candlelight?" That
didn't quite make sense.

"Many things will." Vern didn't explain himself as
he ducked into the bath and retrieved the candles. The
power went out here with every good storm, and she
didn't like to have her reading interrupted.

He set several atop the dresser and lit three of them before returning to sit behind her on the bed.

She couldn't quite mark the transition from admiring the painting to being lost in Vern's arms.

He had apparently retrieved a hairbrush from her bathroom along with the candles and began brushing out her hair. He was gentle, working out small snarls, until he was finally able to make long, clean strokes starting at her part and traveling down to the very tips. No one had ever brushed her hair for her before. It was so sensual that soon the sensations had her eyes sliding closed.

After a long time, probably well past any apocryphal hundred strokes, he put down the hairbrush and began brushing at her face with gentle fingertips. He slowly shifted their position until she lay on her back beside him. His touch following the lines of eyebrows, cheekbones, chin. When they traced her lips, she kissed them, feeling too mellow to do more.

Inch by inch, he covered her with his caresses, by touch and by taste. Their sex had always occurred in stolen moments: from their first frantic encounters at Buck Lake, through the desperate need aboard the Bell 47, and even the ever-so-quiet love they had made that very morning in his bedroom, knowing his mother was down the hall. There had always been an urgency.

There was no haste to Vern's actions now. He slowly unwrapped her from her clothing, as if she were a precious gift, until she lay naked beside him. There was no covering over her, neither flannel sheet nor self-consciousness.

A lethargy had taken her, leaving her open to him, wholly vulnerable and feeling utterly safe. Her sole action was to allow her hands to brush over him; to cradle his head against her breast when he laid it there and listened to her heart for so long; to dig her fingers into his hair as he brushed his lips and tongue over her until the heat pulsed through her in cascading waves. These weren't the hard shock waves of abrupt peak and release. They were a gliding upward until she was so high that she could tumble and tumble with no fear of ever hitting the ground.

The candles were long gone and had been replaced by others before he finally entered her. This time they flew upward together.

Never in her life had she flown so high.

Never in her life had she not worried about the fall.

Here there was only the glory of a man proving how he loved her. A man who she loved back with all her heart.

Chapter 13

"DID EITHER OF YOU SLEEP?"

"Shut up, Mark." Vern wanted to jab the man in the ribs.

Mount Hood Aviation's base camp was very different today than when they'd left it. High noon, there should have been choppers coming in from fires, lunch served, service crews doing maintenance during the pilots' brief breaks—the mayhem of a typical day.

Instead there was a fall chill on the silent air. The three Firehawks, the drone launch trailer, and Denise's service box were the only objects left in the whole camp. The rest of it was empty. The Down Under crew was already gone, taking the four smaller choppers with them. The guide and jump planes were down in a hangar at the airport in Hood River because this camp would soon be covered in snow. They'd dropped their cars off at a garage in town and been shuttled up here. Even the parking lot was empty.

"Yep, we didn't sleep either." Mark winked at him. "Except for the kid who made it through the night without a peep. Our one chance to catch up on our sleep and…" He offered a friendly shrug.

He and Denise had slept…at some point. Watching Denise unravel in the soft, flickering candlelight had been like nothing he'd ever done with or for a lover. She had soared and bloomed, grown and shone until he felt both all-powerful and humbled at the same time. The former because he'd been able to take her to such a place and keep her there for so long; the latter because such an incredible woman could choose to be with him.

But if they *had* slept, it hadn't been for long. He'd dozed off while watching her sleeping face as the candles guttered out. He'd woken to Denise's mane of hair sliding down the length of his body and back so slowly that he couldn't even tell the location of the transition zone where contact and the memory of it met and transformed into shivers of pure fire.

As much of a study of her body as he'd made in the light, she'd made of his in the dark. Using the lack of light to surprise, tease, and taste him, until his release had shattered him and left him gasping for both air and sanity, her hair lying like a smooth, soothing blanket from where she lay, then up over his stomach and chest.

And then later, she'd…

He blinked, trying to refocus. Denise the sexual goddess was gone, and like a cloak of invisibility once more completely intact, the mechanic now covered her as she stood in front of him in the middle of the MHA airfield. Well, there were some holes in the cloak, places where her shy smile shone through with a message especially for him.

"You're looking a bit goofy with that smile on your face, Slick."

"You should know, Wrench, since you're the one who put it there."

Her blush was pure girl, and her response to his hug was pure lover.

In easy harmony they began prepping Firehawk Oh-Three for the hour-long flight to Lewis-McChord and the long flight to Honduras in the belly of an Army C-17 Globemaster III transport jet.

———⁓———

Hot! was Vern Taylor's first thought, and his second and third as he waited for the rear cargo door of the C-17 to open. He'd been mentally steeling himself throughout the flight. Actually, he'd slept like the dead across four of the fold-down chairs along the side of the transport's cargo bay. The deafening roar of the four jet engines, each almost as big as his helicopter, had been no more than a distant lullaby.

So he was trying to make up for it now.

"Hot," he warned his body. He'd changed into shorts and a T-shirt before they landed.

After triggering a warning buzz, the loadmaster hit the switch. The rear of the cargo bay cracked in half. The upper part of the rear hatch lifted up into the ceiling of the cargo bay; the lower half descended to turn into the loading ramp.

A chill breeze slid out of the night and into the transport, wrapped itself about his legs, and sent a goose bump–laden shiver up his spine. It was laced with pine and tropical flowers so dense with scent that it would have been cloying if the air had been anywhere near warm.

"Where are we again?" he asked Mark, who stood beside him in jeans, a denim shirt, and a light jacket.

"Palmerola Air Base, also called Soto Cano Air Base."

"Which tells me nothing." Vern tried to suppress a shiver that just launched five more. "It's feels like fifty degrees. We're south. South is supposed to be warmer."

"You're also two thousand feet up in the mountains." Mark made a show of peering out into the darkness beyond the intermittently lit airfield. "Does feel kinda cooler tonight than usual."

"You could have warned me." As soon as they reached the bottom of the ramp to get out of the load-masters' way, Vern shuffled off to the side and began digging frantically through his pack. He salvaged a jacket, pulling it on first, and then stripped to his underwear as the others hooted and hollered at him. He found long pants and pulled those on.

"Could have warned you," Mark acknowledged in a dry tone, saying that he'd known exactly what was going to happen.

Looking up, Vern saw Denise standing with the others in the group, wearing a big smile and a warm jacket.

"I asked." She tipped her head toward Jeannie, who in turn nodded to Emily. Thick as thieves, these three women. Four women. Carly walked up in a leather bomber jacket that would look damn good on Denise; he'd have to get her one.

He suppressed another shiver and did his best not to feel put upon. Everyone in the crew was appropriately dressed for a cool evening, except him. "Fine," he muttered to himself, then looked around to see what he'd traded a trip to Australia for.

The airstrip was long and in moderately good shape; about half of the runway lights were working. They were at the far south end. Down the west side of the strip appeared to be open fields and a few low trees. On the east side were scattered low buildings and the occasional hangar.

"There's supposed to be an airline terminal mid-field," Mark told the group, "not a row of huts. The corruption and graft on the contract was apparently too blatant for even the Honduran government to accept it. U.S. Joint Task Force Bravo has the use of this building here, mostly medical and rescue, some security work, firefighting when it really hits the fan but it's not their specialty. The First Battalion of the 228th Aviation Regiment flies the Chinooks and Black Hawks you see parked here. We get the last row to the far south."

Vern counted a half-dozen choppers parked in an area designed to hold twenty birds.

"They need to think we're a bunch of firefighter yahoos. No mention of Emily or my background in SOAR, nor yours in the Coast Guard, Vern. We do our work and stay out of trouble."

"Is there a particular reason that we're here?" Denise spoke up before Vern could voice the question.

"If there is, they didn't tell me. So, business as usual. Fly safe and kill fires."

Vern watched the loadmasters rolling the first Firehawk down the ramp and felt a shiver up his back. Last time MHA had flown one of these contracts, they'd come home in one piece, but one of their helicopters hadn't.

What was going to happen this time?

Chapter 14

DENISE COULD ONLY STARE OUT THE WINDSCREEN AND marvel at her new life. Even after a month it was astonishing. The lush, tropical mountain slopes of Honduras rolled beneath their chopper.

Vern hadn't been particularly interested—"they burn about the same"—but she'd learned to identify the types of trees from the air. *Swietenia* big-leaf mahogany punched up through the jungle canopy, over seventy meters tall with crowns forty meters across. The lower rosewoods contrasted sharply with the dark pines and the bright, cheery green of maples.

Almost the whole center of Honduras was tree-covered mountains with low-lying coastal plains on the long Caribbean coast to the north and around the tiny Gulf of Fonseca against the Pacific. Much of the jungle was a cloud forest, like the big California redwoods. Most of the trees were wholly dependent on the damp, heavy fogs for moisture.

It made firefighting in the country's west a real challenge. Over a week, the skies were wholly clear only two or three scattered days. The rest of the time they were dodging fog banks and coastal rainstorms.

"At least it's the dry season."

Vern grunted. "November. The time of year when it's finally dry enough for families to gather together to burn some rain forest."

It was the major cause of fires that they fought. Clear-cutting rosewood and mahogany was illegal, but that didn't matter because the wood brought a good price on the black market and put food on the table. Then the locals would farm the jungle soil for a year or so until it was desperately depleted, then clear-cut another section.

The problem came when they were burning the slash. A five- or ten-acre slash fire didn't know it was supposed to stay at five or ten acres. The MHA team would get the call, usually because Steve had his drone up on daily patrol and not because there was any particularly organized fire-spotting service. And it would be up to MHA to douse the fires.

"Sorry," Vern apologized. "Fifth fire of the day. At least we're getting better at catching them small. Though I may start targeting the illegal harvesters and not the fires if they aren't careful."

Denise let it roll off her. Vern was usually only grumpy in the last hour of the day or if he missed his morning coffee.

Whereas she still felt too much like a schoolgirl on holiday. She was able to fly with Vern almost every day. The maintenance of the Firehawks had turned out to be straightforward. Part of that was because they weren't often flying against big, mature, ash-laden fires that were heaving great masses of char and smoke into the sky. Less carbon in the air meant less wear and tear on her equipment.

Also Vern, who had much more mechanical aptitude than he'd originally admitted to, had become her assistant when they were on the ground. Between the two of them, they could get a lot done fast.

She'd only had to tap the mechanics at the 1-228th once since their arrival.

The chief had been nice, helpful, and had clearly thought he was helping out the little lady who found herself in over her head. All she really needed was his small lifting crane so that she could pull and service one of the engines, though she hadn't minded his help. It was a big job, and they'd managed it overnight between them.

For the first time in her life, she'd let the man think he was in charge and it hadn't bothered her. Vern had certainly been doing good things for her ego.

They'd set up housekeeping in the midsize, on-base studio apartment MHA had rented for them. It had a bed, a sofa, a dresser, and a television that didn't work. Everyone had the same in their quad, a single building of four units, except Jeannie and Cal's television actually worked when there was power. The one station they received clearly was in Spanish, of course, so only Steve could understand it.

Trips into town were rare. And when they went, they went in force, in a group, and stayed close together. Denise wanted to wander through the market, haggle for a fruit she didn't recognize and would never dare eat, and visit the cathedral clock said to be the oldest clock in all of the Americas, built in the 1300s and installed in 1586, decades before Jamestown or the Pilgrims. She did get to visit the clock, but she also learned that Honduras was the murder capital of the world. Every year, one in a thousand people were murdered—twenty times worse than the U.S.

"Next time, let's go somewhere we can actually visit the country."

Vern was good with that plan.

Denise had never lived with a man before. She'd spent many nights of her relationship with Jasper at his place in town, but she'd kept the change of clothes and her toothbrush in a bag in the Fiat's trunk. He also hadn't liked that she had to leave an hour before sunrise to get to work every day. And on-season it was often every single day.

Vern was as easy to live with as he was about everything else. Slow to wake up but fast to arouse. The more time she was with him, the more female she became. It was a startling discovery in her mid-twenties. Half the time when she looked in the mirror, she didn't recognize the woman standing there.

She'd started wearing clothes not because they were the ones that were clean, but because Vern had said she looked nice in them. He held the door for her almost every time. It wasn't that he downplayed her abilities—definitely not when something was broken or needed maintenance.

For the first time in her life she felt attractive. And found that she liked feeling that way. She no longer felt out of place when she was sitting with the other women of the MHA crew with their daunting beauty, long legs, and handsome husbands. For the first time in her life, she fit in with other women. In the lazy evenings after nightfall, when it was still too early on even the most exhausting days, they'd sit and talk and trade stories.

At first it had been about fires and helicopters. But over time, the topics had drifted to old boyfriends. They'd traded stories of first meetings. Hers had been on display for the others to see, but they'd shared their stories, from Emily shooting a laptop computer to Cal nearly burning to death to shoot a photograph.

She'd also finally been told what she was sure was a very sanitized version of what had happened to the original Firehawk Oh-Two. The few details they provided were enough to turn Jeannie sheet white at a year-old memory and to make Denise glad that she didn't know more.

The quad had an *ama*, a cheery and competent woman in her forties named Rosa—how was that for a stereotype—who tended to the shopping and laundry for the whole group. She also introduced Denise's untutored palate to a wide variety of Honduran and Latin American dishes that the whole group came to look forward to. Rosa's mother-henning of them all was a great bonus because they were aloft so constantly and then doing the daily service on the choppers each evening.

One thing that Honduras had aplenty was fires.

The poorer peasants didn't care if their slash-and-burn was on a nature preserve or not. If they were chased out, they repeated their actions somewhere else. If they stayed, they had to move on soon anyway because the jungle soil could only sustain a year or two of crops before being totally depleted of nutrients. The soil had adapted for centuries to nurture slow-growing trees, not fast-growing crops. It took decades of careful husbandry to switch it over once it was clear-cut, a span of time that Honduran farmers with hungry families couldn't wait for.

At any one time, there were dozens and often hundreds of slash fires that had escaped. With the dry season now in full swing, the ones that escaped rapidly became a major problem.

MHA's job was to pound them flat as fast as they could. It was like a massive, dangerous game of Whac-A-Mole.

During the days, Vern had been teaching Denise how to fly. She'd thought herself fairly well versed in the basics; after all, she'd had her rotorcraft ticket for six years. Not even close. She could now pick up a load of water using the siphon without drifting sideways toward an inviting set of trees looming on the riverbank and waiting to eat her rotor blades. And she could hit a flame fairly cleanly, if there were no tricky drafts—though there were always tricky drafts.

The things she really learned from the lessons were twofold.

One, how good a teacher Vern was. She'd worried that a teacher-student role might do a "Jasper" to their relationship, but it didn't. All she had to remember was how sweet he'd been with the kids at the Vashon Cider Fest to know her fears were unfounded.

And two, how really fantastic a pilot Vern was. She'd learned enough to be able to see what he did, even if she had no idea how he did it. She could recognize his mastery from her own ability to drive a car, but she couldn't begin to duplicate it. It was completely in his blood, hardwired right into his nervous system.

"What are you thinking about so hard there, Wrench?"

She hadn't spoken through a half-dozen trips to the latest fire in the Reserva de la Biosfera del Río Plátano. They were dipping water out of the Laguna de Warunta.

She liked using the big lagoon much better than siphoning one of the twisty island rivers. The rivers were brown with silt that was hard on the equipment.

And she didn't like flying down into the narrow canyons of trees, often through an opening barely two rotors wide. Vern could fly in and out of them as if operating in an open cow pasture. But the closed-in nature of those dipping spots freaked her out even when he was at the controls.

"Thinking about you."

"Vile, sexy thoughts, I hope." He initiated his dump run at the coordinates Mark gave him. She now understood the information and could follow it herself.

The joy she found in Vern's body and he in hers hadn't diminished with familiarity. Instead it had increased. Vern was a terribly inventive lover. She'd been mortified when she did it, but she'd finally downloaded a few instructional texts onto her e-reader—without telling anyone, even him—and Vern had seemed very pleased with the results.

"Usually right, lover." She liked saying that word because it meant so much between them. "But not this time."

"Thinking about the job offer?"

"I hadn't been." There was a sudden bitter taste in her mouth. "But I am now."

"You've got to at some point." He rolled a few degrees right and nosed up when she would have nosed down. He hit the release, and she leaned her head into the bubble window in the door to look down at the results.

His drop didn't go straight down. Instead, it caught in a downdraft, which shifted the water dump a half-dozen meters to the side, and the fire-generated wind dragged the water right down onto its own head. It snuffed out like a candle.

"How did you hit that downdraft so perfectly while going a hundred knots?"

"How can you think I'm going to let you change the subject that easily again?"

She sighed. The museum restoration job had been preying on her mind a lot, but she hadn't wanted to talk about it. Apparently jumping Vern whenever he brought the topic up hadn't distracted him sufficiently. And this time throwing her body at him would be a life-threatening distraction.

"Talk it out, Wrench. I'm on your side, you know."

"I do know that." Right down to the core like it was a part of her insides. "We've got something here—"

"Ehhhhh!" He made a harsh nasal buzzing noise over the headset as he slid to a halt back over the lagoon and hit the pump switch. Emily was a hundred yards away also loading up.

"What?"

"No way am I going to be the one holding you back from that job if you want it. I'm not going to be the reason you didn't get your life's dream."

She folded her arms and glared at the console. Vern always slid down about two feet as four tons of water came on board. He'd arrive at eighteen feet, just low enough to sink the end of his twenty-foot siphon hose. She'd be able to tell how full the tank was by how close he came to hovering at sixteen feet.

Denise had watched the others. Jeannie always bobbed a little, the same way she flew; shifting up and down perhaps six inches as she loaded up. Emily's altitude was rock stable. She arrived at eighteen feet, loaded at eighteen feet, and left from eighteen feet—no indicators from the outside as to how full her belly tank was. She peeled away. Ten seconds later so did Vern.

"Damn you."

Vern laughed. She cursed so rarely that he laughed every time she did so aloud—which discouraged her from doing it more often.

"I curse you, evil man."

"So much for the easy way out. Now, Wrench, what's the real reason you didn't leap up and wave both hands over your head the way your dad and Huey were expecting?"

For two more laps of a thousand gallons each, she tried to answer the question to her own satisfaction.

Then for three.

Then she gave in.

"I don't know."

"You don't know?" He did it in one of those I'm-too-cool-and-funny tones, and it set her off.

"No! I don't, Mr. Smarty-pants Pilot." Denise could feel her voice rising but didn't know how to stop it. "Are you happy now? I've spent a month with that question stuck in the back of my brain. I go to sleep with it and wake up with it. I'm sick to death of it. I want this decision to be over so badly that I feel like I'm going to be sick even thinking about it."

"Take it easy, Wrench."

"Go to hell, Slick!"

At least there was no laugh this time.

Vern transported the next few thousand gallons in silence except to respond to Mark's directions from where he and his daughter circled high overhead in a spotter plane.

Okay, he'd deserved that slap-down. It was hard to gauge what to do when a woman was as mild-mannered as Denise. Her idea of a major curse for severely barked knuckles or a banged shin rarely passed beyond a "Darn."

But this was different. There was deep emotional upset here, and he hadn't seen it. Had no idea it had been hiding in there, behind some shield he hadn't even known existed.

"I'm sorry." Her voice was the barest whisper over the intercom. "I—"

"Don't!" he cut her off. "Don't you dare apologize for being human, especially when I was the one being a jerk."

Again, she was silent for a long time. Then she was whispering as if to herself. He could barely hear it over the sound of his own rotors despite the headset. "I don't know. I don't know. I don't—"

"Denise?"

"What?"

"This is not a time to auger in."

"I'm not even touching your helicopter controls. How could I possibly crash it?"

"On yourself, honey. Beating yourself up isn't going to help."

"Then what is?"

Well, he'd had to go and put his foot in it. "I don't know either. But," he cut off her exasperated breath, "maybe working together, we can figure this out. Or at least get closer so you know what the next question is. You game?"

"Hello. Willing to try anything at this point."

"How about sex?"

"Ehhhhh!" She made the nasal buzzer sound herself. "Illegal topic change. Now help me for real!"

"Promise you won't smack me with your wrench?"

"No promises, Slick. Proceed at your own risk." But he could hear the smile. A quick glance as he bounced over a low bluff, looking twice its size because of tall trees, confirmed it. It also confirmed that they had this fire on the run. The smoke output was definitely falling off. Another dozen runs by the three choppers and it should be dead. Then there'd be the next one on today's list.

"Okay, twenty questions." Though he'd wager they'd end up with far more than that. "Any concerns over your ability to do the job?"

—◆◆◆—

Denise scoffed. "Did you see my dining room?" She could picture the hundreds, even thousands, of hours she'd spent studying there.

"A lot of maintenance manuals on those shelves."

"Well, if you'd slowed down enough to check the titles—"

"I was more focused on getting you into bed."

"Do you hear me complaining?" Not for a second. That night of gentle loving still ranked as the best sexual experience of her entire life. One of the best experiences in her life. For in that moment she had discovered a man who thought so much of her, and even more importantly, she'd discovered a woman inside her who could make a man think of her that way.

Back to the topic.

"Those manuals range over the last eighty years of aircraft. It is one of the leading collections outside of a museum; I've spent years building it. And—"

"And you read them a lot. Got the picture, Wrench." He followed the other Firehawk back out to the Laguna de Warunta. "Hey, I'm staying in sync with her."

"What? Who?"

"Me. I'm staying in sync with Emily Beale for number of drop runs. That's so cool."

"Why is that cool?" She squinted at Firehawk Oh-One settling over the lagoon about ten seconds ahead of them, but couldn't see what the excitement was about.

"Why? Because she's the best. Being a six-year stick jockey in the Coast Guard, I know what it means to be a SOAR pilot. Way out of my league, and rumors say she's the best one they ever had."

"Really?"

"Trust me, Wrench. The amount you drive better than me is nothing in comparison to how far out there a SOAR pilot is. It's like me to a professional Formula One racer. She probably trained more hours in a year than I've yet flown as pilot-in-command in my career."

"If"—she couldn't resist—"you don't get your hose down sometime soon, she's going to dust your ass."

"Shit!" Vern hit the control to unreel the siphon hose, but Emily was already pulling aloft. She'd gained thirty seconds on Vern due to his brief inattention.

Now it was Denise's turn to laugh. Sure, there was always someone out there better than you were, even someone as skilled as Vern.

Even someone as skilled as she was.

That was one small piece of her puzzle. If she didn't take the job, the museum would still be okay. Huey had said he had a backup person. There were people who could restore those planes besides her. Maybe not as easily as she could, but they'd get the job done and do it well enough.

She leaned over to kiss Vern on the shoulder.

"What's that for?"

"That's for how much I love you. Ask the next question. It helps."

—⁘—

By the time the sunset chased them from the sky, Vern had chipped away some more of the chaff but Denise could feel that they weren't near the core yet.

Could she manage the problems that would come up with the staff?

She'd been promoted to a lead mechanic slot quickly at Sikorsky and hired as chief at MHA because of her reputation for building a cohesive team. She did it by finding skilled people and giving them the room to do their job, exactly as she'd want to have done for her. Even as a teen, Huey had often had her leading a group of volunteer mechanics on a restoration. So, that was a yes.

The pressure?

"Let's see," she'd answered Vern, "a plane that eventually has to fly three more times in its entire life, from one museum to the next on no fixed schedule. Let's compare that with a helitack chopper, where every six to ten minutes it is out of operation is another thousand gallons that doesn't get to a wildfire. Another home that burns on a bad fire."

The hours?

"Nine to five. Sunday and Monday off."

The pay?

"Not like the chief mechanic at an elite outfit like MHA, but enough to live pretty nicely."

The future?

That one had rocked her back in her seat. When Vern had pushed at her silence, she'd explained the next piece. "Dad is due to retire in about ten years. I'm guessing…he and Huey want to groom me to run the main museum."

Vern's low whistle of surprise had left her with one thing clear. He didn't doubt for a second that she could do that as well. It was one of the top ten flight museums in the country. If you didn't count the museums maintained by the military forces themselves, it might be the best.

When they'd finished the Río Plátano fire, Mark Henderson had routed them to a lightning-strike fire up in the mountains near El Carbón in the Sierra de Agalta National Park. Steve's drone was there an hour ahead of them and had it well mapped before they arrived.

Being up in the mountains made for an exciting visual change with the steep hills and valleys, though it reminded her too much of Missoula and the memory of blistered paint and half-melted hoses. But this was a much smaller fire, less than a day old from some dry lightning the night before.

Despite the challenge of flying among the hills, Vern had continued with his questions, both persistent and supportive, as they puzzled over her reaction to the job offer.

But he'd never made up that lost thirty seconds.

Something she had reminded him of only every ten minutes or so. He was so much fun to tease. She'd never done that to anyone before.

At one point she considered shedding her safety harness, opening her Nomex jacket, and flashing her breasts at him. Then she couldn't believe that she, Denise Conroy, had been the one to think up such an idea. She didn't do it, of course. Distracting your pilot over a fire in rugged mountains was never a good idea.

On their return, as they approached Palmerola Air Base, the tower was very aggressive about their identification. For over a month, there had been times where no one was even manning the tower and the MHA crew simply flew in, not even bothering with a main runway approach, and landed in their southeast corner with no one caring.

Tonight they were very carefully directed. When they came in to land, a landing officer with twin red-lit batons waved them forward to park in the closest open spot on the base. A half-dozen soldiers circled the perimeter. U.S. soldiers she was glad to see.

"Vern?"

"Don't know. Let's take it slow."

Apparently the other crews had the same idea. They timed their shutdowns and exits to match when Mark's small plane rolled up and was also directed to a nearby tie-down.

———

When Mark clambered down—his daughter running over to visit her mother—he headed over to talk to the soldier who had guided them down.

Vern moved in right beside him. Denise followed immediately on his heels. He wished she'd stayed back with the other women so that… A glance over his shoulder proved how stupid a thought that was with this group of women. They were all gathered close to hear what was going on.

"What's up, Sarge?"

The man eyed Mark strangely. "Some of the guys thought you were ex-military. You fly Desert Storm or something?"

Mark grimaced. "That was a quarter century ago, Sergeant. Do I look that old?"

Vern had to grin. Mark and Emily were probably mid-thirties, which would look ancient to the baby three-striper. But there was no way for the sergeant to answer that one safely. Question was, was he smart enough to know that? Vern bet no.

But apparently the sergeant was as he doubled back to the safety of the initial question. "Unrest in the capital. We're tightening up security."

"Your boys in the tower?"

"Yes, sir."

"What assets do you have in the area?" Vern could see Mark was doing a security assessment just as Vern was.

Palmerola was a big, flat strip. A decent horse could jump the perimeter fence; one of the thousands of rusty VW Beetles that seemed to litter the roads here could run the fence down with minimal damage to itself.

The only decent security protocol here was a perimeter guard, which was exactly what the 1-228th was doing.

"Our assets are need-to-know, sir. As you are U.S.

civilian contractors, we will do what we can to keep your aircraft inside our secure perimeter. If you remain in your quad block when on base, that will also be inside our patrol perimeter. Beyond that, you don't need to know."

Vern could see that really ticked off Mark. Himself, he'd had four years at MHA to get used to not having inside access, unlike when in the Coast Guard. It took time for old habits to die. Mark had been out only two years, and he'd been a major. He still came on that way at times, though not many people could shut out a Special Operations Forces major. This time it needed a gentler approach if they wanted insider info. It needed—

Denise stepped forward. "Are we in…danger?" She asked it in such a worried voice that she had to be play-acting. She'd nailed the right tone.

The sergeant did the practiced soothing-a-civilian tone. "We're told not, ma'am." Then he totally softened as he looked down at her. Denise had played the small and cute card. "I've been here a year, ma'am, my com-mander for three. He says they go through this every now and then. Get all riled up, then nothing happens."

"Oh, okay." She clung so pitifully to Vern's arm that he had to look at Mark to not snort with laughter.

Mark's foul expression that Denise's ploy had worked where his own simple question hadn't almost tipped Vern over the edge. He only managed to keep a straight face by pretending this was an official inspec-tion by a commanding officer.

"Are you sure we're okay to go home?" Denise's voice actually quavered, and Vern wanted to pinch her as a warning. The guy wasn't an idiot.

The sergeant nodded to her. Maybe guys always turned into idiots around beautiful females who appeared helpless.

He sure had…except she'd never appeared helpless in his presence.

"And you'll be fine to continue fighting fires," the sergeant assured her. "We're worried about anyone trying to grab our hardware assets. They don't have a single Black Hawk; there are only a dozen choppers in their whole air force that still work—and all but one are transport birds. Between our Joint Task Force and your three craft, we have an equal number of the toughest helicopters ever built. With thirty troops, fliers, and medicos right here, we'll keep you safe, ma'am."

The sergeant grimaced as he realized that he'd told Denise exactly what he'd refused to tell Mark. With that he saluted, looked awkward because none of them were soldiers and no one returned a salute, then hurried away to check his team.

When he was gone, Denise looked up at Mark and batted her eyelashes at him. "The power of a pretty face, boss."

Mark finally shrugged. "It's because he thinks you're twelve, Conroy."

"It's because he thinks I'm cute."

Vern slipped his hands around her waist from behind, pulled her back against him, and rested his chin atop her head. "She got you there, Mark. She's way cuter than either of us."

"Lucky for her with you two ugly mugs." Jeannie joined the conversation.

"Girls rule." Carly offered a fist bump to Denise.

Chapter 15

WHATEVER WAS GOING ON IN THE CAPITAL OF TEGUCIGALPA didn't affect their routine, except for the Joint Task Force maintaining a roving patrol. They didn't fall for Denise's ploys a second time, so information was limited to the daily news from Rosa, none of which seemed relevant beyond the city limits eighty kilometers away.

Denise had felt terribly risqué doing it that one time. She'd never used her sexuality before to get anything. Until Vern, she'd never known she had any sexuality to use. It had worked, but she didn't like the way it had felt afterward. Definitely something she wouldn't be adding to her repertoire.

The next two days were about hard work. Firehawk Oh-One was grounded for scheduled 150-hour maintenance. Every day of flight required a quick inspection before Denise would execute an airworthiness certificate for the next day. Every fifty hours of flight was another level of inspection, and every third one of those included significant work.

Firefighting pushed the choppers to so many in-air hours that she was often doing a major service every two to three weeks on each bird. And with the wear on Oh-One, she'd needed the time to replace a lot of small parts.

The harsh levels of silt in the brown jungle rivers

wore at the pumps. The hardwood ash got into everything. Door hinges, siphon hose reels, even the swash
plate that controlled the angle of the rotor blades as they
spun were showing atypical signs of wear. Thankfully
that was still well within service limits. It would be a
major job that she'd rather attempt back in the States
than under the tropical sun that was no less burning
just because the climate was temperate. This near the
equator, the sun was up almost exactly twelve hours and
passed high overhead.

Vern had bought her a ridiculous floppy-brimmed
straw hat that she'd taken to wearing whenever she
did daytime service out on the tarmac. At least it was
better than the white, straw cowboy hat he'd bought
for himself.

"Ahm jes' a Honduran gaucho," he'd drawl in an Old
West accent.

"Y'all are jus' a drip in a straw sunbonnet," she'd
offer back in her best Southern belle.

By the time Oh-One was back aloft, she took Oh-
Two out of service for a day.

Because she'd been at the base for three days, she'd
been able to see the relaxing of airport security. The
roving patrol went from a half dozen to four to one guard
moseying along the perimeter with his M-16 slung over
his shoulder and looking bored to tears.

The sergeant came over to her as she was signing off
on the final airworthiness certificate for Oh-Two.

"It does seem to have gone quiet with no fuss this
time, ma'am. We're standing down to normal security
after today. Thought you'd want to know, ma'am."

"Denise."

"Yes, ma'am." His smile was friendly and said that he wouldn't be relaxing his formality.

After he left, she had to wonder. Had Vern been as stiff and formal as this sergeant, or even Mark, when he was in the service? She expected they both were. If Vern had excelled in the Coast Guard, he'd probably had to be Mister Soldier in addition to being an exceptional flier. Why hadn't she ever asked him?

Well, they'd be aloft again tomorrow. Time enough then.

Vern came to in his chopper when the first stab of sunlight cleared the horizon and punched him in the face right through the windscreen. At least that's what it felt like as he fumbled around for his sunglasses and pulled them on. The routine had become so grinding that he was functioning on semiconscious autopilot, which was a really bad place to be when flying a five-ton Firehawk against fires.

He double-checked. At least he hadn't tried to take off in his sleep. Everything looked shipshape. He toggled the display and saw that he'd logged the preflight. His hand was on the starter switch for the APU, so he toggled it.

He'd gone to bed with Denise last night, too exhausted to do more than curl against her. Being one chopper short for three straight days had really pushed him. Rather than trading off midday, they'd decided to let the pilot of each grounded bird get a real break while their chopper was in maintenance.

But Oh-Three hadn't been pulled out of rotation yet,

and he could really feel it. It wasn't that restful anyway, since Denise recruited the hands of anyone foolish enough to be caught on the ground to help her with the major maintenance tasks.

Now, he was halfway through his startup cycle and not quite sure how he'd gotten here. As soon as the engines caught and he could shut down the APU, he grabbed his steel travel mug with one hand while nursing the throttle with the other and knocked back a slug of scalding caffeine. That was one of the true blessings of this assignment. Honduras's worst coffee was at least equal to America's best.

The group's *ama* always made sure there was a large pot of it waiting fresh for them each morning, and he always blessed her for it.

The part that confirmed everything was okay was that Denise sat once again in the seat beside him.

Life was good.

"Missed you." He really had. After three days gone, it was like she'd done a leprechaun trick and suddenly reappeared. If he'd been more awake, he'd have asked where his pot of gold was.

Then the sun caught her hair and he knew. But he wasn't awake enough to make the compliment come out right even in his head, so he kept his mouth shut.

The chopper had felt empty, wrong without her beside him. He was beyond gone; she was a part of him now, and he didn't know how he'd survive if they went their separate ways. But he wasn't going to drop a payload like that on her until she'd made up her mind about the job.

"Right. You missed me." Denise's tone was droll.

She'd developed a sense of humor that, while still as gentle and sweet as the woman, snuck out now and then as if she were patting him ever so gently on the head. "I haven't seen you since we woke up together just this morning. No wait, since breakfast. No wait, was it when we walked here from the apartment? Or was it when I preflighted the bird because you were still out on your feet?"

"I've had breakfast? Oh well. As long as I didn't miss any wake-up sex." The coffee must be kicking in. "Did I?"

"I don't think either of us was awake enough for that."

"That's not right!" He keyed the mic and called Mark's frequency. "Boss. We need a break soon. I was too tired for wake-up sex this morning." Uh! Had he really transmitted that?

Denise squeaked with embarrassment from her seat.

"Try having a kid," Mark replied, "and then file your complaint. Though you have a point. We do need a break. I'll work on it."

"Do that," Vern answered lamely as Mark's words finally sank in.

A kid with Denise.

Vern's thoughts hadn't wandered down that particular road yet. Wow! That was a whole other variable. A pregnant Denise was an image to really take his breath away. He was definitely wide awake now.

He was also careful not to look at Denise as he checked that the engines were up to operating temperature and took them aloft to face the next fire. No point in asking for clearance; the control tower was again unmanned.

"Not going to happen, Vern, so don't even think about it."

"What?" He tried to sound innocent, but her mind-reading trick was working as flawlessly as usual. He turned northeast toward PANACOMA, Parque Nacional Montaña de Comayagua. That's where today's first fire was. It wasn't going to take much to find it. The smoke plume rising fifteen miles away was visible as soon as they were clear of the local buildings. This wasn't a small one. The plume was already dark and thick. Even at this distance, he could see the orange brightness of wildfire at the base.

"Kids. I'm never going to have one."

"Why not?" Something medical maybe. Kids and marriage, two topics to approach very carefully with any woman.

"I'm just not."

"That doesn't make any sense."

"It makes perfect sense. Can you imagine me with a kid?"

"Yes!" It was out before he could stop himself. He shouldn't have been so emphatic, but she'd make a great mom. "Two, one of each."

"No way!"

He really needed to learn to keep his mouth shut.

"No, Vern. Just no!"

Okay, keeping his mouth shut wasn't working well either.

He'd started the morning with a full load of water, so he followed Emily and Jeannie toward the blaze. This was going to be a real headache of a day. Water sources were down around five-hundred-meters elevation, but the fire was up over two thousand meters—seven thousand feet. At that elevation, a helicopter carried a much smaller load than it did down in the sea-level lowlands like the Reserva Plátano. And the transition up and down—from fire to water and back—meant they were going to spend the whole day trying to keep their ears clear as the pressure changed every five minutes down to water and five minutes later back above the ridgelines.

"You still haven't said why you don't want kids? Hang on."

Steve's drone took the lead per the new Mountain Protocol they'd developed after Missoula and perfected here in Honduras. It swept in well ahead of them so that Steve could report if they had downdrafts and temperature anomalies indicative of a pending blow-up or a cold-air rotor. Now they consistently had a much better idea of what they were flying into.

His report was negative so far, and the drone passed through clean.

Following the twisting line of water dumped by Emily, Vern and Jeannie came in close behind. Three thousand gallons of water and foam didn't do more than irritate the blaze.

They dove into the valleys seeking a water source. The rivers here were buried in steep canyons guarded by trees so big they often grew right across the river, hiding its track entirely.

Emily found a dipping point near the hamlet of Río Negro along an exposed bend in the river of the same name. Jeannie found a cattle pond on the far side of the town, and Vern was stuck waiting. There weren't any other open spaces. He spun a quick circle of a couple miles to prove it to himself and then ducked down to the river as soon as Emily was clear.

It was a narrow hole in the trees, three rotors across and fifty feet down. He focused on staying dead-center in the hole as he went down.

"Crap, Vern!" Denise was cringing in her seat. He'd forgotten how much he enjoyed their talks and banter as he flew. "You can't be serious. There's no room in here."

"Why no kids?" Vern asked to distract himself and hit the pumps as soon as he could. It wasn't quite a panic spot, but he'd have to stay dead stable for the entire exhausting day.

She didn't answer until he was loaded and had cleared the hole. "Are you serious?"

"Wouldn't ask if I wasn't interested."

"I mean *that*." Denise pointed back to the hole in the forest where they'd been.

"I might check out Jeannie's pond next. See how much it upsets the locals."

Denise was quiet a while—long enough for him to pop his ears a few times, hit the blaze where Mark said, and descend back down for more water.

"My mom." Her voice was soft over the intercom. "I know it wasn't as if she planned it, but I never want to have a child who could lose her mother like that."

"Like you did?"

"Like I did."

Jeannie's pond was about five rotors clear, which was an improvement. It had a feed from the river, so they wouldn't pull it dry. As he hovered there for the forty seconds it took his tanks to fill, he was barely two rotors from a small farm. A half-dozen cattle were up against the fence line looking very unhappy at all of the noise he was making. And the farmer looked even more so. They stared at each other—one man opening a fence made of hand-split rails and herding his cattle through with a wooden staff, the other man sitting in the cockpit of a twenty-million-dollar machine of war converted into a firefighting helicopter.

Vern tried to imagine a whole life bounded by this pasture, this line of fence, and the small house beyond. And what of the woman who shared his life? And the children.

"I think you're cutting yourself off, Denise. Look at Mark and Emily. Can you imagine what their life would be like without Tessa? They're both so damn serious except when their daughter is with them. Then they totally unwind."

"You want children?"

"Oh yeah."

"Why?"

He risked a glance over at her, but she was serious. He waited to answer until he'd hit the business end of the blaze. It was working its way downslope under a steady easterly wind that was sweeping over the ridge and pushing down on the fire. Driving it toward the hamlet far below. If it got too much closer, they'd have to evacuate the farmer and his family. There wouldn't be time to save his cows.

Vern spun downslope, powering the chopper's descent down.

"Is it to carry on your name?" Denise's prompted.

"No. It doesn't even have to be my own blood. We're good people, aren't we?"

"Sure," she agreed.

"No, I really mean this." He'd given it a lot of thought. "Whether it's with each other or someone else, we have a chance to pass on so much. Look at the things your parents passed on to you. I mean, look at you. You're flying over central Honduras as chief mechanic of one of the best firefighting outfits on the planet. And you have an amazing *second* job offer even though you already have a job, in case you were doubting yourself. That's not genetic. Or not only genetic. You did that. But not without your mom and dad, no matter how short a time she was around."

―᎐᎐᎐―

Denise didn't like the feeling of being lectured. She liked even less that Vern was right.

At least he wasn't cocky about it. Again, Vern was only what he showed, no Jasper gamesmanship. Instead, he continued to work them up and down the ridge as smoothly as if born to it.

Her parents had given her so much. Even her dad, who she now understood better as an adult than as a lonely teen, had done the best he could for who he was. He was a quiet man who loved planes and loved his museum. And his daughter. She would deny it if she could, but he did love her as well as he could manage.

Denise's seat dropped out from under her. In a moment they went from the trees being a lumpy carpet a few hundred comfortable feet below to flying so close to the treetops that she pulled up her feet.

Vern didn't swear or curse; he simply pulled up on the collective and tipped the nose forward for more speed. "All pilots," he called out over the radio. "We now have a downdraft of about two hundred FPM developing."

Denise's fingers ached from where she'd latched on to her seat cushion. She checked their instruments. They'd actually only dropped about fifty feet, but it felt like a lot more.

"Roger that," Mark replied. "Everyone, flight levels up another hundred feet and keep loads at ten percent less until we see how it develops."

"Sorry." Vern spoke softly as he lined up and dumped his load, spraying it directly on a line of pine trees that looked more like torches than trees.

"I'm okay. You scared me."

"Huh?" He looked around as if he hadn't really noticed the plunge toward the trees. "I meant I was sorry for getting up on my soapbox. If you don't want to have kids, that's your choice, of course. Not mine to say."

"Damn it, Taylor. I'm trying to be mad at you. Stop being so considerate."

"Oh, sorry." He didn't sound the least put-out. "Not working, huh?"

"Not working."

"I'm a hard guy to stay mad at. All the best women say so." He aimed one of those sassy grins at her. "Does this mean I can get wake-up sex tomorrow?"

The laugh bubbled up inside her. "Only if you can wake up in time."

"Harsh."

What was harsh was how Vern felt two exhausting days later. The PANACOMA fire had battled them back and forth. This was a country that didn't have smokejumpers, so there was no one to cut firebreaks. Only the U.S. typically fought fire with retardant, so aerial application of retardant-based firebreaks weren't in the battle plan either.

The only way to stop the fire was to beat it to death from the air. There were people on the ground: armed with rakes and shovels and wearing sandals and thin shirts, not armed with chain saws and water pumps and wearing Nomex gear. They didn't have a single trained firefighter on the ground. They didn't even have radio communications, so the efforts were wholly uncoordinated.

But still, they beat it. Sunrise to sunset, two days in a row. The only breaks were to refuel. Meals were a gobbled-down sandwich or an energy bar.

Vern now hovered above the black, looking for any remaining hot spots. He was the last one aloft. Steve had his drone's infrared camera on a feed that Vern could watch on his terrain map screen.

"There's one." Denise pointed toward his screen. "Lower right corner."

There was. For the hundredth time in two days, he blessed that she was along. He was so tired that he wouldn't have trusted himself to fly solo, but she kept him on his toes. Served as an extra set of eyes, did some of the simpler flying so that he could at least shake out his hands every now and then.

"I think it's the last one. Punch it, Vern."

He slid over what had once been a cluster of

rosewood trees and punched it. A thousand gallons of water fell from the sky in a hard deluge, hard enough that he could see it crater the char, then create a small wave of runoff. The hot spot was extinguished so fast it didn't even have a chance to release smoke in complaint. It was simply gone.

And with that, he was done and done in.

"How's your fuel?" Mark called over the radio.

He had to squint to see, then he remembered. "Topped off half an hour ago. I'm near full."

"Good. New coordinates, Vern."

"I'm wiped out, boss."

"New coordinates." Mark's voice was stern as he read them off.

Denise punched them into the nav system for him and Vern turned, cursing Mark. Maybe he'd take the museum job. Or if Denise took it, maybe he'd get a job doing flight tours somewhere nearby. Or driving a taxi. Nah. He hated traffic; he liked flying over it. Air taxi?

He slid down over the cloud forest, already wrapping itself in a soft evening fog. No flame, little smoke. Unlike in the U.S., there was no Type II or III incident response team to make sure the fire was well and truly out. Also no habitat stabilization and restoration team hot on their heels. If the fire reignited, they'd have to come back and fight it again.

The nav directions led them back down over the hamlet of Río Negro, a town that had known little silence for the last two days because of the reloading choppers in constant circulation.

But the coordinates weren't to the pond; they were to the farmer's field. It wasn't on fire.

He radioed Mark. "Care to explain?"

"Just set it down. Off to one side. We'll be there in a minute."

Doing as he was told, he slid as close to the trees as he dared and settled the Firehawk. There would be room for one other big Firehawk.

He and Denise had the bird shut down and filled out the flight logs. Still no one. So, they clambered down and collapsed. The grass here was lush and—once they'd checked it to make sure it was clear of any cow patties—very comfortable to lie down in.

Five minutes later, Firehawk Oh-Two arrived above them from the direction of the air base rather than the fire and settled onto the other side of the clearing. Once it was on the ground, the rest of the MHA crew stumbled out. Jeannie must have followed Emily back to base and picked up Mark and the Oh-One crew.

Denise sat up, inadvertently placing an elbow in his gut as she did so. Vern didn't even bother to try and sit up; he simply lay there and grunted.

"Six weeks." Mark strode up as if it was the beginning of the day, not the end. "I think after six weeks, we get a day off."

It sounded glorious. Vern could really do with a day of not having his butt pounded by his chopper.

"Maybe even two."

"For two days off, Mark, I'm going to have to marry you." Vern sagged with relief. He'd get to spend some conscious time with his girl.

"Why here?"

Yep, that was his Denise. Sharp as a tack that woman, he thought dreamily. His eyes half closed as the last of the sunlight drained out of the late-afternoon sky.

"Here," Mark said, "is right up Vern's alley."

Vern reopened one eye to look up at his boss.

"We are parked in the back field of the Finca Río Negro—the Negro River Estate. In addition to having some very comfortable tree-house bungalows specifically set up for well-heeled tourists, it is also considered to be one of the finest producers of artisanal coffee in the country."

Vern closed the open eye. Someone had just transported him to heaven.

Chapter 16

VERN KNEW HOW HE'D GOTTEN HERE, BUT THAT DIDN'T MAKE it any less surprising.

David, pronounced Da-veed, wasn't some young dreamer entrepreneur. He was a small, wiry man who could have been anywhere on the far side of sixty, unless he was on the far side of seventy. Last night he had served them a simple platter of roasted chicken, black beans, rice, and fresh-made flour tortillas to wrap around it, with french fries on the side. Stream-chilled beer with dinner, and a mild coffee liqueur that he distilled himself, and fresh-sliced mango topped off the evening.

With all of them limp from the exhausting day, David led them to four bungalows. Each was a small tree house perched between five and fifteen meters in the air on a group of *Swietenia* trees.

"Tourists, they cancel when they see the big smoke you put out," David informed them in his heavily accented English. "I tell them too late for to refund. So I am paid, but they yours for saving my farm." He sniffed the air deeply; whether to deride the feeble tourists or prove that the air did indeed bear no scent of smoke, Vern couldn't tell.

They had protested the gift to no avail. Finally, Vern had traded a glance with Mark. They'd leave him a really serious tip.

Inside the tiny tree house had been a squat-hole that led to an under-hung bucket, a couple of bottles of water, and a beautiful queen-size bed on a hand-carved rosewood base. It had a mosquito net that draped lightly around it. Good linen sheets and a thick blanket of geometrical weaving in golds and greens, blacks and yellows that made it look terribly cozy once they'd climbed up into the tree house. Outside the window on a tiny balcony stood a pair of narrow chairs, also carved, with a view out at a long bend of the Negro glinting in the moonlight.

Closing the trapdoor, he and Denise were in their own oil-lamp-lit bubble in the jungle.

For the first time in ages, they settled into sleep rather than collapsing.

Now, some evil habit had him awake at first light. Or not so evil. Denise slept as she usually did, curled up inside the curve of his arm, her cheek on his shoulder. He rested his cheek on her hair and listened to her gentle breathing. He could imagine her lying right there a year from now, a decade, a lifetime.

It was so strange. Vern had never doubted he'd settle down someday. He had his parents' example, so how could he think otherwise? But Denise was unlike any woman he'd ever gone out with.

He'd consistently picked up women who were tall, funny, and outgoing. Between them, they'd be the life of any group, but it never lasted. Some great women. He was still friends with several, had casual email friendships with others, but the serious, love-bound relationship had never happened.

Instead, his feet had been kicked out from under him by a short, tentative, utterly brilliant introvert. His

mother, with her infallible instincts, had liked Denise
right away. But Denise was more like his dad—the quiet
sailboat mechanic. Of course almost everyone was qui-
eter than his mom. She was the life of every—

He jerked with the shock of it, and Denise murmured awake.

"Wha'? Fire?"

"Shhh." He brushed a hand over her hair. "Nothing.
It's okay." He waited until she'd snuggled back to sleep
before returning to the scary thought.

He'd spent a lifetime looking for his mother.

Well, not quite, but close enough to be kinda weird.
He was always drawn to tall, extroverted, creative
types. It never mattered what their art was; one of his
longest relationships had been with the assistant brew-
master at the big brewery in Hood River—a true artist
with flavors.

Denise was a magician with mechanics, but even
when he tried to, he couldn't quite twist it under any definition of being a creative artist. She created order—the
perfect order of a machine performing at its engineered
peak. He'd learned that in any group of more than three
or four, she went silent.

Even after MHA's two months together at the quad of
Palmerola Air Base apartments, if all eight of them were
around the table—as they often were—she rarely spoke
unless directly addressed.

How bizarre. If she agreed—though he wouldn't ask
until she'd decided about the job—this was the woman
he'd be spending the rest of his life with. With or without children didn't matter. He had his preferences, but as
long as she was there, the rest was less important.

With that decision, he came one step closer to understanding Denise's father and the terrible loss the man
had tried so hard to keep from his daughter. Whether
or not they both would have been better off if he'd had
a breakdown and then restarted, rather than locking it
away inside, was now ancient history.

But his daughter was so full of life. It was only that
she didn't see it.

He did.

And he'd count himself very lucky to be with her.

He drifted back to sleep, until he was woken in a terribly delicious way by the love of his life.

———— ∽∽ ————

They hadn't made it to breakfast. Denise observed that
no one had, except for Mark, Emily, and Tessa, who
were returning from a hike in the woods.

Lunch was a major meal here, the biggest of the
Honduran day—quite different from the firefighter's
usual quick bolting down of calories. It wasn't fancy,
but it was good and it was substantial. The *pastelito* had
shredded beef, avocado, beans, and potatoes wrapped in
a flour tortilla and deep fried. On the side was coffee.

She'd never really acquired the taste, despite growing
up in Seattle, so she asked for hot chocolate. Honduran,
fresh-ground hot chocolate didn't have the big, milky
punch of American hot chocolate. Instead it was light
and so pure. David was only too glad to explain.
Fermented and roasted cocoa beans ground fine with
roasted fresh cinnamon, then built up with sugarcane
juice and hot water. Pure heaven.

But watching Vern with his coffee was fun—he went

completely nuts. He found out that David was something called a Q cupper.

Vern was decent enough, despite his excitement, to explain to her as they went. "There are only a thousand Q cuppers in the world. They are highly trained and tested graders of specialty coffees. They rate everything from the bean to the final product and the eight steps in between."

Nothing would satisfy but that they follow the whole process, from the donkeys carrying the heavy bags down from the steep hills of the thousand-acre farm. The beans were then dumped into water; any that floated were thrown away as defective. The depulping removed the bright red hulls from the precious inner bean. Though done by a grinder, the process was finished by hand. Fermenting tanks led to long, drying tables set out in the Honduran sun. Denise wished she'd thought to bring her straw hat, but it was hanging up in her service container.

Then the beans had the final hull removed before they were sorted by size so that each batch would roast evenly in the same amount of time.

"Only light roast," David had insisted. "Dark roast is done to hide bad coffee. Good coffees only use light roast."

Vern was nodding as if this made perfect sense.

Denise had drifted off, wanted to go exploring. David's wife, who looked as ancient and wrinkled as her husband, had given her a small map of the local trails. It had drawings of waterfalls at various places. The woman spoke no English, and always being on the base or in the air, Denise had picked up woefully little Spanish. Her high school French was of no use whatsoever.

But the woman had pointed at her, then at Vern, raising her eyebrows and offering a smile that meant she knew exactly what Denise was looking for. She took a pencil and drew in another trail. She drew in a stream, even a small bridge, and finally another waterfall. Then she tapped the beginning of the trail, pointed around the back of the roasting house, and winked.

Denise winked back and took Vern's hand. He tried to lead her inside a large shed to follow the packing process, but she dragged him aside. David offered her a knowing smile. Half of the afternoon had spun away.

"Sorry, I don't know what happened to me. It was like a drug."

"I thought coffee was one."

"Only to some of us," he'd scoffed at her hot chocolate.

As they entered the canopy of the forest, he kept bubbling on about what he'd learned, only slowly becoming aware that they had left civilization behind. Denise had gone hiking a few times around Mount Hood. The tall Douglas fir and aspen forest had little undergrowth beneath the dense canopy other than ferns.

Here, the jungle super-story was far above them. A massive *Ceiba* tree did that jungle thing she'd always seen in movies, where its base split in waves of high, thin ridges for the last ten feet to the ground. She could stand between two waves of the base and not see Vern in the next one.

The thing she hadn't been ready for was how much life was here. Ferns grew under low frondy bushes that were overshadowed by some type of palm tree which snuggled in between rosewood. All the lesser growths stared upward at the *Ceiba* and *Swietenia* with dreams of grandeur.

"Look!" she practically screamed in surprise, startling both Vern and the brilliant red-and-blue feathered macaw parrot that had merely been going about its business. It aimed a sharp complaint at her before soaring off behind one of the palms. She kept waiting for it to reappear. It didn't.

Further on, Vern pointed out a bird with a big, yellow beak almost the size of its body. "A toucan."

In the mile walk along the trail, they spotted dozens of creatures. Birds, salamanders, bugs, and a snake that Vern flicked into the bushes with a stick.

"My hero," Denise cooed at him.

"Hey, for its sake, I hope that it was less afraid of me than I was of it. Snakes are freaky strange animals."

They'd been following a stream lost in the brush off to their right most of the way. The trail crossed a fallen log that must be the bridge in the drawing and then dipped down to a small pool. A waterfall, perhaps ten feet high, trickled down and splashed over rocks to make the pool sparkle where bits of the afternoon sun reached the surface. The pool itself was a dozen feet across with a smooth rock bottom.

She dipped in a toe. Warm. Very warm. Maybe there were hot springs upstream. The trees surrounding the pool were shrouded in flowers as big as her head, vibrant with yellows and reds. "That does it. I'm moving here."

"Anything you say, Ms. Conroy."

"Anything?" She smiled up at him.

"Anything."

Well, she'd see if he was as good as his word.

—⁓—

"You touch me, I stop."

Vern looked down at her. "I don't see how those two can coexist in the same universe. How am I supposed to find the control not to touch you?" He held up their still-joined hands from their walk.

"Figure it out, Slick." She pulled her hand from his.

He sighed deeply but was grinning. Beautiful man in the jungle primeval.

Well, Denise was feeling very primal, even if she wasn't sure either how this was going to work. Vern was always taking her to new heights and new sensations. He was a lover very focused on making her body exquisitely happy. It wasn't that she felt a need to give that back; their satisfaction was clearly mutual. It was more that she wanted to be…

What? She wasn't sure. The idea had simply popped into her head and she'd gone with it. She was learning that when she stumbled on something that wasn't how her mind typically worked, that was a good enough reason to go with it. Vern had expanded her thinking of herself almost as much as he'd expanded her thinking of her body.

It wasn't about being dominant. Vern had no more of those games in his lovemaking than he did in who was driving the car.

She slid his T-shirt up and off. The sunlight dappling down through the forest canopy wove shifting patterns across his skin. Parrots and other creatures of the jungle offered a fading background soundtrack that slowly drifted from her attention.

"I could—"

"Shh, No talking allowed either." Denise circled him without touching, only admiring. She let him wait as she studied the lines of his shoulders and back, admired the definition of his powerful body. When at long last she ran a fingertip down his spine, he shivered.

With touch and caress, she brushed over him, never once moving back into his line of vision. Reaching around, she dropped his pants until he stood like a magnificent naked god at the edge of the jungle pool.

Me, was all she could think. *He is here for me.*

He hissed with frustration as she brushed her hair down his back, jolted when she pressed her bare breasts against his back, moaned when she slid her hands between his legs and cupped him from behind.

She wanted…so much. She wanted to understand inside herself that somehow she deserved this. No, she knew that already. The thought that she was unworthy of this intimacy had also long gone by the wayside and morphed into acceptance. Yes, she was worthy. She knew that now.

Denise felt his building shivers as she lay against his back and investigated his chest, belly, and thighs with arms wrapped around from behind. She held off as long as she could stand it before she began to caress and stroke him in a way the caught his breath up short.

Vern began cursing quietly under his breath as his body's tension built and built like a wildfire slowly consuming more and more of him. If the jungle residents were still chattering, Denise didn't hear them. All she heard was the effect she was having on his body.

Did she want to somehow confirm that she could do this to a man like Vern? That was a laugh. The way he reacted to her slightest touch, and she to his, told her all she needed to know about that.

Vern groaned as if in agony.

She teased him to the very cusp and kept him there, stilling her hands and leaving a line of kisses down his back.

Then she knew what she wanted, why she was doing this.

Denise Conroy wanted to do something that she had very little experience with. She offered back to Vern what he gave her so freely.

Pure, undiluted, joy.

"I've been thinking—"

"You were thinking while we were doing that?" Denise cut him off.

Vern looked back at the innocent-seeming pool as he pulled on the last of his clothes. His skin was wrinkled, the sun was westering toward dinnertime, and he prayed his knees were working sufficiently to get him back to the little resort. "That would be no, Wrench. That was totally mind-numbing. Wherever in your imagination you're thinking this stuff up, please don't stop. You're gonna kill me, but I will die a very, very happy man."

Denise offered one of those beaming smiles but provided no explanation to keep it company.

"You look like this sweet, innocent woman. In fact, I

know you are. But"—he waved a hand helplessly—"you are far and away the sexiest and most sensual woman I've ever met."

At that a look of surprise brushed across her features, but it was gone so fast he had trouble being sure of it.

The slightly smug look that replaced it almost had him dragging her back into the pool where he'd spent a long time proving that turnabout was fair play.

"You were thinking?" she prompted him.

"Right. Before this. There's something that I don't want to be a factor in your job decision."

"What's that?" They headed back down the trail. This time she didn't squeak in surprise when the scarlet macaw swooped low to inspect them.

"If you take the job at the Restoration Center, I'll be there. Test pilot, errand boy, tour guide—I don't care. As long as we're together, everything else will work out."

"Is that a proposal?"

"Huh!" He hadn't quite meant it that way. Or maybe he had and simply hadn't gotten that far. "Let's—" He had to clear his throat and start again. "Let's say it's certainly down that track. You're the woman I want to spend my life with—which sounds even more like a proposal—but I'm not ready for that yet."

"Good. Because neither am I." They were almost back to the farm before she spoke again. "But, yeah, I'm way down that track too."

Chapter 17

DINNER HAD BEEN A CONVIVIAL AFFAIR. EVEN DENISE HAD joined in. They were no longer three couples plus Vern and Denise; they were four couples. Everyone felt the change.

Mark had given them a second day off, but everyone needed to be back on the base by nightfall. David had paying tourists arriving that night.

After lunch, Firehawk Oh-Two loaded up, and Vern went looking for Denise.

"No need to hurry," Mark told him as he climbed aboard. "See you back at base."

Vern couldn't find her. Neither could he find David or his two sons or his wife. The cows looked placid enough, but no one was in the packing barn or up in the tree house. The place was utterly deserted.

He looked up, but Firehawk Oh-Two had long since passed out of sight beyond the trees. No way she was aboard there.

He ducked into David's house. It was a simple, clean adobe building with a tin roof. In the dim light from the couple of windows, he could see that the floor was well-worn wood, the furniture simple but solid. The kitchen, two bedrooms, and generous pantry were deserted.

Stepping back into the sun, he had to squeeze his eyes shut against the blinding light.

When he managed to blink them open, Denise was standing right in front of him.

"There you—" He didn't get to finish his sentence.

Her eyes were huge.

Beside her was the most villainous man he'd ever seen, short and dark like most Hondurans.

He was pressing a massive gun against Denise's temple.

A twitch, still there from the Coast Guard, moved his hand a half inch toward his hip, but there was no firearm there to grab.

The man eyed him carefully.

Vern tried to swallow and couldn't. His throat was too painfully dry.

Slowly, he shifted his hands out to the side and focused on staying very, very still.

Chapter 18

"QUÉDESE DONDE ESTÁ!"

Vern was pretty sure that meant "don't move," mainly because the man had pointed at the ground and waved his gun in Vern's face.

Like they had a choice. They'd been pushed down to sit with their backs against the two posts holding up the outside corners of the thatched porch on the main house. Each post was a stout length of tree trunk, debarked and polished smooth, but still stout.

Then they'd been gagged with foul-tasting bandannas, and their hands had been bound behind them around the post. The posts looked as if they were just resting on a piece of stone. But even if Vern could free himself from this one, he'd have no time to free Denise before the man with the gun would be on them.

Denise was on the side away from him; he was facing her bound wrists. At least she was in the shade. He could feel the midday heat cooking his brains.

The man with the massive gun came over and shoved Vern's cowboy hat down on his head, hard. It was a relief, but he felt utterly ridiculous.

Denise could easily have shifted around the post so that they were facing each other, but she didn't seem to realize that. So all he could see were her back and hair as she cowered. With no training for anything like this, she must be terrified.

The man had rattled off some Spanish that Vern didn't understand, but he'd caught the words "*el jefe*." He'd read enough Tom Clancy novels to know that meant they were waiting for the chief to show up.

He wanted to comfort Denise, but the gag made that impossible. At least they weren't blindfolded.

They didn't have long to wait. A light-skinned man with a ragged, blond beard and mustache arrived in a Jeep that had seen far better days. He jumped down lightly and came over to them. He wore a black T-shirt and camo pants. He was armed with a knife, two pistols, and a rifle.

While the man who'd kidnapped them looked villainous, this man simply looked lethal. His dirty blond hair hung long and had been bound in place with a sweat-stained bandanna. He crossed in front of Denise, barely looking down at her, and knelt in front of Vern. His blue-gray eyes looked right through Vern as if he were a bug being assessed before it was squished.

His accent was rough, but his English was clear. "*Amigo.* You the pilot?"

Vern grunted.

The man jerked off the gag hard enough to hurt.

Vern swallowed against a dry mouth. "I am."

"Who's your *amiga*?" He nodded toward Denise, still gagged and bound to the other post. They hadn't touched her yet, thank God.

"Copilot and mechanic. I can't fly without her. So if you touch her—"

The man slowly turned his light gaze back on Vern. Stone-cold killer.

Vern reached as deep into his training as he could and met the guy eye to eye. "Just don't."

The man smiled at something for half a moment, then shifted back to his feet in a smooth motion. Ex-military. And Vern thought he'd been getting to like Honduras, or at least the Hondurans. That—

The man shouted something at his crew. They scrambled for the Jeep and began lugging supplies over to his helicopter.

A five-gallon drum of paint? Rollers and trays?

Vern looked at the man. But he didn't bother explaining.

"MHA?" he asked even as the company logo disappeared beneath medium-blue paint. It was a color used by the Honduran Air Force.

Vern didn't see any point in answering, until the man kicked him.

His boot hit Vern in the thigh, but totally missed the obvious charley-horse pressure point that every soldier learned to use in basic training. But the kick was hard enough to hurt plenty even without that.

"I speak, you answer. *Comprende*?"

"Yes, Mount Hood Aviation."

"Boss's name?"

"Mark." Vern didn't include Mark's last name, and the man didn't ask. It was an odd question, but for some reason he looked as if he liked the answer.

A shift of Denise's hair showed that she was listening rather than simply cowering as he'd thought. She too must have thought the question odd.

"How much fuel?"

"Three hours." That would be obvious as soon as the chopper was powered up. Maybe he could dump fuel along the way to wherever this guy wanted to go. Force a landing.

The guy looked up at the sky, then shouted at his crew painting the chopper, "Twenty minutes!" and began walking away.

"Hey, at least take off her gag."

The man kept walking.

—⁓—

Denise was thinking very hard. The panic had gone down after the gunman with the bad breath had tied them up and then left them alone.

She hadn't turned to face Vern. If she did—and saw him tied up as she knew he was, the panic would crash back over her. A helpless Vern didn't fit into her new world order. And if she panicked, she wouldn't be able to think.

She had almost broken down when Vern defended her, even if the threat was merely a verbal warning from a powerless position. Threatening the most dangerous-looking man she'd ever seen. It was crazy. It was stupid. And she loved Vern for it.

They'd tied her to the post facing the chopper. From behind the shield of her hair she could see what they were doing. Four men with rollers were painting the whole helicopter as fast as they could. Medium blue above, white belly, and a light blue wavy stripe down low in the medium blue.

The Honduran Air Force craft were a hodgepodge of camouflage patterns. This paint job was far from perfect, but it was the colors of the Honduran President's personal transport.

The unrest in the capital city hadn't been controlled as well as the sergeant at Palmerola Air Base believed.

Painted presidential blue and white, the Firehawk would be able to fly anywhere with no one questioning their presence. These thugs could fly right into the presidential compound.

And then what?

The leader returned to the Jeep. He wasn't a big man, but he picked up a large machine gun as if it were merely another paint roller and carried it to the chopper. He set it inside the open cargo-bay door, then fetched a second one, and finally several big steel cases that must be ammunition and looked immensely heavy.

Denise knew from the aircraft she'd studied that these were M240 machine guns—possibly the "B" variant, though she was too far away to tell. They shot NATO 7.62 mm rounds at over eight hundred a minute. These weren't cute little rifles; these were weapons of war.

This time, the leader didn't go to Vern, but came up right in front of her. His muscles rippled as he squatted in front of her. Around the edges of his sweat-stained tank top, she could see that he'd led a rough life. There were several scars showing, a pair of them circular ones like bullet holes in his shoulder.

"No more hiding in the hair," he snapped at her.

With a twist of her head and a dip of her shoulder, she managed to get one eye in the clear.

"I remove the gag, you do not scream. I untie you and you run, your pilot, *muerto*." He looked over her shoulder for a long moment toward where she could feel Vern glaring at him, then back to her with a hint of a smile. "You run, your *amante*, your lover, he is dead. *Comprende*?"

She nodded.

"I need guns mounted. You *mecánico*? You know how?"

She nodded. She'd mounted enough weapons on vintage warplanes at the restoration shop to know she could do it.

"You make mistake or hurt the weapons, I know. You will no like what happen."

That much she believed.

Chapter 19

Vern's wrists hurt from where he'd bucked against the rope when the man freed Denise. He'd been unable to hear what he told her, but he hadn't liked the man's evil smile as he'd contemplated Vern over Denise's shoulder.

She had the guns mounted by the time the paint job was done. The guy had been watching her like a hawk.

They'd been totally set up. The sergeant back at the air base had said that they were safe, but the helicopters weren't. He hadn't said a word about what would happen if they were caught alone with the helicopter.

Denise was placed in the copilot seat. Vern could see a man position himself directly behind her in the cargo bay with his gun drawn.

This time, the *jefe* had his knife out when he knelt in front of Vern. It wasn't some utility knife. It was a big, military blade with an edge that gleamed in the late-afternoon light. He twisted it to flash a reflection of sun in Vern's eyes, forcing him to blink. By the time he opened his eyes, the knife was in the man's other hand and a half inch from his eye.

"You any *problema*? Any at all?"

"No, sir."

"You fly military, *amigo*?"

According to Vern's training, you never admitted to military training. Foreign thugs liked to think they could best U.S. military people. They'd go out of their way to prove it, even when the military person was bound and gagged. The history of the 1985 TWA Flight 847 hijacking was pounded into every U.S. military trainee's brain. The hijackers killed only one of their 150 hostages. They'd identified him as a Navy SEAL, beat the shit out of him, shot him in the head, and dumped his body on the tarmac. You didn't—

"Respuesta!" The knife moved closer.

"Coast Guard pilot. Search and rescue." Vern spat it out. Hopefully that sounded neutral enough.

The man smiled. *"Bueno."* When he leaned in to cut Vern's bonds, he spoke quickly and quietly in perfect English. "Do your preflight. We leave as soon as you can get the engines hot. You will not transmit the hijack code on your transponder. You will not tap out an SOS on your microphone."

He acted as if he was laboring over the knot, even though Vern could feel his wrists were already free. Vern noted that the man's back was to the other men.

"The girl would have been safer if we'd left her here, but your announcement that you needed her to fly—at least two of my men would understand that. No choice now. She flies." He hauled Vern to his feet and whispered a last instruction. "You stay scared. Really scared. But do what I say and we just might all get out of this." Then he nearly crashed Vern to the ground when he grabbed Vern's arm and hauled him toward the chopper.

Vern tried not to be sick as he stumbled through the preflight inspection. Pretend to be scared? Not a problem! He was fucking terrified! By his own actions he'd dragged Denise right into harm's way.

He held himself together for Denise's sake and soon had the chopper running. He grabbed her hand for a moment when he was pretty sure no one was watching. She looked okay, unharmed at least. Her gaze didn't skitter or her hand shake like someone on the edge of panic or entering shock.

"They look for you soon." The man's English was again broken and Spanish accented. "Raise your *jefe* on radio. Then you say what I say. Exact what I say."

As soon as the radio was hot, Vern dragged on a headset, leaving the inner-side muff slid off his ear. It was uncomfortable, but that was the least of his problems at the moment. He didn't want the man on the system, but he had to be able to hear. The man was leaning forward between their seats.

"Mark? You out there? This is Vern."

"What's up? Why aren't you back yet?"

"Uh…" He paused, but the man crouching beside him didn't give him any guidance. "We're both okay."

"Who else is there?" Mark tried to sound casual, but Vern could hear the soldier voice come over him. In the background he could imagine frantic signals to start warming up choppers.

"Tell him," the man leaned in and whispered, "the cave and the Silver Star." Then he leaned back and began talking loudly to his men in rapid Spanish, and the last of them began clambering aboard with paint-scarring bangs and thumps.

So Vern repeated the message verbatim, keeping his voice low so that he couldn't be heard in back over the man's shouting.

Denise looked at him strangely; she was the only

other one wearing a headset, but she had both earphones on and hadn't heard what was being said. She pulled one ear cup aside.

"Really?" Mark sounded surprised.

"That's what I was told to say." Good. Now Mark would know that they were being held against their will.

"Remember what we talked about that night in the middle of the runway?"

That wasn't the response he'd been expecting, not even a little. Confused, he looked at Denise.

She rolled her eyes at him, and then he remembered before she mouthed, "Second contract."

"Yes, I remember."

"You're in it, buddy. Try to find out if he wants us in the air."

As soon as Vern clicked off the radio, Denise whispered to him over the intercom, "*El jefe* must have a reason for hiding who he is. I'm guessing we can't be giving him away."

Vern nodded his agreement and tried to catch his breath. These vicious mercenaries were the *good* guys? Then what the hell did the *bad* guys look like? Even scarier?

"Oh"—Mark clicked back in—"tell him he should go take a jump."

"No way!"

"Trust me."

The man stuck his head back up between the seats. "Eh?" he grunted and waved his gun in front of Vern's face. Vern noted that the finger was alongside the barrel rather than on the trigger, a military man's safety—no finger on the trigger, it doesn't shoot.

"My boss told me to tell you to go jump."

"*Excelente!*" The blond man grinned at him. "*Vámonos!* Go south! To capital!"

"Just one chopper?" Vern kept his voice low, but could feel his nerve shrivel at taking Denise into the capital on some unknown but clearly hazardous flight.

The man hesitated for a moment.

Vern could see he was thinking quickly.

"*Sí. Vámonos!*" He left enough space between the words that Vern was sure of the message.

Under cover of the liftoff, Vern transmitted a single word to Mark. "Solo."

"Roger that." Mark didn't sound happy.

Which he supposed was okay, because Vern didn't feel real happy at the moment himself.

Chapter 20

DENISE FELT ABOUT AS USEFUL AS A BUMP ON A...ROTOR blade. She was glad she hadn't found a way to sabotage the guns, though she'd felt awful while mounting them on her precious chopper's frame.

If this was the "home team" working under the scope of the second contract, she could afford to relax. She'd been trying to scheme a way to break the chopper without getting them both killed.

Now it sounded like if she just appeared completely cowed for a while, they'd be fine. There were a hundred questions she wanted to ask Vern, twice that many ideas of why their chopper had been painted presidential blue and what might be going on, but he'd already made it clear that they were to keep chatter to a minimum.

For lack of any other way to look useful, she rested her hands on her set of flight controls and took comfort in Vern's smooth corrections.

The museum job was suddenly looking very, very good. Vern was sweet, but she couldn't drag him away from MHA to follow her to the museum. That was ridiculous. He sounded sincere now, but a year from now? Two?

She almost laughed at the absurdity of her thinking. She was used to such a limited scope.

They had both spoken about a "lifetime." Not two years but twenty. Forty. She couldn't imagine such a thing, someone wanting to be with her for a lifetime.

Yet she didn't doubt Vern for a second. The more she thought about it, the more confusing the whole situation became—not even counting being hijacked in a foreign country on the brink of a coup.

They hadn't even cleared the national park when she noticed something on the screen in front of her. She'd been tinkering with screen modes during the last couple fires and found one she liked. The layers of information were far more complex than something she could have understood two months ago, but now they made sense.

She had two large LCDs in front of her matching the pair Vern had in front of him. There was also one in the center that gave them both a display of the terrain immediately ahead of them.

She'd set her left-most screen to give her engines, pressure, and HUMS status. Everything she wanted in a single glance—from operating temperature on the turbines to flight hours on this set of rotor blades. On her second screen, she'd set up an overlapping image of flight corridors and other air traffic, which had proven very useful over fires. She'd also overlaid the infrared image from Steve's drone so that she could see hot spots.

Now, as they entered the standard flight corridor south of Palmerola toward the capital of Tegucigalpa, the readout was abruptly overlaid by an image of hot spots. The strip of paved road to the west became a shining strip on her display. In moments, she could see the heat signature of their own helicopter as it rushed south.

Denise kept her voice to a whisper. "Vern. IR readouts."

She saw him glance in front of her, then he started clicking through screen modes using the controls on his collective until he brought up the feed from Steve's drone.

"What's that?" *El jefe* stuck his head up between the seats.

Damn him!

"Nothing," Vern responded.

Good. Served the man right for hijacking them.

Then the man growled. It was low and feral, and left her wondering if he really was the "home team." He sounded as if he just might cut their throats and fly the mission himself.

"Infrared feed. From above," Vern answered.

His voice wasn't steady. Denise stared at him. Vern's jaw was clenched and his hands were white-knuckled on the controls. Vern never flew with a tight grip. Even in crisis his touch on the cyclic was light and quick, mostly wrist action. At the moment he looked as if he was preparing to rip out the joystick by brute force and beat someone with it.

"Civilians with drones. Shit!" And then he was gone again.

"Vern?" she whispered over the intercom. He glanced over at her but offered no reassuring smile.

Denise's pulse rate escalated to a pounding in her ears. Vern knew something. Knew they weren't safe and just out flying some little secret errand.

He was scared!

Anything that scared a man with Vern's vast experience terrified her. They really were in horrible danger.

"Easy on the controls, Wrench."

She jerked her hands off the controls she'd been gripping so hard her hands ached.

They were at risk of—she swallowed hard—dying. And Vern had made a joke for her sake. If they got out of this, she was marrying him and to hell with the consequences.

The man reappeared between them so abruptly that she cried out.

"*Aquí!* Here!" He jammed a scrap of paper into her hand. Coordinates had been scratched on it in a hasty scrawl.

Her hands were shaking so badly that she could barely key the latitude and longitude into the navigation system. She also hit a switch that sent the data feed up to the drone.

In moments, Steve was flying ahead of them. They'd been hijacked a twenty-minute flight from the capital, and ten of that was already gone. But any advantage the drone could give them, she'd take.

It only took a minute before Steve was zooming in on the target and sending the data feed back to them.

Sometimes Denise hated being right.

They were carrying a half-dozen mercenary soldiers on a helicopter painted in the presidential colors. And they were flying to the Honduran presidential residence.

They weren't in the middle of a coup d'état. They *were* the coup!

Chapter 21

"JEFE!" VERN SHOUTED OUT.

Denise flinched.

When the man stuck his head forward between the seats, Vern wanted to hit and strike and beat him for what was about to happen. But he knew that even if he could surprise this man, the half-dozen others aboard would make sure neither he nor Denise survived. So he clamped down on his rage and did his best to keep his voice steady. "We did *not* sign up to kill the president of a foreign nation."

The blond man clapped him hard enough on the shoulder that Vern almost bobbled the controls. "We no here to kill him, *señor*. We here to save him."

Vern had to process that one, but not Denise. She got it right away and was already nodding her head by the time he saw through his haze of red fury.

They weren't the coup. They were a rescue mission! That he understood. He'd flown hundreds of them in far worse conditions than a clear afternoon. Though this was the first time he'd done it with a gun to his head. "Well, I think we may be arriving too late."

Even as he spoke, Steve's feed showed dozens of vehicles quickly converging on the massive edifice of the presidential residence. It was a two-story structure with a traditional red-tile roof. It was built in the form of two connected boxes with open courtyards in

the middle of each, forming a large, red figure-eight
from above.

A tall office building occupied the far end of the compound with a parking lot and a barren field in between.
In the field was a large square with a giant *H* painted in
the middle to indicate a helicopter landing area.

A perimeter wall encircled the whole area, which was
tight between roads on every side.

Two of the racing vehicles parked in the middle of
the H, blocking his landing zone. He'd lay good money
that these weren't the good guys. He could easily land,
it was a big field, but he'd wager they'd shoot him dead
before he could shut down the engines.

"*Mierda!* How good are you, Coast Guard?"

"He's the best!" Well, at least Denise believed in him.

"We'll see. Put us inside the north courtyard."

"We have an incoming helicopter." Denise was
paying more attention inside than he was; the incoming
craft showed on the edge of the radar screen—five miles
out and it was moving fast.

Vern appreciated the extra set of eyes because his
were too busy bugging out as he flew into the heart of
the capital.

"*No problema!*" the man insisted. Easy for him to say.

Steve's feed showed that the square north courtyard was completely within the building. It was
perhaps a rotor-and-a-half across. While he could
technically fit in there, a Firehawk was not only the
size of its rotor disk.

The tail rotor of the chopper stuck out another
eleven feet.

He'd have to land diagonally and make sure the

rear rotor lined up into a corner of the square court-yard. Even five feet out of place, and they'd clip a wall and plummet to the ground in a spray of shat-tered helicopter.

And he couldn't be sure of the necessary precision if another helicopter was coming in to help. Any blast of downdraft from above could send him veering into a side wall. Then they'd be lucky if any of them could so much as crawl away.

The man had given Denise another radio frequency. "Do you have encryption?"

They did, which he'd always thought strange in a firefighting helicopter. It sure made sense now.

Denise, who of course knew everything about every-thing, locked in the encryption circuit. Then she did a trick that took him a moment to figure out. She tied the second radio signal into the first so that they'd be trans-mitting encrypted to Mark at the same time.

Yet another reason to appreciate the woman.

"Two kilometers out," Vern announced.

"Transmit," the blond man said, "Desert Girl. Arrive hot. Going hot."

A microphone click was the only response he received.

Vern wanted to warn Denise but didn't have time. The man had just ordered weapons live in both helicopters.

Battle was imminent.

Most of the chopper's armor had been stripped off when it had been decommissioned from the Army. They weren't wearing bulletproof vests.

He had to protect Denise as much as he could.

So, rather than coming in high to the presidential

residence and then descending into a hail of gunfire, he put the chopper down on the deck and opened up the throttle.

He roared up the street, slaloming around buildings and hopping up just high enough to clear his wheels over the electrical lines crossing the four-lane road.

The Firehawk was moving at close to two hundred miles per hour when he popped over the residence's perimeter wall and descended until his wheels were barely above the cars in the parking lot.

By the time any gunmen saw him, he'd be gone before they could take aim.

Denise's "Yikes!" as she braced her hands against her seat made him smile. This wasn't flying to a fire, at least not the kind of firefight she'd been exposed to. But he'd flown to gunfire more than a few times, sneaking up on unhappy drug runners racing for the coast through rough seas.

The first rounds pinged off his windshield when he was a hundred yards from the President's residence. It was painted in white with dramatic, rounded white arches down the whole side.

The harsh *brap* of the M240s mounted in the cargo bay answered the gunfire, but he was too busy to do more than register the noise.

He flared the nose up hard. The helicopter climbed abruptly, dumping speed for height.

If he did this right—

He shoved the nose back to level right as he lost all forward speed.

They were hovering fifty feet above the north court-yard. Kicking the rudder pedal to shift the rear rotor to line up with a corner, he settled down into the area shadowed by the westering sun.

The gunfire ceased as he dropped below the roof peak. One story down. One to go.

"Vern, there's a fountain," Denise called out.

"Where?"

"About to clip you on the port-side cargo bay."

He looked at the walls of the tight courtyard, his rotor disk an invisible shining circle with indefinite edges.

Dirt, plants, a stray towel, all whorled violently in the enclosed space. He could hear the roar of the turbines off the walls, echoing until it was deafening.

Five feet? That was his best estimate of the distance from his rotor tips to the mezzanine-level walkway's railing.

He shrunk it to three...and they didn't hit anything. "We clear?"

"Barely, yes," Denise called out.

He descended the final story blind in his own dirt storm. The air was so turbulent that it was a miracle he was still flying.

That's what had happened to the stealth Black Hawk that crashed in the bin Laden compound. The weather had been hot, and they'd been at high altitude and heavily loaded. Then, as they flew down into the courtyard surrounded by a towering wall, any smooth air had turned into a maelstrom and the rotor blades had lost all lift.

He sagged in the seat once the wheels hit.

He'd made it down.

"Keep it spun up," the blond man shouted while his men jumped off the helicopter. He raced after them.

Vern had made it down.
But he had no idea if he'd be able to take off again.

Chapter 22

THE RELATIVE PEACE WAS SHOCKING.

Denise could feel her ears popping as she tried again and again to adjust to the sudden stillness. The turbines still roared and reverberated off the walls, but it was a calming, steady sound after the violence of their passage.

Vern's voice was a visceral shock over the headphones. "You okay?"

"I think so. A bit too much to process."

Vern had flattened the rotor blades so they were simply whirling without moving any air. The detritus in the courtyard that had been blowing in their own personal tornado had slowly settled back to the terrazzo floor. Small chairs and tables had been slammed against walls or sent skittering down long hallways.

"You better add some negative lift." At least some part of her mind was still functioning.

"I'm worried about being able to take off, not staying in place."

"Vern. Your exhaust is currently 580 degrees centigrade. That's"—she paused to do the conversion—"1,076 Fahrenheit. You're going to be igniting walls soon if you don't circulate the air."

"Oh." He lowered the collective. By giving the rotor blades a negative tilt, they sucked up air from any open passageway in the building and drove a column of hot air upward.

It wasn't enough to do more than stir everything scattered across the courtyard, but she could feel the air temperature dropping in the cabin. It was only after the reek of the exhaust fumes was being forced up and out that she noticed its absence. Her senses were moving through thick mud.

"Why does it feel so peaceful?" She really felt quite content to sit here with Vern all afternoon if that's what it took. Beyond the laminate windshield was a very ornate and stately building. Doors of rich mahogany led to rooms that she imagined to be well-lit, professional, and cozy by turns. Wide, open-plan hallways led off in various directions, looking cool and inviting with dark tile and arched white passages.

She glanced back into the cargo bay. The edge of the large, open door was actually inside one of the cascading levels of the fountain. A cheerful stream of water washed through the cargo bay and out the far door as if it had been designed that way.

It was actually quite pretty. Maybe they should add it to every chopper design so that—

"Maybe it seems peaceful because no one is shooting at us."

"Someone was shooting at us? Really? It was just—" Choking her by the throat.

"Easy there, Wrench. Easy. They're done with that now." Vern had taken her hand.

She could feel him holding it, but it was far away.

His voice was fading until all she could hear was a distant call of, "Hey! Hey. Hey…"

When she came back, she'd have to remember to tell Vern that he sounded like a scarlet macaw winging through the jungle and squawking to others that there were humans swimming in their private pool below the waterfall.

A bright, sharp sensation pierced the warm cocoon she'd been pulling around herself.

It was Vern.

Kissing her.

Hard.

"Ow!" She pushed him back and rubbed at her lips. "What was that for?"

"Seemed better than a slap." He was grinning at her.

She was sitting in Firehawk Oh-Three in the middle of the presidential residence in Tegucigalpa during a coup d'état. And they were shooting at her.

Very slowly she turned to look at the two guns she'd mounted in the rear of their craft. The fountain's flow through the cargo bay was washing a dirty, rattling clutter of spent brass bullet casings out the door and scattering them all over the palace's terrazzo floor. These were added to the hundreds more that had spilled down while the Firehawk was flying and firing above the courtyard.

Holes. There were holes in the hull where daylight was filtering through places it wasn't supposed to filter through.

Boeing Museum Restoration Center, here I come.

"Vern. I—"

A rattle of gunfire cut her off. She spun to face forward. The gunfire was coming from a hall directly in front of the helicopter. She flinched and ducked down, trying to make herself smaller in her seat.

A group was rushing toward them down one of the corridors. A small man, a big woman, and three girls in their teens ran at the front. A half-dozen others raced close behind. Then at the rear, the mercenaries led by *el jefe* were doing a staged retreat.

"Hang on, honey." Vern's voice was steady over the intercom. "This is where it gets rough."

Denise turned to Vern, aghast. "*Now* it gets rough?"

Chapter 23

VERN LISTENED FOR THE SIGNAL, UNSURE WHAT IT WOULD BE.

He pulled up the collective until the chopper was practically dancing on her wheels.

The signal was a hard punch on his arm from behind, which worked fine. With the escalating gunfire—the bright flashes of rounds pinging off the military-grade laminate windows—he couldn't be sure of hearing a hand slap on the hull.

He was so tensed for flight that the punch made him jerk up on the collective. They practically bounced five feet straight up. He had planned on easing upward inch by careful inch to get clear of the courtyard.

Through the chopper's foot-well windows he could see people spilling into the courtyard, bearing machine guns and pistols that flashed with fire. A few in military uniforms, others in ragged street clothes.

So, he went with it and kept the collective pulled up for a fast rise.

He slewed the cyclic to shift a few feet to the left as he rose.

He felt a slight jar that he hoped was running into the top of the fountain and not gunfire striking some critical system.

An alarm buzzer went off, but he didn't have time to deal with it.

"Denise!"

On his second shout she responded.

"The alarm. Deal with it."

The alarm stopped. "We're okay."

That's what he wanted to hear.

Whether by skill, chance, or blind luck, he cleared the roof edge without catching a rotor blade. He'd been afraid that with the rotor turbulence in the confined space, he wouldn't be able to maintain the needed amount of lift. Probably just as well he'd climbed fast.

The problem was—now that he was in the clear—he had flown out of one level of hell and into another.

He could go straight up, but that would make him a sitting duck for everyone in both the courtyard and the cars and military vehicles that had been in the large parking lot of the compound.

So, he twisted east and dove down into the city streets.

The rebels had the streets covered, of course. A big military truck was parked a few hundred meters up the main avenue.

He was committed now, but this wasn't going to be good.

As the troops around the truck were raising their rifles, a rain of gunfire drove down on them from the left, sending them diving for cover. The truck exploded upward in a brilliant fireball. A tiny MD500 chopper whipped by not two rotors ahead of him.

He punched through the flames and kept going.

The attack helicopter's model was the only thing it had in common with the MD500 he'd flown to fire for MHA. This tiny machine was flat black with no markings. It carried machine guns and rocket pods mounted on small winglet extensions to either side, rather than a bright orange Bambi bucket dangling beneath.

As Vern drove his Firehawk down the Boulevard Juan Pablo II, the small chopper danced around him for a moment and then disappeared. Whoever the pilot was, he was damn good.

"You still with me, Denise?" Vern called over the intercom.

"I think so." Her voice was giddy with nerves.

"What was the alarm?"

"Don't try to use the brakes when you land. You don't have any."

"Oh. Okay." At least she was still with him. He'd worried when she went shocky in the courtyard. "Check yourself for injuries. Your adrenaline is probably so high that you won't feel them."

"Not even a gunshot?"

"Probably not."

He could detect frantic motion off to his side, but he was too busy staying low and fast. A mile out, he eased up into the air, finally clear of the wild ride down between the buildings.

No one shooting at him.

No more firing from the big guns mounted in the back.

Winding back the moment in his mind, he had heard them pounding away at the soldiers who had bailed out of the shot-up truck.

A quick scan of the display. The feed from Steve's drone and his own radar showed nothing else airborne but the one other chopper and a big passenger jet climbing out of Toncontín International on the south side of the city. How normal it looked climbing out.

"What next?" Denise must be thinking again. As usual, she arrived at the question before he did.

"Damned if I know."

Chapter 24

DENISE JUMPED WHEN THE BLOND MAN JAMMED A PIECE OF paper into her palm without speaking.

By the time she turned to look, he was gone again back into the cargo bay. She had an impression of red blood and immediately turned back to the forward console. There was a bloody thumbprint on the scrap of paper she was clutching.

As before, she keyed the coordinates into the nav system. Then she looked up and saw Vern.

He sat at the controls as if nothing unusual was happening.

"How can you be so calm?"

He shrugged, checked his screens, and began turning the chopper to take them where she'd keyed in. "I think the Coast Guard trained panic out of me."

"What about before? I thought you were going to strangle the cyclic."

He managed a weak laugh. "That wasn't panic. I was so goddamn pissed at myself for forcing *el jefe* to bring you along. I nearly got you killed."

"You'd have gotten yourself killed if I hadn't been with you."

He nodded a little. "You are good, Wrench. So damn good."

"Until I panicked." Denise held her own hands out in front of her to inspect them. They weren't shaking either. There'd been gunfire and terror. Her mouth had a bitter taste in it that might be adrenal letdown and of blood-copper from where she'd bitten the inside of her cheek. But her nerves were steady. For the moment.

"For your first firefight, you did great."

"Can I never do that again?"

Vern kept silent, and she had to think about it. Firehawk Oh-Two had been downed. Firehawk Oh-Three probably had a lot more than thirty-four holes in it now. She'd think about the future…in the future.

"Where are we headed?" Denise looked out and saw that they had passed out of the city and were climbing up the hills.

"We'll know when we get there."

She was going to make some joke about how that would be a good description of their relationship at the moment as well, but Vern sounded suddenly exhausted.

Digging around in the small day bag they'd taken to keeping in the cockpit, she found an energy bar and held it out for him to bite off a chunk. She took her own bite right over his, and they both chewed for a moment in silence.

"We appear to be going way up."

That worked for her in both ways. Up was always a good direction in a relationship as well.

The coordinates were leading them up a mountain to the east of the city. Tegucigalpa sat in a bowl of mountains. To the east, high up, was perched a group of tall transmitting towers.

Denise looked back and was glad to see less red. One of the soldiers had a white bandage wound around his leg, but he also had a gun in his hands and was watching out the door. The President and his family were huddled in the rear.

"President. Transmitting towers," she said over the intercom.

"Television station," Vern finished. "We're not only a rescue mission. We're supposed to be stopping the coup as well."

The blond man was back. Denise pulled back the earpiece so that she could hear his conversation with Vern.

"Get on the radio, the encrypted one, not the cross-feed you set for Mark."

Well, Denise thought, so much for being sneaky and subtle.

"The message is: 'Trish? We set?' Send it."

Vern transmitted the question.

A bright, cheery woman's voice came back. "My man is inside and in control. He reports he has a small studio set up and ready to splice into the main feed. LZ is cold and solid, *jefe*." The last word was dripping with humor and sarcasm.

Denise would bet the woman was a handful. Then she spotted the source. One chopper had been circling around behind them, some kind of rearguard action. A new one was hovering low in a hole among the trees not far from the transmitting towers. Invisible to radar or anything but a close inspection from above, but ready for immediate action.

A woman who flew attack helicopters. Denise wasn't sure why she found it surprising, but it was.

"And your wife is circling around somewhere nearby," Trish continued.

Two women pilots. Wait!

"Your wife?" Denise spun to face the cruel-looking blond man who'd made their last hours hell. Someone had married this man?

His expression softened, making him seem only dangerous but no longer scary. He had a smile that tugged up one corner of his unruly mustache. "Best pilot there is other than Emily."

A mercenary leader who knew Mark and Emily. That meant…

"Get us down there," he ordered before withdrawing.

As Vern settled down in front of the transmitting towers, they whispered to each other over the intercom. "SOAR. Special operations."

This was a U.S. Army operation. Then why were they in the middle of it?

And how would they get out back out?

Vern dropped them at the transmitter. There was nowhere big enough to land, but he managed to hover close enough to a small, rocky bluff that everyone could jump out.

The blond *jefe*, who still hadn't given his name, hesitated a moment before jumping. "Now get the hell out of here. And thanks."

Once he was gone, Vern pulled back aloft.

Denise leaned over to inspect the back. "Hey, they took their machine guns and ammo as well. That's what we get? A near-death experience, a shot-up helicopter, and 'Thanks, little lady,' as if he were John bloody Wayne?"

Vern had never heard Denise so worked up. It was

as if she'd come to life somehow. Comfortable enough with herself to let that deep brilliance of hers slide out into public.

"Oh my God! They made a total mess of our helicopter. There are holes and bullet casings everywhere." She was on a roll, and he didn't try to stop her as they flew north along the face of the ridge, headed back toward their base. "Who the hell were those people? I need to know who to send the bill to because—"

Vern was on the verge of laughing—

A rattle of gunfire struck his bird.

"Shit!" He slammed to the right, turning the chopper almost on edge as it carved a turn. That got Denise above him, another layer of protection as he then dove for the hills. "Trish? Desert Girl?" he called over the radio, but there was no response. "Mark?"

Silence.

"Denise. Get me back some radios."

He'd only managed a glimpse as he'd maneuvered. Their passage up the mountain hadn't gone unnoticed. A line of military vehicles were racing up the narrow road that threaded its way back and forth across the mountain's face as it climbed.

This was a whole world of hurt headed for the mountaintop.

"Radios are dead. I think they cut the antenna lines, of all unlikely things."

Not what he needed to hear right at the moment.

"Water!" Denise shouted at him.

"Water?"

—◆—

"Get a load of water, Vern. Fast." Denise figured she was either about to be brilliant or remarkably stupid.

But Vern didn't question her. He'd slammed over the controls and was diving down into the outer reaches of the city. The only river was too far away. She looked right and left. No cattle ponds here. Just endless rows of hovels.

Vern slowed so abruptly that she slammed against the safety harness.

He was descending down and backwards even as he unreeled the siphon hose.

Only when she stuck her head into the bubble in the door's window did she see what Vern had spotted. "A swimming pool?"

"Water is water, with or without chlorine."

"But it's full of people!" It was a community swimming pool, and it was packed solid with Hondurans both in and around the water.

"They'll move." He backed right over it without even leaning out to check.

Well, Mr. Hotshot Special Forces *jefe* wasn't the only one married to an amazing pilot.

Married? She laughed aloud, and it was a wonderful feeling. Even if they weren't married, hadn't said the words, it felt as if they were. There was no longer any doubt about their future. Whatever it might be, it would be together.

"What?"

"Nothing. I'll tell you later, you amazing hunk of a man."

Vern had been absolutely right. The swimming pool had cleared rapidly as the large helicopter came to a stable hover eighteen feet over the water.

He fired the pumps. They both took turns making sure no one got pulled toward the siphon hose and desperately willed the load gauge to hit a thousand gallons faster.

"The pump is reading okay, but it's slow. I bet the tank is full of bullet holes and we're leaking like a sieve. I'm going to take an extra hundred gallons because I'm sure we'll shed at least that much in flight."

The moment it registered eleven hundred gallons, Vern simultaneously shut down the pumps and began reeling in the hose as he shot for the skies. He pounded upward so fast she could feel the G-force driving her into her seat despite the heavy load.

"Where are we going?" Vern had them right up to the edge of the never-exceed speed and climbing fast. "If we try to drop right on the military column, they're going to shoot us again."

"Better than that. Take us a couple hundred yards below the transmitter."

It took him a moment, but then Vern laughed and they continued to climb.

Chapter 25

"It was a thing of beauty," Vern admitted.

Victorious, they'd flown back to the Finca Río Negro. No one had shot at them. Vern had deemed it inadvisable to land a shot-up, blue-and-white-painted Firehawk Oh-Three right in front of the Joint Task Force 1-228th. Reaching the same conclusion, the rest of the crew had come up in Firehawk Oh-One without needing to be called. They brought along selected items from Denise's tool kit, service supplies, and ten gallons of gloss black paint. Again.

Once night had settled, the two tiny Night Stalker helicopters joined them, landing around the other side of the house and again upsetting the cows.

Introductions had gone around: Trisha—a red-haired fireball even smaller than Denise; her husband—a really big guy named Billy who was clearly a patient man; "Desert Girl," who was named Claudia—a very striking brunette; and her husband, Michael—the heretofore nameless *jefe*. No last names. No ranks.

Under the shadow of darkness and a small campfire, David and his wife had set them up with meat-stuffed masa tamales steamed in banana leaves and deep cups of decaf coffee heavily laced with guaro—a local cane-sugar liquor that was clear, sweet, and lethal. Exactly what Vern needed.

"Denise was the one who spotted it." And was

currently curled up against him in a chair not really made for two and therefore about perfect, to his way of thinking.

"The bridge supports over that highest canyon leading up to the transmitters were probably laid down by the conquistadors in the 1500s. They certainly looked that way." She joined her own story despite the size of the group listening.

"We arrived at the bridge over the ravine about two hundred meters ahead of the attack group. Denise showed me where to hit it. A thousand gallons as a single fist-punch almost took the bridge out. No time for a second load or to find a way to rally support from your choppers, but it wasn't needed."

Denise turned her face into his chest at the memory as he described the next part.

The first truck—with the coup's leader, the head of the opposition party—rolled onto the bridge and then tumbled over five hundred meters down the hillside when the weakened span collapsed.

An armored personnel carrier transporting the general who supported the coup attempt had followed too close on his leader's heels and also gone down.

With the head of the coup and the military leader dead, and the President broadcasting with his family on national television, the bid for power had rapidly collapsed.

"Why us?" Vern asked the *jefe*. He couldn't quite imagine such a dangerous man being named Michael. Such a common, normal name.

The man studied the fire for a few moments before speaking. "It wasn't supposed to be you. Our

best intelligence said we had a week before they took
action. We had assets inbound, but when it went down,
I needed a heavy transport bird in a big hurry. We
couldn't exactly call up the Joint Task Force and ask
to borrow one; there couldn't be a hint of U.S. involve-
ment in this. That's why we painted you with presidential colors. They may not have a Black Hawk, but no
one will be able to unravel that as soon as you repaint
this bird."

Michael tossed a branch on the fire. "We considered
stealing one, but the 1-228th would notice and they'd be
plenty efficient about hunting us down." He shrugged.
"We were going to approach MHA, knew you guys did
some specialty work, but didn't know if your Honduran
team was a part of the covert ops group. I guess someone who knew about the op had your team placed down
here but forgot to tell us."

"That doesn't add up." Denise was back in the conversation. "Why us, Vern and me?"

Vern liked the way that sounded. "Vern and me."
His mind was drifting. Despite how casual he'd tried
to sound for Denise's sake, the day had really taken it
out of him.

Michael's voice was gentle now that there was no
military action under way. He had the casual non-accent
of the Pacific Northwest.

Vern also noticed that he sat very close to his quiet
wife. He'd bet that they had the type of conversations
where neither of them ever spoke.

"One of my assistants," Michael continued, "received
a tip that you were parked here off base. He caught you
here flat-footed. He didn't think he had the forces to

control two choppers, so he grabbed one and called me in. I had to find out if you were part of MHA's covert arm, so that's why I asked for your boss's name."

"Then what was that cave and Silver Star stuff?"

Vern had thought Denise past speaking, but maybe she'd drunk less than he had. The guaro was definitely working its magic on his system.

"Past mission. And, no"—Michael held up a hand before she could ask—"I can't tell you about it. But it did include me taking a jump. A leap of faith." He nodded toward Emily with great respect.

The scene slowly shifted before Vern's eyes. Mark and Emily had fought wars with these folks. They'd trusted each other with their very lives. He'd hate to leave their company. They weren't only the best fire-fighters he knew, they were also the best people.

The talk drifted late into the night. Mark, Michael, and Carly were soon deeply involved in discussions of fishing, of all odd topics. Claudia and Trisha joined Emily and were talking helicopter formation tactics at a level even Vern couldn't follow.

He suspected that even if the guaro hadn't done its work, he probably couldn't follow where they went. As it was, Vern wasn't sure he'd ever move again.

At some point past midnight, the military types took their leave and went aloft. "Have to be offshore before first light."

Before he left, Michael came up and shook Vern's hand. "That was one of the top ten piloting jobs I've ever seen. Well done." Then he was gone before Vern could respond.

By the startled look Mark turned on him, Vern got

the idea that Michael didn't give compliments lightly. Added to the glow of the guaro and the woman beside him, he'd found a seriously happy-Vern place.

The night was quiet for a long time after they'd gone. Geckos creaked, frogs peeped, and somewhere far off a monkey screamed out a call, moved, and called again into the darkness.

"So, Mark"—Denise stirred lazily in Vern's arms—"where are we going next year?"

Something pinged in Vern's brain.

"Hard to say until it gets here. Back to Oregon in another month, then hopefully a quiet season from there. Hard to say."

The ping in Vern's head had gotten louder. It almost drifted off with the lethargy that had overcome his system—contented just to be sitting here with Denise mostly in his lap.

Then the ping stumbled on too much guaro and nearly drowned. He glared down at his coffee mug looking for the answer, but it had long since shifted from mostly coffee to mostly cane liquor, so the answer wasn't there.

"Say that again." Vern managed to speak.

"Which part?" Mark asked.

"Not you. Her." Denise was curled against his shoulder so he couldn't really see her and had to point to show who he meant.

"Which part?" she asked as sweetly as could be. He wasn't buying that innocent, I'm-so-helpless tone for a moment.

"The part where you asked where we're going next year."

"Oh, that part. Why?" She was up to something.

Vern glared at Mark, the campfire, then Emily, but found no greater insight. None of the others were offering any guidance either.

"*We*." He managed to latch on to the word. "Next year." Two more words that somehow linked to... "Ha! Next year we're going to be in Everett, Washington, at the Boeing Museum Restoration Center."

"What?" Mark looked perplexed. "The hell you are."

"Yes!" Vern spoke slowly to make sure his words were clear. "We are. At least she is. No idea what I'll be doing yet."

"You are?" Mark was now sitting up and looking at Denise intently. Everyone else, at least those still able to, had leaned forward enough to be lit by the fading fire's glow.

Vern could feel the slick slide of Denise's hair against his chin as she shook her head no.

"We aren't?" Now Vern was really lost.

"Nope."

He tried to push her upright so that he could see her face, but the size of the chair and their positions weren't cooperating. He finally managed to wedge her free and get her perched beside him so that he could face her.

"What the hell, Wrench?"

"I'm staying with MHA."

"Because of me. You can't. I already told you that you can't do that because I won't—"

"Shut up, Vern."

He sputtered but stopped talking.

"I love you. And I'm going to marry you."

That brought applause and cheers from around the circle, which he ignored.

"Hello." He raised his eyebrows in what he hoped was a wise gesture. "I already knew that."

"You did?"

"Duh!"

She laughed and gave him a quick kiss that he was moving too slow to capitalize on. "But"—she placed her hand over his heart—"you've got to stop talking nonsense."

Now he really was lost.

"You break the birds, Slick, and I'll put 'em back together. It's what I do. Though I never want to go through"—she helplessly waved a hand at the outside world—"that again."

He felt her shudder at the memory.

"I've been in a museum my whole life. Now I want to go places. I want to help people. Did you see the President with his family? His wife and three beautiful girls. The whole time he made sure he was between them and the danger. Every single step of the way. Even between them and the men rescuing him."

"But—" Why the hell was he protesting? This was the woman he'd fallen in love with, suddenly aflame with the life shining from her. Not hidden behind a shield of silence, caution, and shining hair.

This was a beautiful woman facing a dangerous world. She didn't need his protection. Nor the museum's. Not anymore.

"This is what I want, Vern. All of this. Even children that I will love as much as the President loved his. Your children, Vern. Will you go there with me?"

He grinned at her. He couldn't help himself; he loved this woman past reason. He saluted and clumsily on purpose hit his forehead hard, knocking his head into the back of the wooden chair with a solid thunk.

Actually too hard.

It hurt.

"Whatever you say, ma'am, Wrench, sir."

He considered dragging her against him and kissing the living daylights out of her. But something more was needed. Something…

He raised his hand, thumb pointing to the sky. Made the sideways "I love you sign" plus the little helicopter tail with his fingers. And he swung his hand up and out.

For the first time he'd ever seen, Denise was crying. Tears were sliding down her smiling face faster than he could brush them aside.

She nodded once, her hair swinging forward and back in a shimmering swirl. Then she fell into his arms and gave him a salty kiss to bind the promise.

Wherever they flew, they would fly there together.

He didn't feel the pain where he'd hit his head for long.

Read on for a sneak peek at *Target Engaged*, the first book in the explosive new Delta Force series by M.L. Buchman

CARLA ANDERSON ROLLED UP TO THE LOOMING, STORM-fence gate on her brother's midnight-blue Kawasaki Ninja 1000 motorcycle. The pounding of the engine against her sore butt emphasized every mile from Fort Carson in Pueblo, Colorado, home of the 4th Infantry, and hopefully never again the home of Sergeant Carla Anderson. The bike was all she had left of Clay, other than a folded flag, and she was here to honor that.

If this was the correct "here."

A small guard post stood by the gate into a broad, dusty compound. It looked deserted and she didn't see even a camera.

This *was* Fort Bragg, North Carolina. She knew that much. Two hundred and fifty square miles of military installation, not even counting the addition of the neighboring Pope Field Airport.

She'd gotten her Airborne parachute training here and never even known what was hidden in this remote corner. Bragg was exactly the sort of place a tiny, elite unit of the U.S. military could disappear—in plain sight.

This back corner of the home of the 82nd Airborne was harder to find than it looked. What she could see of the compound through the fence definitely ranked "worst on base."

The setup was totally whacked.

Standing outside the fence at the guard post, she could see across the compound a large, squat gray concrete building, incongruously cheerful with bright pink roses along the front walkway—the only landscaping visible anywhere. More recent buildings—in better condition only because they were newer—ranged off to the right. She could breach the old fence in a dozen different places just in the hundred-yard span she could see before it disappeared into a clump of brush and low trees drooping in the June heat.

Wholly indefensible.

There was no way that this could be the headquarters of the top combat unit in any country's military.

Unless this really was their home, in which case the indefensible fence—inde-fence-ible?—was a complete sham designed to fool a sucker. She'd stick with the main gate.

She peeled off her helmet and scrubbed at her long, brown hair to get some air back into her scalp. Guys always went gaga over her hair, which was a useful distraction at times. She always wore it as long as her successive commanders allowed. Pushing the limits was one of her personal life policies.

She couldn't help herself. When there was a limit, Carla always had to see just how far it could be nudged. Surprisingly far was usually the answer. Her hair had been at ear length in Basic. By the time she joined her first forward combat team, it brushed her jaw. Now it was down on her shoulders. It was actually something of a pain in the ass at this length—another couple inches before it could reliably ponytail—but she did like having the longest hair in the entire unit.

Carla called out a loud, "Hello!" at the empty compound shimmering in the heat haze.

No response.

Using her boot in case the tall chain-link fence was electrified, she gave it a hard shake, making it rattle loudly in the dead air. Not even any birdsong in the oppressive midday heat.

A rangy man in his late forties or early fifties, his hair half gone to gray, wandered around from behind a small shack as if he just happened to be there by chance. He was dressed like any off-duty soldier: worn khaki pants, a black T-shirt, and scuffed Army boots. He slouched to a stop and tipped his head to study her from behind his Ray-Bans. He needed a haircut and a shave. This was not a soldier out to make a good first impression.

"Don't y'all get hot in that gear?" He nodded to indicate her riding leathers without raking his eyes down her frame, which was both unusual and appreciated.

"Only on warm days," she answered him. It was June, in North Carolina. The temperature had crossed ninety hours ago and the air was humid enough to swim in, but complaining never got you anywhere.

"What do you need?"

So much for the pleasantries. "Looking for Delta."

"Never heard of it," the man replied with a negligent shrug. Something about how he did it though told her she was in the right place.

"Combat Applications Group?" Delta Force had many names, and they certainly lived to "apply combat" to a situation. No one on the planet did it better.

His next shrug was eloquent.

Delta Lesson One: *Folks on the inside of the wire*

didn't call it Delta Force. It was CAG or "The Unit." She got it. Check. Still easier to think of it as Delta though.

She pulled out her orders and held them up. "Received a set of these. Says to show up here today."

"Let me see that."

"Let me through the gate, and you can look at it as long as you want."

"Sass!" He made it an accusation.

"Nope. Just don't want them getting damaged or lost maybe by accident." She offered her blandest smile with that.

"They're that important to you, girlie?"

"Yep!"

He cracked what might have been the start of a grin, then he opened the gate, and she idled the bike forward, scuffing her boots through the dust.

From this side she could see that the chain-link was wholly intact. There was a five-meter swath of scorched earth inside the fence line. Through the heat haze, she could see both infrared and laser spy eyes down the length of the wire. And that was only the defenses she could see. So...a very *not* inde-fence-ible fence. Absolutely the right place.

When she went to hold out the orders, he waved them aside.

"Don't you want to see them?" This had to be the right place. She was the first woman in history to walk through The Unit's gates by order. A part of her wanted the man to acknowledge that. Any man. A Marine Corps marching band wouldn't have been out of order.

The man just turned away; spoke to her over his shoulder as he closed the gate behind her bike. "Go ahead and check in. You're one of the last to arrive. We start in a couple hours," he said, as if it was a blasted dinner party. "And I already saw those orders when I signed them. Now put them away before someone else sees them and thinks you're still a soldier." He walked away.

She watched the man's retreating back. *He'd* signed her orders? *That* was the notoriously hard-ass Colonel Charlie Brighton? What the hell was the leader of the U.S. Army's Tier 1 asset doing manning the gate? Duh…assessing new applicants.

This place *was* whacked. Totally!

There were only three Tier 1 assets in the entire U.S. military. There was Navy's Special Warfare Development Group, DEVGRU, that the public thought was called Seal Team Six—which hadn't been named that for thirty years now. There was the Air Force's 24th STS—that pretty much no one on the outside had ever heard of. And there was the 1st Special Forces Operational Detachment—Delta—whose very existence was still denied by the Pentagon despite four decades of operations, several books, and a couple of seriously off-the-mark movies that were still fun to watch because Chuck Norris kicked ass even under the stupidest of circumstances.

Total Tier 1 women across all three teams? Zero.

About to be? One. Staff Sergeant First Class Carla Anderson.

Where did she need to go to check in? There was no signage. No drill sergeant hovering. No—

Delta Lesson Number Two: *You aren't in the Army anymore, sister.*

If that meant she had to take care of herself, well, that was a lesson she'd learned long ago. Against stereotype, her well-bred, East-coast, white-guy dad was the drunk. Her dirt-poor half Tennessee-Cherokee, half Colorado-settler mom, who'd passed her dusky skin and dark hair on to her daughter, had been a sober and serious woman. She'd also been a casualty of an Afghanistan dust-bowl IED while serving in the National Guard. Carla's big brother Clay now lay beside Mom in Arlington Cemetery. Dead from a training accident. Except your average training accident didn't include a posthumous rank bump, a medal, and coming home in a sealed box reportedly with no face.

Clay had flown helicopters in the Army's 160th SOAR with the famous Majors Beale and Henderson. Well, famous in the world of people who'd flown with the Special Operations Aviation Regiment, or their little sisters who'd begged for stories of them whenever big brothers were home on leave. Otherwise totally invisible.

Clay had clearly died on a black-op that she'd never be told a word of, so she didn't bother asking. Which was okay. He knew the risks, just as Mom had. Just as she herself had when she'd signed up the day of Clay's funeral, four years ago. She'd been on the front lines ever since and so far lived to tell about it.

Carla popped Clay's Ninja—which is how she still thought of it even after riding it for four years—back into first and rolled it slowly up to the building with the pink roses. As good a place to start as any.

"Hey, check out this shit!"

Sergeant First Class Kyle Reeves looked out the window of the mess hall at the guy's call. Sergeant

Ralph last-name-already-forgotten was 75th Rangers and too damn proud of it.

Though…damn! Ralphie was onto something.

Kyle would definitely check out *this shit*.

Babe on a hot bike, looking like she knew how to handle it.

Through the window, he inspected her lean length as she clambered off the machine. Army boots. So call her five-eight, a hundred and thirty, and every part that wasn't amazing curves looked like serious muscle. Hair the color of lush dark caramel brushed her shoulders but moved like the finest silk, her skin permanently the color of the darkest tan.

She looked powerful. And dangerous. Her tight leathers revealed muscles made of pure soldier.

Ralph Something moseyed out of the mess-hall building where the hundred selectees were hanging out to await the start of the next testing class at sundown.

Well, Kyle sure wasn't going to pass up the opportunity for a closer look. Though seeing Ralph's attitude, Kyle hung back a bit so that he wouldn't be too closely associated with the dickhead.

Ralph had been spoiling for a fight ever since he'd found out he was one of the least experienced guys to show up for Delta Selection. He was from the 75th Ranger Regiment, but his deployments hadn't seen much action. Each of his attempts to brag for status had gotten him absolutely nowhere.

Most of the guys here were 75th Rangers, 82nd Airborne, or Green Beret Special Forces like himself. And most had seen a shitload of action because that was the nature of the world at the moment. There were a couple SEALs who

hadn't made SEAL Team Six and probably weren't going
to make Delta, a dude from the Secret Service Hostage
Rescue Team who wasn't going to last a day no matter how
good a shot he was, and two guys who were regular Army.

The question of the moment though, who was she?

Ralph walked right up to her with all his arrogant
and stupid hanging out for everyone to see. The other
soldiers began filtering outside to watch the show.

"Well, girlie, looks like you pulled into the wrong
spot. This here is Delta territory."

He thought about stopping Ralph, thought that someone should give the guy a good beating, but Dad had
taught him control. He would take Ralph down if he got
aggressive, but he really didn't want to be associated
with the jerk, even by grabbing him back.

The woman turned to face them, then unzipped the
front of her jacket in one of those long, slow movie
moves. The sunlight shimmered across her hair as she
gave it an "unthinking" toss. Wraparound dark glasses
hid her eyes, adding to the mystery.

He could see what there was of Ralph's brain implod-
ing from lack of blood. He felt the effect himself despite
standing a half dozen paces farther back.

She wasn't hot; she sizzled. Her parting leathers
revealed an Army-green T-shirt and proof that the very
nice contours suggested by her outer gear where completely genuine. Her curves weren't big—she had a lean
build—but they were as pure woman as her shoulders
and legs were pure soldier.

"There's a man who called me girlie earlier." Her
voice was smooth and seductive, not low and throaty,
but rich and filled with nuance.

She sounded like one of those people who could hypnotize a Cobra, either the snake or the attack helicopter.

"*He's* a bird colonel. He can call me that if he wants. *You* aren't nothing but meat walking on sacred ground and wishing he belonged."

Kyle nodded to himself. The "girlie" got it in one.

"*You*"—she jabbed a finger into Sergeant Ralph Something's chest—"do not get 'girlie' privileges. *We* clear?"

"Oh, sweetheart, I can think of plenty of privileges that you'll want to be giving to—" His hand only made it halfway to stroking her hair.

If Kyle hadn't been Green Beret trained, he wouldn't have seen it she moved so fast and clean.

"—*me!*" Ralph's voice shot upward on a sharp squeak.

The woman had Ralph's pinkie bent to the edge of dislocation, and before the man could react, had leveraged it behind his back and upward until old Ralph Something was perched on his toes trying to ease the pressure. With her free hand, she shoved against the middle of his back to send him stumbling out of control into the concrete wall of the mess hall with a loud "klonk" when his head hit.

Minimum force, maximum result. The Unit's way.

She eased off on his finger and old Ralph dropped to the dirt like a sack of potatoes. He didn't move much.

"Oops." She turned to face the crowd that had gathered.

She didn't even have to say, "Anyone else?" Her look said plenty.

Kyle began to applaud. He wasn't the only one, but he was in the minority. Most of the guys were doing a wait and see.

A couple looked pissed.

Everyone knew that the Marines combat training had graduated a few women, but that was just Jarheads on the ground.

This was Delta. "The Unit" was Tier 1. A Special Mission Unit. They were supposed to be the one true bastion of male dominance. No one had warned them that there was a woman coming in.

Just one woman, Kyle thought. The first one. How exceptional did that make her? Pretty damn was his guess. Even if she didn't last the first day, still pretty damn. And damn pretty. He'd bet on dark eyes behind her wraparound shades. She didn't take them off, so it was a bet he'd have to settle later on.

About the Author

M. L. Buchman has over thirty novels in print. His military romantic suspense books have been named Barnes & Noble and NPR "Top 5 of the Year" and *Booklist* "Top 10 of the Year." He has been nominated for the 2014 Reviewers' Choice Award for Romantic Suspense by *RT Book Reviews*. In addition to romance, he also writes thrillers, fantasy, and science fiction.

In among his career as a corporate project manager he has rebuilt and single-handed a fifty-foot sailboat, both flown and jumped out of airplanes, designed and built two houses, and bicycled solo around the world. He is now making his living as a full-time writer on the Oregon Coast with his beloved wife. He is constantly amazed at what you can do with a degree in geophysics. You may keep up with his writing by subscribing to his newsletter at www.mlbuchman.com.